CW00665154

# GREAT BRITISH HORROR II

# DARK SATANIC MILLS

# Great British Horror II
## Dark Satanic Mills

*Edited by*
Steve J Shaw

BLACK
SHUCK
BOOKS

First published in Great Britain in 2017 by

Black Shuck Books
Kent, UK

TOOLS OF THE TRADE © Paul Finch, 2017
FRAGMENTS OF A BROKEN DOLL © Cate Gardner, 2017
THE CARDIAC ORDEAL © Andrew Freudenberg, 2017
THE LIES WE TELL © Charlotte Bond, 2017
OUR LADY OF WICKER BRIDGE © Angela Slatter, 2017
THE CHURCH WITH BLEEDING WINDOWS © John
Llewellyn Probert, 2017
SLEEPING BLACK © Marie O'Regan, 2017
SATIN ROAD © Gary Fry, 2017
NON-STANDARD CONSTRUCTION © Penny Jones, 2017
THE NIGHT MOVES © Gary McMahon, 2017
/'DƷʌST/ © Carole Johnstone, 2017

Cover design and interior layout © WHITEspace, 2017

The moral rights of the authors have been asserted in
accordance with the Copyright, Designs and Patents Act, 1988.
All rights reserved. No part of this publication may be
reproduced or transmitted in any form or by any means,
electronic or mechanical, including photocopy, recording, or
any information storage and retrieval system, without
permission in writing from the publisher.
This book is a work of fiction. Names, characters, businesses,
organisations, places and events are either the product of the
author's imagination or are used fictiously. Any
resemblance to actual persons, living or dead, events or
locales is entirely coincidental.

978-1-913038-04-5

*Dedicated to the memory of Sir John Hurt*

*Tools of the Trade*                                        9
    Paul Finch

*Fragments of a Broken Doll*                               49
    Cate Gardner

*The Cardiac Ordeal*                                       59
    Andrew Freudenberg

*The Lies We Tell*                                         77
    Charlotte Bond

*Our Lady of Wicker Bridge*                               103
    Angela Slatter

*The Church with Bleeding Windows*                        121
    John Llewellyn Probert

*Sleeping Black*                                          141
    Marie O'Regan

*Satin Road*                                              167
    Gary Fry

*Non-Standard Construction*                               189
    Penny Jones

*The Night Moves*                                         215
    Gary McMahon

*/'dʒʌst/*                                                235
    Carole Johnstone

# Tools of the Trade
## Paul Finch

One thing that always irritated Adam was conspiratorial behaviour by his informants.

Okay, quite often they were whistle-blowers, guys who were breaking rank to pass quiet confidences which, if they stood up sufficiently to make it into print, would definitely mean trouble for someone. But there was trouble and then there was trouble. This was a small town by Lancashire standards, a nameless smudge on most people's maps, so even exposing shenanigans at the highest level of the local authority wouldn't make too many waves. Woodstein and Deep Throat it wasn't. And yet, when Adam arrived at the railway station forecourt that unseasonably mild November lunchtime, Dick Wetherby was sitting in one of the bus shelters, his overcoat fully buttoned, its collar turned up to conceal half his face, the rest of it hidden behind an outspread copy of *The Times*. The one or two other commuters present ignored him, but they'd doubtless spared him at least a glance or two, wondering what he was up to.

"You realise it's ten degrees?" Adam said, slumping onto the bench alongside him. "And yet you look like someone who's about to go polar trekking. It's a bit of a give-away."

"My job could be on the line with this one," Wetherby replied tightly.

Given to nervousness, he often said things like that. Wetherby was aged in his late forties, and was a tall, gangling beanpole with a mop of limp yellow hair, watery eyes and a pair of steel-rimmed glasses perched on a protruding woodpecker nose. Adam was a similar age, but by contrast shorter and stockier, with a shaved head and a reddish moustache and goatee. It was a slightly thuggish look even in a jacket and tie, as now, though that misrepresented the truth. Adam Croaker *could* be a bruiser, but only in intellectual terms. Not that he felt peacefully inclined towards Wetherby at present.

"Dick... because you're insisting on keeping this thing quiet, I've had to come here during my lunch-break. Everyone at the office thinks I nipped home because I forgot my butties. Please tell me this is going to be worth so much trouble."

"It's about *that*." Wetherby nodded across the main road. Adam glanced over there, puzzled.

Tunbridge Railway Station wasn't situated in the most salubrious corner of town. Oh, on paper it was a hotspot: officially part of the town centre and located on Tunbridge Hall Road, a key thoroughfare; and it wasn't as if the station itself serviced an unimportant railway – the elevated line traversing the town's rooftops and chimneys, and in fact passing over an arched bridge not one hundred yards to the left of where they now sat, was part of the West Coast Mainline, the most direct route between London and Glasgow. Directly behind the railway sat the bus station, which was never less than heaving. If nothing else, this district was always busy. But transport hubs rarely attract the more upmarket standard of boutique, on top of which the Recession hadn't been kind to Tunbridge anyway, so much of what passed as retail property in this always rather functional zone having suffered considerably. A lot of it was now 'to let', while what remained would have been unappealing at the best of times. The row of shops indicated by Wetherby was a case in point: cycle repairs, a tattoo parlour, a scruffy takeaway and a thrift store, all their signage decayed, all their windows filmed with layers of dust.

"Which unit am I looking at?" Adam asked irritably.

Wetherby tutted. "Not the shops, you prat… though God knows, they add to the bloody eyesore. The Great Northern. Or what's left of it."

Slowly, the penny dropped. Sandwiched between the tattoo parlour and the takeaway, a padlocked grille blocked off a broad, rectangular recess with a grimy brick arch over the top. The grille itself was old, caked in rust and hung with scraps of waste-paper – but not as old as the recessed entry it denied access to. This was so dark you'd never know that six yards into it stood a heavy oaken door, also locked, and that on the other side of that a flight of stairs led up to what had once been the reception area to a very elegant hotel. Adam's gaze roamed up and across the dilapidated façade of the once fine Victorian building.

A relic from the age of railway hotels, the Great Northern's baroque-style terracotta frontage had once been the first sight to greet weary travellers when they emerged from the railway station opposite, its handsome bay windows ablaze with warm and welcoming lamplight. Now, those same windows were either broken and boarded, or covered by drab interior hangings. The fact they still boasted fanlights and balustrades added to their air of faded grandeur. Pale shadows of the ornate painted lettering that had once adorned the structure – GREAT NORTHERN HOTEL – had been visible up until a few years ago, but now the damp, the soot and the general dinginess that crept over everything in the heart of a post-industrial town like Tunbridge had accounted even for those.

"Okay," Adam said, his interest pricked a little – the Great Northern had been a bone of contention at Council meetings for as long as he could remember. It was listed, so it couldn't just be demolished, but no-one ever seemed to want to buy it and spruce it up, and if they did, it soon ended up back on the market. "Tell me more."

"You know we had a vigil there last week?" Wetherby replied. "Well... something happened that ought to be of interest to you."

"You had a *what* last week?"

"A vigil. You know, we sit in all night, set our equipment, take readings, see if we can make any kind of contact..."

"Just a bloody minute!" Adam was well aware that Dick Wetherby, though a serious-minded person in his professional life, was also very keen on his hobby, which was paranormal investigation. "Are you saying you've brought me here in your capacity as ghost-hunter rather than officer of the Council?"

"The Council don't know anything about this." Wetherby lowered his voice further. "And they must never know. They're quite close to Degley & Sons, who own the damn place. If word gets to old man Degley, he'll move in and take all the credit, not to mention the profit."

"What's this about, Dick?" Adam glanced at his watch. "Because I'm telling you, I've got a stack of stories to write today, most of them piece-of-crap press releases that came in this morning. I don't particularly want to do it, but as you know, we haven't got half the news team we used to, so someone has to..."

"This is your way out of that," Wetherby interrupted. "We're not just talking a front page lead here, Adam. This'll be something you can sell to the nationals... but that would be a waste, in my opinion. If I were you, I'd be looking to write a book. I assure you, this is hot stuff."

"Ghosts are ten-a-penny, Dick." Adam stood up. "Especially if you haven't got any proof. Even if you *have* got proof, it's going to need be better than a few midges masquerading as orbs, or the odd creaky floorboard which suddenly becomes 'electronic voice phenomena'..."

"It *is* better than that."

"There are haunted houses everywhere. It wouldn't surprise anyone in Tunbridge if the Great Northern had one or two spooks. Nor would it particularly bother them..."

"Jack the Ripper."

"I mean... what?"

Wetherby peered up at him with po-faced sincerity. He even had the good grace to look a little unnerved by the information he was imparting. "Jack the Ripper, Adam... that's what we're talking about here."

"Jack the Ripper?"

"Are you denying that's the one murder case the whole world still talks about? The one that everyone on the planet would love to see solved? How would you feel about being the man who achieved that?"

"On the say-so of a ghost? That'd boost my credibility."

"On the say-so of DNA. Yeah... that's right, Adam. Modern forensics. No-one'll be able to argue with that, will they?"

Adam pondered this, refusing to allow himself even a tingle of excitement. "Let's get a coffee," he finally said. "I feel more than a little conspicuous standing arguing with you in this bus shelter, and I've got to get something inside me... at present I'm running on fumes."

"Are you telling me that building has been empty since 1889?" Adam asked, incredulous.

"No, course not." Wetherby stirred his latte. "It's been used for other things since then... British Restaurant during World War Two, stand-in Council Chamber when the Town Hall was being refurbished in the 1960s. There was even a flea-market there in the '70s."

"Think I remember that." Now it was mentioned, Adam had some vague recollection of going upstairs into the building as a kid, seeing collapsible stalls set up amid shabbiness and dereliction, selling second-hand records, paperbacks and other bric-a-brac.

"But it ceased to operate as a hotel in the summer of 1889," Wetherby added. "No reason was ever really given except that guests stopped staying there. We can only surmise, I suppose."

"You mean because it was haunted?" Adam did his best not to sound too scornful.

"The Victorians were very superstitious about suicide. As far as they were concerned, if anything was likely to cause ghostly activity, it was that."

Adam glanced again at the bits of paperwork Wetherby had pushed across the coffee shop table. Ironically, most of them were printouts from 1888 editions of the *Tunbridge Gazette*, his own newspaper, and related to the "dreadful self-destruction of a London Jew" in an upper room at the Great Northern Hotel on November 9th that year. It seemed that one Julius Baczkowski, who had arrived in Tunbridge that evening having ridden north on the all-day train from London, had cut his own throat with a razor blade – not once, but twice – and subsequently died on his hotel bed amid gouts of blood.

"Have you noted the date?" Wetherby asked.

Adam shrugged. "November 9th. What's special about it?"

Wetherby sipped from his cup. "November 9th 1888 was the day on which Jack the Ripper's last victim, Mary Jane Kelly, was killed. Her mutilated corpse was discovered at 10.45 that morning, the foul deed having been committed during the early hours. More than enough time for Baczkowski to catch an early morning train from London Euston and head north."

Adam eyed him sceptically. "I hope you've got a bit more for me than this."

"I've got a lot more if you'll hear me out." Wetherby sipped again, noisily. "When we first went into the Great Northern last week, on November 9th..."

"The same date on which Baczkowski died?"

"Of course. It was his ghost we were trying to contact. Bear in mind, all we knew about him at the time was that he'd committed suicide in his room in the Great Northern. We didn't know he was a Ripper suspect... in fact no-one did. He was never officially named as such, though I looked into his past afterwards and it wasn't too hard to find some suspicious details. To start with, he was a Polish Jew. Remember, at the time the police were strongly convinced the Ripper was of Polish/Jewish descent. In addition, Baczkowski was a boot-mender. You must have heard all that stuff about Leather Apron?"

Adam nodded, but still wasn't finding any of this persuasive.

"Baczkowski lived in Southwark," Wetherby said. "Which is across the Thames from Whitechapel. That may have explained why he was never fingered for the crimes – the coppers were convinced the Ripper was a local man who knew his way around, but apparently Baczkowski's ex-wife lived in Whitechapel, and he regularly used to turn up there drunk and causing trouble. He probably got to know the neighbourhood pretty well..."

"Just tell me what happened at the hotel the night you went in," Adam interrupted.

"Well... it's a bit of a dump, as you can imagine. The building's doors last closed in 1983 and it's been empty ever since. But we finally found the room where Baczkowski took his own life, and held a séance in it."

"I thought you paranormal investigators were all supposed to be scientists."

"We take a scientific approach... we *always* do." Briefly, Wetherby looked affronted by the implied slight. "We set up all our usual kit, temperature gauges, tape recorders, the lot. But if you're trying to contact spirits of the dead, there are some tried and tested methods."

"And did they work?"

"At first we got nothing. I mean it's a rickety old building, there were creaks, taps... all the usual things that TV mediums get so excited about when it should be plain to anyone with half a brain that town centre structures are constantly on the move. We heard all that stuff, but nothing particularly unusual. Until just before midnight – about quarter-to in fact, which was the estimated time of Julius Baczkowski's death – when there was a scratching sound. Really loud. From all around us." He paused, awaiting a response.

Adam gazed at him blankly. "Dick... I'd be more surprised if the Great Northern did *not* have its own rat population."

"Bollocks, Adam! These *weren't* rats. I worked in the Planning Department for eight years. I've been in more than my fair share of condemned buildings. I know the sounds rats make. This was nothing like that. What we were listening to were human fingernails, or something very similar, being drawn over a rough surface in long, slow movements. And it just went on and on, getting louder and louder..."

"Human fingernails?"

"For sure. Like I say, all around us... but with no visible sign of the cause."

"Someone was hiding. Someone who'd got there ahead of you and was trying to scare you."

"We considered that possibility, though it seemed unlikely. Degley's firm had provided us with the keys to go in. They knew what we were doing, but they weren't particularly interested. They're not even based in Tunbridge, they own dozens of similar buildings across the Northwest. As far as they're concerned..."

"Could anyone else have known? Someone at the Council maybe?"

"No-one I told," Wetherby said. "I don't make a big deal of this sort of thing... not at work, anyway. People might think it a bit weird."

"I wonder why?" Adam replied.

"Hey, do you want this information or not. I mean, you're not the only journalist."

"Go on... there was a scratching sound."

"Yeah. We couldn't trace it, but we really searched. Like I say, the place is mouldering to its foundations and crammed with rubbish, but we checked everywhere. All the adjoining rooms and passages. There was nobody hiding. Anyway, then it stopped – bang on midnight. After that there was nothing, no more phenomena of any sort... and we were in 'til seven the next morning. But the really spooky thing is what happened the next day, when I went back there."

"You went back?"

"Yeah. Alone." Wetherby finished his coffee. "I was

supposed to return the keys that afternoon. After the vigil, I'd obviously gone straight home and tried to get some shut-eye, but I couldn't sleep. I kept thinking about what we'd heard, trying to work out what it might have been, and then something occurred to me. The one place we hadn't looked when we were hearing those terrible sounds... under the floorboards."

Despite his innate doubts, Adam found himself listening with increasing interest.

"I intended to return the keys to Degley's agent in the afternoon, as planned," Wetherby said. "So I went back to the hotel just before lunch. It was still a scary old place, even at midday, especially with what I thought I knew about it – namely that someone had been concealed under the floorboards in that room."

"Perhaps going up there alone wasn't too smart a plan, Dick."

"On the contrary. Going up there alone has worked out perfectly for both of us. Or it will."

"How so?"

Wetherby leaned forward, intense of expression. "Because of what was lying under those floorboards when I lifted them."

"You actually lifted them?"

"Not all of them. Most were solid, but I found a few loose ones in the corner of the room where the bed would once have been. What I found under there, Adam, is what sent me scurrying off to look a lot more deeply into this Julius Baczkowski character..."

"Don't tease me, just tell me."

"It was a pair of knives."

The few diminutive bristles of hair remaining on Adam's scalp began to stiffen.

Wetherby sat back again. "Vicious looking things, they were... I'm not talking penknives, if you know what I mean. But both were very old and caked in rust."

For the first time that day, Adam couldn't form words, either scathing or otherwise.

Wetherby regarded him unblinkingly. "That's right, Adam. I found Jack the Ripper's knives."

Adam didn't get much work done that afternoon. At least, none that he was supposed to be engaged in. As official chief-reporter, he tended to be given a lot more leeway at the *Gazette* than would normally be the case. For example, he was more senior both in age and experience than the news editor, while the overall editor was a distant, omnipotent force responsible for several other titles at the same time, whom he rarely saw – so when, instead of transforming the usual raft of ho-hum press releases into reams of compelling column inches, as was his usual duty, he immersed himself in the known facts of the 1888 Jack the Ripper investigation, no-one actually noticed, or if they did, they didn't comment.

As Dick Wetherby had said, nowhere in any of the suspect lists did Julius Baczkowski's name appear. Which was perhaps surprising given how many suspects there'd been, though it was noticeable that a large number of these had been fingered for reasons verging on the ludicrous.

For example, Richard Mansfield, the eminent actor,

was connected to the crimes because of his hypnotic portrayal of Mr Hyde in the West End that summer. Similarly incomprehensibly to modern eyes, the wife-murderer Frederick Bailey Deeming was the subject of much speculation, even though it was known he was in South Africa at the time of the Whitechapel slayings. In addition, there were the usual conspiracy theorist suspects whom everyone already knew about: Prince Albert Victor, the Duke of Clarence; Sir William Gull, private physician to Queen Victoria; and even children's author, Lewis Carroll – in none of whose cases was there a shred of even circumstantial evidence. Perhaps more serious were the accusations levelled at the likes of Serewyn Klosowski and John Pizer. These had been persons of genuine interest to the police at the time, and for pretty good reason. Klosowski was a Polish immigrant to Whitechapel, a barber by trade, and had a violent antipathy towards women – he was later hanged for three different murders. Polish Jew John Pizer was another Whitechapel resident with a history of violence against the fairer sex; he'd previously been convicted of slashing prostitutes with knives. Present-day researchers had done their bit too, tossing a few other viable names into the hat: Aaron Cohen was believed to have contracted syphilis from a Whitechapel prostitute, and his subsequent violent behaviour led him to be incarcerated in Colney Hatch lunatic asylum – at which point the murders mysteriously ceased; Alexander Pedachenko was a Russian-born medical man and Czarist secret agent, who for a brief time was thought to have been at large in London on a mission to embarrass

Scotland Yard. Neither of those suspects impressed the modern-day 'Ripperologist' community – but both involved that Eastern European and/or Jewish factor again. Apparently, this stemmed from the alleged anatomical skills demonstrated by the murderer. Though the notion that he might have medical knowledge was jettisoned at an early stage of the enquiry, it was felt that he might be a butcher, slaughterman or furrier, skilled professions which in Whitechapel during the 1880s tended to be monopolised by immigrants.

But no matter how determinedly Adam perused the lists of names, there was no trace of a Julius Baczkowski.

Was that good or bad?

He simply wasn't sure. No-one had been prosecuted at the time. Even now, one hundred and twenty-nine years on, the case was still officially open, which meant that the police's preferred suspects must have had solid alibis. One footnote appended by a famous criminologist to an investigators' forum caught Adam's attention:

*The problem with the roll-call of Ripper suspects is that it reads like a Who's Who of 1880s London society. The reality is almost certainly that Jack the Ripper was nobody; that he was utterly faceless to the wider public. A street-sweeper maybe, a dustcart driver, a bricklayer or ditch-digger; a working class person of no fame whatsoever, who could move easily and anonymously through the teeming multitudes of Whitechapel, who could drink in the local pubs without causing a stir, and maybe even mix on familiar terms with the street-*

*women. The sheer ordinariness of this person would have been his greatest shield. That is why he wasn't apprehended at the time, and why he has never been named and shamed since.*

*Until now perhaps*, Adam thought, sitting back from his computer.

Briefly, he allowed his mind to wander.

Was it possible? Could it actually be...?

One thing Dick Wetherby had said was definitely true. If those were the Ripper's knives, and they'd been concealed under those floorboards on the same day Mary Kelly died, possibly there'd be DNA traces on the blades. According to Wetherby, Mary Kelly's grave was still visible in St. Patrick's Roman Catholic cemetery in Leytonstone. How difficult could it be to get a court order for an exhumation under these circumstances? It didn't help of course that Adam wasn't a police detective attempting to close a case. He was a journalist on the make, but it wasn't like there wouldn't be widespread interest. There could certainly be a book in this, and potentially a very lucrative one. Wetherby had mentioned the 1992 publication, *The Diary of Jack the Ripper*, which had controversially named Liverpool cotton merchant James Maybrick as the killer. The theory had been debunked since, but the book had still gone on to sell a million copies. Of course, in that case the author had been able to protect his position because all he'd needed to do was present a diary he'd claimed to have found and yet withhold it from public view until he'd struck a deal with a publisher. There'd been no necessity to dig up a dead body, no suggestion that he was in possession of a murder weapon the police might still have an interest in.

Of course, before Adam and Wetherby could work out any strategy, they had to retrieve the knives, which for some bewildering reason the council clerk had left in situ. In explanation, he'd muttered something vague about not wanting to leave his fingerprints on the weapons and trying to avoid interfering with something that might be classified as a crime scene – not without first consulting a 'professional' like Adam.

"If nothing else, I have to look at them," Adam had told him. "They're still under the floorboards in that upper room, yeah?"

"Right at the top of the building," Wetherby had replied. "I can find my way back to it easily enough. The only problem is, we'll have to go tonight... after dark."

"Why would that be?"

"Because we've no longer got permission to be in there. I've had to return the keys, like I said."

"So how do we get inside?"

"I made a copy of the keys first."

Adam had only just managed to keep a lid on his exasperation. "Well... if we weren't on the verge of committing illegal acts before, Dick, we almost certainly will be now."

"So do we just leave it? The find of the century?"

"No, we bloody don't. We'll go after dark. Where do you want to meet?"

"Same place as earlier."

"Not conspicuous at all, then?"

"It's a bus stop, Adam. There're loads of people coming and going there."

"Okay... what time?"

"How does eight suit?"

"Eight's fine."

Adam glanced at his watch. It was now nearly five. His shift was almost over. He had plenty time to go home, have a shower, get some tea, fabricate some not entirely untrue story to Angie that he was chasing an interesting lead, and then maybe sit on his bed for half an hour, agonising over whether this was a sensible course of action. To boost his courage, he leaned forward and tapped on his keyboard, calling up again the webpage concerning *The Diary of Jack the Ripper*.

That figure hit him again, right between the eyes.

*One million copies sold...*
*One million copies...*

And that find hadn't even solved the case, whereas this one might. He snorted with laughter. It was truly an amazing concept – that studious, bespectacled, ever-cautious and methodical Dick Wetherby might have made both their fortunes with some crazy ghost-watching stunt. But stranger things had happened.

The ghostly aspect of all this was another problem, Adam told himself as he walked from the car park to the railway station, pulling on a pair of leather gloves. It was ten to eight now, dark, dank and noticeably colder. A stiff breeze had picked up, whipping dead leaves along the pavement. Rush hour had ended, and it being a weekday, there was almost nobody around.

Mention ghosts and people would automatically snigger. It wasn't as if there couldn't be other more rational explanations for scratching sounds under the floor. Most folk would jump to the same conclusion he had – rats. Perhaps that was the story they should adopt: that Wetherby had been drawn to the corner where the floorboards were loose by local wildlife? No-one would particularly question that, except they might find it a tad convenient he'd then found these amazing artefacts. That said, claiming that supernatural forces had been at work might add some colour to the story. Okay, the usual sceptics would scoff, but it was curiously logical in a Gothic, romantic kind of way. The Great Northern itself would garnish the tale with hints of the esoteric.

Tunbridge boasted lots of town centre buildings that harked back to a more opulent era: towering edifices of industrial brick, but handsome too, decked in the mock-classical style with Italianate cornicing and traceried stonework. Even those now converted into office blocks or carpet warehouses, or simply standing empty and desolate, hinted at venerability. But none quite matched the Great Northern in terms of lost glory. It was no architectural gem – not by big city standards. But it had overlooked Tunbridge throughout the rise and fall of the 'muck and brass' empire and ever since, slowly gathering grime, its extravagant rooms filling with dust and decay. The thought that it had been partly used as a flea-market while the rest of it stood gutted and silent was shudder-inducing. Could the original architect ever have envisaged *that*?

Now, of course, it wasn't even a flea-market. Just a hulking outline in the Lancashire night. The dim lights from the one shop still open on its ground floor, the takeaway, failed to conceal the scabrous façade rising overhead. For the first time it struck Adam that they were heading inside there, that they were actually going to wander – or more likely *blunder* – through that warren of abandoned rooms, passages and stairwells with nothing but torches.

Wetherby was waiting at the bus stop, as promised. He was even in the same seat and had the same rolled-up copy of *The Times* jutting from his raincoat pocket.

Adam sat down alongside him. "Why did you decide to hold a vigil in *there*?" he asked.

"The shopkeepers downstairs had been complaining," Wetherby replied. "About noises from the supposedly empty floors overhead. Substantial noises... as if people were moving around."

"Why didn't the police go in?"

"They did. Not enthusiastically, I have to say. I mean, what was the worst they could find? Squatters? A bunch of kids looking to vandalise a property that had already rotted beyond recognition because its absentee owners couldn't be bothered looking after it? It was hardly a priority for them."

"And?"

"They found nothing. There was no sign anyone had been up there in decades."

"How thoroughly did they check the place out?"

"So thoroughly that when further complaints were made, they didn't bother going back."

Again, Adam's eyes roved the high, barren frontage. "You remember where the room is? I mean *exactly* where it is? So we won't be inside any longer than necessary."

"I remember." Wetherby glanced sideways at Adam, his thin mouth crooked into a half-smile. "Not scared, are we? The man who reports fearlessly on police and local authority cock-ups, on establishment corruption, on frauds and embezzlers and child-abusers?"

"Let's just say that none of that will help if you and me get caught breaking into this place. Quite the opposite."

"Well..." Wetherby stood up. He didn't seem half as nervous as he had done that lunchtime. "That's why I said meet me here at eight. It's a bit quieter now."

And that was true. Aside from people arriving at and departing from the railway station, there wasn't a great deal to attract anyone to this part of town with business hours over. Beyond the railway bridge lay the Hexley ward. That had always been rough. Row after row of crumbling terraced houses originally built to accommodate the population of Tunbridge's mills and coalmines, but, like those ancient industrial structures, the terraces and their occupants were long gone now, leaving empty lots and the odd derelict shell. The only folk to be found over there these days were dealers and good time girls.

Wetherby set off across the road. Adam pulled up the hood of his anorak before following. He didn't think there'd be any surveillance cameras trained on the entrance to the Great Northern, but you never knew.

They stopped on the far pavement, in front of the grilled entrance. The only person in view from here was the young Asian guy in the takeaway next door. He leaned on the counter, his uniform baseball cap worn at a jaunty angle, but his face disconsolate. He gave no indication that he'd noticed them, and they were quickly able to step out of his line of vision.

Satisfied, Wetherby produced a key-ring with two keys on it and attacked the lock. Even though he'd opened this same padlock earlier that week, only after much grunting and twisting did the thing spring apart. The grille opened outward with a dull groan. Wetherby stepped through, Adam bustling after him, eager to be away from prying eyes. The recess on the other side would normally be littered several inches deep with chip wrappers, curry cartons and the like, but Wetherby having been in here twice recently, all that had been cleared aside. Faded black-and-white tiling was just about visible in the exposed floor-space.

While Wetherby re-locked the grille behind them, Adam pressed forward, hands extended, until he'd reached the hotel's main door. It was made from heavy oak and had once been painted black, but said paint was now peeling off in scales, and where the great brass knocker had hung, only the corroded nubs of screws protruded through clots of oily dust.

Adam's eyes gradually attuned as Wetherby pushed up alongside him, prodding around the lock and attempting to accommodate the larger of the two keys in the finger-sized hole he finally located. Surprisingly, given that this lock was much older than the first, and therefore presumably much rustier, it opened quickly and easily, but with a dull *clunk*, which Adam fancied would echo through the entire building. The door pushed inward stiffly. After about three feet, it jammed, but that was sufficient for Wetherby to slide his gangling body through. Thanks to his stockier build, Adam had a little more trouble, but no sooner was he inside than Wetherby pushed the door closed again. There was another shuddering *clunk* as its catch reconnected, a sound that echoed and re-echoed through the empty rooms and passages above. Adam fumbled his torch from his coat pocket, but before he could switch it on a man spoke to them.

Or whispered. Semi-incoherently.

It was no more than three or four words, possibly "serve thine master". But it was delivered directly into Adam's right ear, as if whoever the fellow was he'd been waiting just inside the door. Adam reacted violently, swinging around, half shouting as he lashed out with the torch rather than actually switching it on.

"What're you playing at?" Wetherby hissed. He apparently hadn't heard anything, but now hit the button on his own torch.

It flooded their immediate area with light. The space was tight: enclosing walls turned scabrous and damp, the stairs that rose into blackness in front made from stained, uncarpeted wood. There wasn't room for anyone else to be standing there.

"I heard something," Adam said. "Right in my ear."

Wetherby pondered this, but didn't seem unduly surprised. "This place'll play lots of tricks on you. The main thing is... when we go upstairs, go quietly. We don't want that bloke in the kebab shop calling the police again."

To Adam's mind, the police turning up no longer seemed quite so ominous. But he understood the need for caution.

"You're sure there isn't already someone up here?" he asked as they stealthily ascended. "You know... dropouts, druggies?"

"We've just come in through the only entrance," Wetherby replied. "And we gave the place a thorough going-over the last time we were here. There's no-one... apart from that spirit. Assuming that's what it was."

*Yeah*, Adam told himself. *The spirit of Jack the Ripper. Hooray.*

The stairway was steep, the darkness at the top so intense that it might have been a black lid firmly closed. However, on the hotel's first floor there was more light than they'd expected. Here, they were back in the realm of windows, and though many of these were covered with dingy sheets or slanted boarding, the sodium glow of the streetlights outside managed to filter through, creating a brownish, almost sub-aqua gloom.

Adam had half expected to find the remnants of a once-fine carpet, perhaps an old reception desk with a bell at one end, maybe a chandelier suspended overhead, dangling cobwebs so thick with dust they were more like rotted drapery. But of course, all the hotel fixtures in this place had been removed long ago, as had any relics of its days as a restaurant and/or stand-in Council chamber. Again, he recollected how as a small child he'd come in here with his father when it was doubling as a flea-market. But there was no sign of the temporary stands and stalls that had been erected on that occasion either. All he saw now was a cavernous space that ran perhaps thirty yards to his left and thirty to his right. In the wall directly facing him there was a tall, arched window with fragments of stained glass remaining, though its former image was no longer recognisable.

The beams from their torches speared left and right as they pivoted at the top of the entry-stair, but did little to penetrate the dimness, exposing only sticks of broken furniture, scraps of fallen plaster and more dust-heavy floorboards. Adam sniffed. The air wasn't as foul as he'd expected; tainted by decay, naturally, but fresh breezes blowing through various apertures brought relief from this. Then his torch winked out. Only momentarily; but he had to shake and fiddle with it before it came on again.

"That thing not working?" Wetherby asked, keeping his voice low.

"Who's got a torch that works properly?" Adam replied, still fiddling with the device, as if the mere act of twisting it more tightly together would compensate for it being old and worn-out. "There's one under every sink in every house, but how often do they have bulbs or batteries? It'll be alright. Loose connection or something. Just goes on and off from time to time."

"Use the light on your phone maybe?"

"This'll be fine." Adam tried to keep the snap from his voice, but it wasn't easy given how irritated he was with himself for not having brought a better torch. So much for the investigative reporter. "Anyway, where to?"

Wetherby gave this some thought; it took several seconds longer than it perhaps ought to have. Adam shone his torch up into the council officer's face, which seemed curiously pensive.

"You're not telling me you've forgotten already?"

"I've not forgotten," Wetherby replied. "The thing is, Adam... we're *really* going to rewrite criminal history here. Have you considered that?"

Adam was briefly puzzled as to why Wetherby was bringing this up now. But then the truth struck him. "What you actually mean is how are we going to split the profits... yeah? Even though I'll be writing the book, you want an equal share, maybe more. And unless I provide you with some kind of confirmation of this, you're not going to show me the evidence. Is that right?"

Wetherby shrugged. "I obviously can't make you sign a contract or anything that's legally binding. Not at this stage. But it would be good to know your thinking on this."

"Look, Dick... we wouldn't be here at all if you hadn't found this stuff." Adam understood the guy's need to protect his interest, but nonetheless was frustrated that here was someone else expecting to make a fortune out of a book when they couldn't string two words together themselves. "But ultimately, you can't write the damn thing... and if you don't mind me saying, that's going to involve a lot more work than you and your mates spending one night in here as part of a vigil."

Though they conversed quietly, their voices echoed,

reverberating through the shadows. It was vaguely distracting in that it made it difficult to imagine that someone wasn't lurking nearby, eavesdropping.

"All that said," Adam added, "I can't do this thing alone either. We've got to convince people – agents, publishers, newspapers and the like – that what we've got here is real. And that's going to involve us making a very professional case."

"I can definitely help with that," Wetherby said. "I mean okay, I'm just a civil servant… but in the ghost-hunting community I'm widely respected."

"*Whoooaaa*, wait up! If we go big on the ghost-hunting stuff, people are *not* gonna buy it. It's the criminologists we want to appeal to. The obsessives who spend every waking moment trying to work out who Jack the Ripper was. For that, we need to be factual, we need to use science."

"Alright, but we keep this a two-man deal, yeah?" Wetherby said.

"I'm *not* going to cut you out of this," Adam replied. "I couldn't even if I wanted to. Suppose these knives are what you say they are. Suppose there's visible blood on the blades that can be traced back to the Ripper's victims? Even then we'll have lots of hoops to jump through. Interviews to give, phone-calls to field, articles to write. It's going to take at least two of us to handle all that crap."

Wetherby nodded glumly, as if this reassurance was the best he could realistically hope for. He offered his gloved hand. "Let's at least shake on it… a two-man deal."

Adam shook. "A two-man deal."

Wetherby strolled on, heading left. Adam followed,

stabbing his torchlight every which way. They entered a passage, which, without windows, was virtually black. At the end of it, they turned right and commenced climbing a wooden stair so narrow they could only ascend in single-file. From the top of this, rather than find themselves in another corridor, they had to progress through a trio of odious little rooms that had been stacked almost to head-height with furniture and other hefty oddments, many of these draped in mouldy sheets. Adam shook his head as they sidled their way around and between. Despite all he knew about civic matters and the hard-headed characters involved, it still amazed him that certain money-men would resist spending their cash to spruce up a premises like this and get some new companies into it, because that wouldn't alter its long-term value, which stemmed mostly from the mere fact it was a town centre property. To avoid risking a minor loss, they'd prefer to be owners of a crumbling ruin filled only with grot.

Then his breath caught in his throat – so sharply that it hurt.

They'd just entered the third room, and his gaze locked onto its far corner, where a figure clad in dingy white and wearing a tatty old clown mask was seated on a stool.

For half a second, Adam was frozen with shock.

Wetherby chuckled, an unusual sound for him. "Sorry, Adam... should have warned you." He grinned broadly, which was equally unusual, and perhaps with good reason, as it revealed an unsightly row of longish yellow teeth, all browning at the root.

"Christ almighty..." Adam stuttered, staring at the corner.

Wetherby edged his way over there, pushing junk aside. "This is probably a leftover from that flea-market you remember."

Clearly it was a mannequin, life-size and dressed in some kind of ancient Pierrot costume. Adam could even make out the pompoms down the front of it. But the really weird thing was that it seemed familiar. He wasn't sure whether it was possible to remember detail from so long ago – what would he have been, six years old? – but suddenly he was sure that he'd seen this thing before.

"Here you go." Wetherby pinched the clown's face by its nose, and lifted what was evidently a very old rubber mask with a mop of greenish, moth-eaten fur on top to serve as hair. Underneath it lay a featureless polystyrene head.

Adam still couldn't speak. He was now certain that he remembered the object, or at least the costume. He'd come in here with his father one Saturday morning. Well... not *here*, as in this crammed upper room, but downstairs, in the main lobby, where the flea-market had been set up. One of the stalls had been selling off old circus props or pantomime gear, or something like that. The woman behind the counter was a gypsy type with long grey hair and dangly earrings, wearing a big, multi-coloured poncho. But there'd been someone else with her too, standing alongside the counter rather than behind it – wearing this very same Pierrot outfit. Of course, it had been in good condition then, whereas now the clothing was dirty and threadbare, the mask yellow where it should be white, orange-lipped where it should be red.

At least the eye-holes were empty now, unlike that day back in the 1970s, when...

Adam shivered.

*"Nothing to worry about, m'dear," the gypsy lady said when he tried to hide behind his father. "All trickery. All façade."*

*The figure wearing the mask stared down at him, the white-gloved fingers meshed together across its belly. And those eyes glinting like pinpoints of fire...*

"When we first saw it, it was covered by a sheet," Wetherby said, letting the mask drop back into place, where it hung slightly askew, seemingly turned in Adam's direction. "We recognised its human outline though. Scared the crap out of us. Course, we had to uncover it to see what was underneath. There're a few other bits like this in here."

He turned to a smaller object on his right, positioned on what looked like an old office bureau. The featureless cloth draped over the top of it resembled a hangman's hood, especially when Wetherby whipped it away to reveal another polystyrene head underneath, this one still smeared with fragments of garish make-up, creating the impression of a face that had distorted in agony.

"You alright?" he suddenly asked, seeing how pale Adam had turned. "It's just bits of rubbish. Stuff no-one wants."

"Let's... let's get on, eh?" Adam said.

"Yeah, sure. We're almost there."

Wetherby sidled back through the junk, setting an old rocking chair creaking noisily, before reaching the next doorway and stepping through it. Adam backtracked in pursuit of him, but halted before the doorway, hovering there, peering with fear and fascination at the costumed form, in particular at its shadow-filled eye sockets, which still looked to be fixed on him. He wondered what he would do if he glanced away for a second and when he looked back found the mask's upward-curved smile curved downward into a frown. Of course none of that happened, though it must have been a trick of the light that the shape of the mannequin appeared to have adjusted slightly, as if it had shifted its whole body to look at him more clearly.

Adam reached out to still the rocking chair, then turned and passed through the door, jabbing his torchlight in front of him. It revealed a junction of three passageways lined with closed rooms and floored with mildewed planks, all leading off into darkness. But no sign of Wetherby.

He listened, expecting to hear the Council officer's receding footsteps as he plodded off into the distance. But there was no sound at all. At first. Then... abruptly, there came a faint rustling of aged cloth, as if something was stirring to life in the room behind him.

It was the perfect time for his torch to wink out, plunging him into Stygian blackness.

Adam almost shouted, though in truth he hardly dared. He listened, horrified, to what sounded distinctly like movement across the room he had just vacated, as if something was lurching its way through the jumble.

He jerked his way forward blindly, groping in every direction, cursing aloud as he dropped his torch and heard it roll away from him – and heard something else at the same time: the arthritic creak of the rocking chair again: once, twice, three times as something forced its way past.

"Wetherby!" he choked as he stumbled on, arms outspread but hands finding nothing he recognised. "For Christ's sake!"

Behind, he could now hear clear sounds of pursuit. Whatever it was, it had come out into the passage. With shuffling footfalls, it blundered along in his wake.

"*Wetherby!*" he all but shrieked.

If anything, that rustling tread behind came on with greater firmness.

Adam knew he was proceeding down an open corridor, and so drove himself forward recklessly, on the verge of running, sweat beading his eyebrows. At any second he would connect with something, even if it was the facing wall of a T-junction. But where would he go from there, left or right? As he deliberated, the stumbling, lifeless form at his rear sounded closer. Surely it would reach out for him now and latch a dirty-gloved paw onto the back collar of his coat? He'd been in the process of digging through his pockets for his phone. Now, by instinct, he gave up on this and dodged sideways, moving no more than a couple of feet before caroming backward from a heavily fastened door, toppling and landing with a *crash*.

Despite a darkness so dark it blotted out all vision, he sensed a tall, thin figure totter to a halt directly to his left. It towered over him, stationary yet within touching distance. Adam struggled to breathe, the air rasping through his chest, which had tightened like a vice. And then... a searingly bright light glared to life on his right.

It filled the immediate area of passage, revealing – nothing.

"Had a fall?" Wetherby enquired, emerging around the next corner.

"Jesus wept!" Adam jumped to his feet. He gazed back along the corridor towards the doorway connecting with the junk-room. It was bare of life; there was nothing there. "Dick by name, dick by nature! What the bloody hell do you think you're doing, scooting off when you know my torch is on the blink?"

"Sorry, mate... thought you were right behind me."

Wetherby sounded genuinely contrite, but Adam wondered if there wasn't some veiled amusement in his tone. He glanced back along the passage. His own torch lay close to that dark doorway. Only vague, indistinguishable shapes were visible beyond that – none of them moving, but he knew he hadn't imagined those sounds of pursuit.

"Which direction have you just come from?" he demanded.

"From round that corner," Wetherby said. "I was only a couple of dozen yards away. I heard you take a tumble."

"I could have... shit, I could've sworn there was someone behind me!"

"I told you, this place plays..."

"No, this was no trick. There was someone there. I *heard* them. They came out of that room."

"Adam, there's no-one else here, I assure you."

"I know that... that's the problem."

Adam's eyes remained fixed on the doorway as he walked back down there and bent over to retrieve his torch – he only realised that a diminutive grey-furred form had darted past him, vanishing into the room, when it brushed his arm with its whipping tail.

"Good Christ!" he yelped, jumping backward again. But Wetherby only chuckled, something he seemed to be doing regularly now, even though Adam had heard never him do it previously.

"There you go," Wetherby said. "That's your problem. A rat."

"A bloody rat..." Adam twisted his torch, and immediately its wavering beam was restored, the effect of which was to plunge what little he could see of the junk-room into deeper darkness. However, he knew he couldn't press on from here without at least checking. He ventured back to the doorframe and glanced through, torch held in front of him like a weapon. Nothing met his eyes except the sheet-covered heaps of lumber and the made-up dummy head and clown mannequin in the far corner, the latter still perched where he'd left it, mask hanging askew. Dust motes fluttered around it in the glow of the beam, but they fluttered everywhere in this place merely from the passage of air.

"A rat," he said again, under his breath. Listen though he may, no scuttling or scampering sounds came to his ears. No rustling of old rancid cloth.

They turned and pushed on, Adam urging Wetherby forward, telling him he didn't want to spend any longer in this decaying heap of brick than he had to. Round the next corner, they came to a broader stairway than the previous one. It had balustrades on either side, though again was made from bare wood, so it was impossible to prevent their feet from clumping as they ascended. Twice Adam spun around, spearing his light down behind him, convinced the echoes of their footfalls was someone following. On the first occasion his light revealed nothing, just the bare boarding at the foot of the stairs. But the second time there was a rat there; a horrible twisted little thing, sitting upright on its haunches, peering after them. In the glare of the torch, its tiny eyes glinted like points of flame.

Adam continued to watch it as he climbed – until he half tripped.

"Careful," Wetherby said from in front. "You're an accident waiting to happen tonight."

When Adam looked back again, the rat was nowhere to be seen.

"This place is a shithole," he asserted.

"Make a good opening for the book, won't it? The terrors we braved sniffing out the tools of the Ripper's trade."

Adam didn't laugh.

At the top of the stair, they joined another corridor. This, having not been involved in any of the temporary uses to which the Great Northern Hotel had later been put, was vaguely plusher. It possessed a carpet, though it slid beneath their feet and was green with rot. The tarnished relics of brass lamp fittings hung at head-height every ten yards or so. There was much dripping of water up here. It stained the doors and walls, while the plaster ceiling had entirely collapsed, exposing sodden, skeletal lathes.

"Cost millions to fix this place up," Adam said. "No wonder no-one's ever tried."

"It'll get a new lease of life when *we're* finished," Wetherby replied, halting. They'd come to the last door on the corridor. "Anyway, this is it."

Adam watched while his guide turned the handle. The door swung inward, and a foul blackness – fouler and blacker than it had any right to be, even in this place – exhaled outward. Adam had some fleeting vision of a vast but decayed presidential suite: tattered hangings on every wall, the immense Gothic skeleton of a four-poster bed, a colossal hearth deep in stone-cold ashes. But in fact, it was nothing more than a poky little room stripped of any ornament: damp, plaster-strewn floorboards; peeling walls; yet more exposed rafters.

A few lumps of half-melted candle were all that remained of the séance Wetherby and his cronies had held here. Behind the single narrow window, which still contained grubby glass, the brick buttress of a protruding left-hand wall afforded only the narrowest of gaps, beyond which lay the opaqueness of night, though even in daylight you'd have seen no more from here than the desolate waste of the Hexley ward. Oddly, it struck Adam that it wouldn't have been much better back in 1888: parallel lines of rain-wet roofs stretching to a distant horizon where a row of factory chimneys belched smoke and soot, the sky beyond them red with the hellfire of foundry and furnace. If Julius Baczkowski was the Ripper, he'd have fled one Whitechapel only to arrive at another, or at least a near-exact replica.

"So what do you think?" Wetherby asked.

"What do you expect me to say, Dick? Yeah, it's horrible."

"You could write an entire chapter on this room alone, eh?"

"Let's get real,' Adam retorted. 'It's just a gutted bedroom... probably not even safe to enter. The sooner we find these knives – or whatever they are – and get out of here, the happier I'll be."

Wetherby pointed to the farthest corner. Adam strode over there and hunkered down. When he prodded at the floorboards, they were indeed loose. Hefting the torch in one hand, he reached with his other and, one by one, lifted them, half expecting another rat to emerge – right in his face, maybe an entire pack of them.

Instead, he exposed an underfloor cavity and inside this a wad of dust-web so thick that it was more like a cushion, though as Wetherby had said, this had already been thoroughly rummaged. What had been retrieved from it now lay on top: two items side by side. A shadow flickered across the room – a fleeting ripple effect, nothing more, yet surely unnatural in electric torchlight. But this only distracted Adam for a fleeting millisecond. He gazed down at the knives. There was nothing exotic or ornate about them; they clearly weren't museum pieces. But they weren't toys either. If anything, they looked like basic butchers' knives; curved, heavy-bladed, bone-hilted, and more than capable of slicing open a human body. In keeping with this ugly thought, they were both spattered with age-old reddish/brown stains.

Adam's scalp prickled. Could it be? Was it actually possible after all these years?

"I can't believe it," he said slowly. "I cannot bloody believe it."

"I told you," Wetherby replied. He sounded strained with excitement.

"But, wait... these are in such good nick. They look sharp enough to cut even now. How could they have been preserved so well?"

Wetherby shrugged. "If they were down there all that time, undisturbed..."

"That's not good enough, Dick. People will say they look too good to be of nineteenth century manufacture. They'll accuse us of creating a hoax."

"I'm sure there's some test we can have done to prove it."

Adam hadn't yet touched either of the two weapons. He was long in the habit of doubting good fortune when it showed up – mainly because the occasion was so rare. But Wetherby spoke the truth. They didn't need to go public with this until they'd found some lab guys to back them up. Warily, he reached down, nudging the hilt of the first knife with his gloved thumb. He wasn't quite sure what he'd expected to happen when he did this. No raddled, bloody claw burst up from underneath to snatch his wrist. The knife didn't crumble to dust. In fact, when he caressed it properly with his fingers it felt solid: the blade didn't drop out of the hilt; its edge was indeed razor sharp. Eventually he took hold of it properly. It was heavy in the hand, but well-balanced. For all its length – the blade was maybe ten inches – he fancied it would be easy to manoeuvre at close-quarter.

It was only when Adam stood up that he went dizzy.

The floor of the bedroom tilted, the walls cavorting around him. He thrust an arm out to try and steady himself, but tottered against the window, face pressed on the grimy glass, seeing again those parallel rows of dingy Victorian terraces, jumbled chimneys, rain, mist. Briefly he could even smell it: the dank stink of winding brick alleys, of smoke, sulphur, urine, the foulness of diseased breath, of ragged clothes mouldering on emaciated frames.

"Christ!" he said, shaking his head as he forcibly jerked himself out of it.

Wetherby chuckled. "This place, I'm telling you."

Adam was startled to see that he'd jammed the knife into the wall. It had penetrated several inches into the rotted plaster. "Shit... look what I've done!"

"It'll be fine."

Adam tugged on it, waggled it, tugged on it again. He gripped the hilt tightly, fiercely... and with a dull grating of metal, the blade slid free, apparently undamaged.

"Good quality knives, these," Wetherby commented, approving.

The gash Adam had inflicted on the wall looked gruesome. A deep cleft; a trickle of greenish moisture ran freely down from it. He probed at it, even took his glove off to fully assess the smooth wetness of the incision.

"There's life in this old building yet," he observed, sniffing his fingertip.

Wetherby approached, bent down and scooped up the other knife. He adjusted it in his palm, as though he too appreciated its weight and balance. "Here's to the future, Adam. Our two-man show still on, or what?"

Adam didn't bother to answer, not even as they headed downstairs – just pulled his glove back on as he descended from floor to floor with quick, sure steps.

The stench of the place no longer bothered him. They saw no more rats. Even if they had, it wouldn't have mattered. That was the way of it. These vermin-ridden places, these blots on the landscape; they were loaded with foulness but also with memory. They were anchors to the past, which, grim and sordid as it often was, was the tale that underwrote all their lives. Speaking of which, they dallied in the junk-room no longer than they needed to. Adam was amused by the scare he'd had earlier. The unknown, frightening though it seemed at the time, should never be as daunting as the actual known. Because though he *knew* they had good times ahead, it would still involve an awesome challenge. When they left the building, Adam waited in the shadows while Wetherby closed the grille and fastened the padlock. It was late evening now, cars still passed and occasional figures could be spotted on the railway station forecourt, but what did that matter? Most likely they wouldn't notice anything. People didn't. That had been proved hundreds of times.

Once the building was secure, they set off walking.

"Keep that blade safe," Adam said.

There'd been an unspoken agreement between them to take one knife each. If nothing else, it would ensure that neither could gain an advantage over the other.

"Don't worry." Wetherby dug into his coat pocket. "Wrapped it in this." He drew out the bundle of cloth that had served as the hangman's hood in the junk-room. By accident, the knifepoint had torn two rents through a single fold so that when he opened it out, they resembled eye-holes.

Adam nodded as they passed under the railway bridge.

He'd been very careful stowing his own blade, wadding it in a handkerchief and placing it in a different pocket from the clown mask. The mask was neatly folded, but would need a new string. But that was no problem. An old shoelace would do. Anything they could find before they reached the Hexley ward, where all these years later the street-girls still plied their lonesome, night-time trade.

# Fragments of a Broken Doll

## Cate Gardner

Razor wire pinged. Howls echoed both without and within the city, shaking in the hollow of her belly. Trill pulled the tatty rag-doll to her chest, dragging at its limbs to dislodge grey and black and green stitching, her fingers working at the stuffing. The room was dark. It was always dark because she wasn't allowed a candle and the electrics didn't work, but her eyes had adjusted and she could see outside; find what was causing the razor wire to scream.

The house backed onto the prison, rents were cheap and either they lived here with a leaking roof, dodgy plumbing and the smell of death or in a cardboard box in a doorway. Harry had forbade her from working. She was too frail, or too young, or too old, or mentally incompetent. Always a different reason. Floodlights revealed most of the prison yard but the wall surrounding the prison was dark: a dull and pitted concrete topped with razor wire. Wood creaked as Trill opened the window. The doll's belly burst, throwing a ball of cotton stuffing into the wind that dropped onto the bleeding hand of an escaping man.

They regarded each other. Trill held her breath until it seemed her throat would explode. Harry told her the

*49*

prisoners were locked up because they'd murdered children and women and girls, always girls, and Trill knew she was both of those things, or was, or would be. Harry kept her safe. Harry and his uniform. Trill released her breath to spit on the floor. Now she couldn't find the man. He'd dropped from both wire and wall, probably onto the nest of old mattresses that the dossers slept on. If he'd landed on cobbles he'd have smashed a bone.

Good.

Trill crept down the stairs, which were determined to betray her. Harry didn't like her having the highest room in the house because she'd tumbled down stairs when she was very little. Age four or five or maybe sixty-two. He allowed her the attic because she screamed if all she could see from the window was wall. Snores echoed from the ground floor. Harry didn't like heights.

The keys hung on a hook beside the front door. Trill grabbed them, although she didn't want to open that door, but if Harry found them gone, he'd check the street and not the back yard. In the kitchen, rusted bolts left orange welts on her hands. If the prisoner were still in the alleyway he'd hear the scrape and he'd run. He'd hear the scrape and wait to murder her.

For a moment, the back yard seemed darker than her bedroom and her foot found the shovel she'd left out to trip Harry when he went for a smoke. She didn't like him smoking. Father smoked. She recalled puffs of orange hair and tar stained fingers, the strike of his belt, and the cough that echoed in the courtroom where mother pinched Trill's arm and then pulled her sleeve down to hide the bruises.

*Trill is clumsy.*

Something clattered in the back alley. The escaped prisoner was still there. The murderer. This had to be one of the silliest things she'd done and that included stitching her skirt to her knee when fixing her rag doll and telling her school friend that bleach tasted like apple juice. The latter proving the only time father was proud of her.

*Daddy's girl.*

Trill pressed her ear to the door out to the alley and then her eye to the gaps in the slats but she couldn't see and she couldn't hear anything. Her breaths came in jerks and she wasn't certain if it was due to exertion or laughter. Oh, she wanted to laugh so loud and so hard. People always laugh when they're nervous. She'd laughed when Katy screamed that her throat was burning, when Katy knocked the apple-juice-bleach onto her school skirt and a pale wash grew across the fabric. The back gate proved a struggle. Her fingers refused to work this evening, perhaps they were tired and needed to rest while the rest of her wanted to dance and whoop and catch a killer. A siren awoke within the prison. Its shrillness galvanised her hands and she pulled the door open. The wood splintered. The door hit her in the face and caused her to fall back. The killer pushed through the door and undid her hard work by bolting it. Now *his* breaths came in jerks.

The thing that worried Trill most was her nightdress. It was floral and ugly and she was certain it twisted above her Tweety Pie knickers. Her back hurt. The edge of the shovel dug into her shoulder; if it drew blood, she'd need another Tetanus injection. The killer did something unexpected. He helped her up.

"A little lady like you shouldn't be lying on damp cobblestones."

He sounded like he'd stepped from an old movie, the kind with steam trains and black and white streets, and where everyone wore hats. Blood dripped from his hand.

"They'll smell your blood," she said. "The dogs."

She pulled at the lace that cuffed her sleeve and wound it around his hand.

"Thank you for your kindness."

Then she whipped the lace off causing him to wince. She'd hurt someone who had sliced and throttled and stabbed women and children and girls. She'd kick him in the balls too but her knee didn't reach that high.

She showed him her fists. "So I can persuade the dogs to hunt elsewhere. Don't make me fight that back gate again."

She'd disarmed him, just as she had Daddy when she'd dragged her doll to the police station and for the price of an orange lollipop had given up the bodies in the chest freezer, including Katy.

"You can lock the gate."

She had the keys.

Wheels scraped along tarmac, sirens blared as the prison gates opened fast enough to rattle the bones from her skin. Dogs barked. Trill had traced the blood cloth against the outer prison wall, along the alley and out onto the main street. They wouldn't find the killer in her kitchen or buried under her bed. It's tiring when you need to move faster than cars and men and dogs, especially when you should have been tucked in bed hours ago. She should have warned the killer about Harry and his uniform.

Harry took care of her. Harry would take care of them both if the killer didn't throttle him. She kept to the side roads, like the killer would. Ideally she'd run along the alleys but they'd put gates up and she hadn't the skill or the time to climb over them. She'd get as far as she could and hope it enough distance.

Goosebumps peppered her arms and, despite the chill, tiredness caused her to close her eyes so that she moved as if sleepwalking. She wandered onto the High Street. Chaos woke her. The sirens couldn't compete with the noise erupting from the pubs, the drunks spilling out to join the taxi lines, the shouts, the hollers. She pressed her hands to her ears and screamed but no one heard and whether she was young or old no one came to her aid. If Harry would let her have a mobile phone she'd ring him to come and get her, she'd ring him and get him out the house before the murderer ate his liver.

*There are Coco Pops and Chocolate Mini Rolls in the cupboard and surely anyone would eat them before a man's liver.*

Trill dropped the bloodied lace in the collection tin of a man sleeping in the doorway of an abandoned shoe shop. She wanted to curl up next to him and sleep, but resisted. If the police found her wandering they'd take her home and find Harry's innards hanging from the lampshade.

There were cars parked outside the prison gates and chaos almost equal to the High Street. Trill passed in the shadows, her nightgown dirty at the hem and sleeves, but still white enough that they should have noticed her passing. They probably supposed a killer wouldn't wear flannelette.

Despite the reverberating shake of Harry's snores, the killer sat in the kitchen nursing a mug of tea and nibbling stale toast.

"You can't hide in the attic 'cos I hide there. Goodnight then. Oh, and please don't eat my Harry's heart."

Trill slept soundly.

The killer slept on the floor beside her bed. He clutched the tattered remains of the rag doll. She stepped on him as she climbed from the bed. Well it was a silly place to lie.

He awoke with a start and grabbed her ankle. If he snapped the thin bone, he'd trap her in the attic forever or until it healed. This didn't worry her. Outside the window, the prison remained alight and awake is if they still expected to find him lurking beneath a bench or camouflaged against the wall. She waved.

"What the fuck?" the killer said. "Get down."

"If I were harbouring a killer why would I wave at the guards, silly?"

"You look like you're signalling for help."

"Oops!"

She waved again.

He dragged at her nightdress, wrenching her away from the window and pressing his hand to her mouth. He tasted of blood and cigarettes. He shook her off.

"Did you just lick my hand?" He wiped it on his shirt. "Should have run last night, shouldn't have hid."

The killer paced the room. He'd attract Harry's attention, Harry would put on his uniform and blow his whistle, and they'd both hang from a noose. *They don't hang people these days.* Daddy had hung by the neck, tongue hanging from his mouth, a wet patch at his crotch. She hadn't seen it, of course. You weren't allowed to watch the dead swing no matter how much you loved or hated them. Mummy died in prison when her breasts rotted and no one cared, no one cared.

"Would you like a cup of tea?"

He paused.

She continued, "Before you murder me."

"I'm..." He crumbled then. Fell to his knees and sobbed so loud the dogs in the prison kennels would catch it.

"You don't like tea?" *Am I four or forty-five? Am I nine or ninety?* "Coffee then."

"I don't know why I... What came over me? Is it too late to go back?"

"It's always too late to go back."

She should go downstairs before Harry came upstairs and paraded his starched uniform and polished buckles. If the killer let her leave. If she were the killer then she wouldn't trust a child to keep a secret or an adult not to scream of murder.

Harry climbed the stairs. With each step discovery, with

each step a twitch of the killer's limbs as if she had injected a poison into his veins and he was about to slip into a fit.

A long breath to the window and Trill began to write HELP in the steam. Well Harry would have to think her kidnapped. Although, didn't Harry know her better than that?

"What sort of name is Trill?" the killer said, his pleasantness evaporating, nerves taking control. "You sound like bird food."

"Dad kept parrots that used to scream of murder until Dad froze them and served them to the neighbours as turkey sandwiches. Mum wore their feathers to the party. I remember laughing 'cos the neighbour's wife was a Polly and the husband wore an eye patch."

"You couldn't make it up," he said, pulling the door ajar and peering down the dark staircase. "Who's Harry?"

*Who's Harry?* "Harry is my"—*brother, son, uncle, grandfather*—"family. Harry will blow his whistle and the roof will fall down on all of us. You should hide in the wardrobe or under the bed or throttle my scrawny neck before I tell on you."

The killer had no time to consider this and chose an alternative solution. He hid behind the door. Harry was dressed and his hair slicked back with oil.

"There's been trouble at the prison. Keep the doors locked and if the police call, pretend you're not home. Stay away from the windows."

He glanced towards the window then but her breath had faded. In a moment he would turn and leave and either see the killer and cause a murder or leave her with the killer.

"You hear me, Trill?"

"Bring, bring, there's a voice on the line but the static is interfering with its message."

"I've no time for this."

A floorboard creaked. A heartbeat dragged out waiting to discover the outcome of the killer's movement. He had no weapon, no tie with which to strangle Harry. He had surprise but that only went so far. A swift turn to Harry's heels and the game was set.

Harry held his arms out to his sides and tried to keep Trill behind him. His mind would be whirring and the more it whirred the more the steam would fog until all conclusions ended in disaster.

"Let me call from the window," Harry said. "It's best for all if I alert the authorities to your location. You won't get away. You won't leave this house and see your family again. You don't want to stay here. Even we don't want to stay."

With no weapons between them, the men were evenly matched, although Harry had the hindrance of trying to keep Trill behind him. She giggled.

"I just need space to breathe," the killer said. "I'm innocent. Miscarriage of justice."

Trill spat at the word *justice*. Her spittle landed on Harry's shoulder. He didn't notice. Trill waved her hands at the killer who seemed to want to ignore her. *Pfft!* After she'd mislead the police and their vans and their dogs. She'd wave her nightie from the window and invite the dogs in for supper. *Yum, yum, killer's bum.* Harry pressed his elbow against her chest, urging her back, caging her in. She stomped her foot in the manner of a three-year-old and felt the pain of a seventy-year-old shoot up her leg.

With Harry distracted by Trill's strop, the killer punched him in the side of the head and Harry fell down.

"Oh!" Trill said. "Well that was rather naughty."

"I didn't mean. I just... I can't go back. I don't belong there. Have I killed him?"

"Possibly." She stepped over Harry's prone body. *No blood.* "Would you like some apple juice?"

"I just... I just... I just..." He played like a broken record.

Trill understood why Katy had drunk her apple-juice-bleach, she was little and stupid and trusting. This man though, this supposed killer. He lay slumped across the kitchen table. Harry picked up the killer's arm and allowed it to flop to his side. Then he sobbed. Trill sobbed too for it seemed the thing to do. Then she gathered the torn bits of her doll onto her knee and began to sew it together, this time careful not to thread the needle through the paper-thin skin at her knee.

# The Cardiac Ordeal

## Andrew Freudenberg

"Daddy have some?"

"No honey, that's yours. You eat it up."

Shane forced a smile as Linda attempted to get another spoonful into their daughter's mouth. The little girl wriggled and squirmed in her seat, always eager to find something more entertaining than eating. She would get round to it eventually but, at nearly two years old, saw no future in hurrying anything. A grubby hand reached out for her cup and swiped it onto the floor. Her laughter and delight subdued any anger her parents might have felt; she was just too cute to stay cross with.

"Do you want me to try and feed her?"

"You've got work. Don't worry about it. We've got all morning to eat breakfast."

Shane glanced at his watch and looked out of the window at the grey skies. It seemed like months since the weather had been anything approaching pleasant – probably an exaggeration, but he missed the summer months. At least then they could go and relax in the park on weekends. For the rest of the year they were virtual prisoners in their tiny home. They'd done their best to make it comfortable of course, but this aging council flat wasn't exactly bursting with potential.

"I need a holiday."

Immediately he regretted saying the words out loud. There was no mileage in complaining, and he couldn't face another argument.

Linda looked up from where she was sponging spilled milk from the ground. She looked tired, he thought. There were shadows under her eyes and her skin looked pale and dry. If anyone could do with a change of scenery, it was her.

"*We* need a holiday," he corrected.

"Maybe we'll be able to afford it next year." Her voice was a half whisper. "I should be able to work part time when Emma goes to nursery."

Living in the City did not come cheap. As well as the obvious things like rent, taxes and everyday bills, they both had student loans for degrees that somehow hadn't turned into lucrative jobs. *At least we found each other* he thought, scrabbling for a silver lining.

"Love you Daddy".

Then there was Emma. She was what kept them together and gave them the will to keep going. Throwing off the shadow of gloom that was enveloping him he reached across the table and grabbed her hands.

"I love you too pumpkin. To the moon and back..."

"Moon!" she shrieked and giggled, pulling her fingers free from his.

He pulled a face and swigged the remains of his coffee before standing up. His chair screeched as it dragged across the worn vinyl flooring.

"I'd better go."

"OK. Cheer up. How can you be sad when we have a little monkey like this in the house?"

"I'll be fine. I'm just tired."

"Say goodbye to Daddy, Emma. He has to go to work."

"Bye bye Daddy, bye bye."

He leant over his daughter and kissed the top of her head, breathing in her scent as if it might sustain him through the day. She smelled of freshly baked biscuits and it lifted his heart.

Shane arrived at work out of breath and out of sorts, barely swiping his entry card in time to avoid losing an hour's pay. The gate clicked and he was inside. He dashed to the cloakroom, where several acquaintances were donning the long blue lab coats that the company insisted on.

"You look like you had to run mate. Alarm not go off?"

"Somebody jumped in front of the train again."

"Poor bastard. I can sympathise."

"With me or him?"

"Ha, both I suppose."

"Well I'm alright, even if I did have to stand all the way. I expect they're still scraping him off the tracks."

"It might be my imagination but it seems to be happening more and more often these days."

"I think you're right. Hard times..."

"What a way to go though. I often wonder if they plan it in advance. My theory is that they're just standing there one morning, look around at all the miserable faces, and the urge just takes them. Screw it. Boom! They've traumatised some poor driver for life. Game over."

Before Shane had a chance to respond, a loud bell signaled the beginning of their shift. Like obedient

Pavlovian dogs they padded out into the massive warehouse and went to work. It was repetitive and thankless labour; robots retrieved stock from the darkened recesses of the building and he then transferred it by hand to the packaging department. There was a supervisor but Shane had only spoken to her once or twice; he took his orders from a small scanning device that hung from his belt. It was a twilight existence, dimly lit and smelling of oil and plastic.

That morning was like any other. He walked back and forth until another bell announced that it was lunchtime. His work coat was barely back on its hook before his mobile phone started ringing. It was Linda.

"Shane? Shane... she's gone."

Once the police had finally left they found themselves sitting opposite each other at the kitchen table. It had been a madhouse when Shane got home, a maelstrom of questions and activity. Now that they were gone the silence was palpable and there were only the darkest of thoughts to fill that void.

Linda was clearly in shock, her tear-stained face pale and drawn. Shane could think of nothing to say that hadn't already been said, or that wouldn't make it seem as if he blamed her. Of course he couldn't help but do exactly that. He hadn't been here after all, and anyway, how could anyone lose a child in their own flat? How could Emma have disappeared in the brief moment that her mother had turned away? Had something unthinkable happened that she just couldn't admit?

"You blame me, don't you?"

"No, of course not."

They both looked at the empty high chair at the same time.

Shane lay in bed staring at the ceiling. He felt brittle, as if he might shatter into a thousand pieces at any moment. Where was she? His mind raced through the possibilities, never settling on anything. Linda lay beside him, unconscious thanks to the ministrations of a police doctor. She had been hysterical while they went about their business and the sleeping pills were an act of kindness. Now she lay on her back like a corpse, arms by her side.

He listened to the sounds of London, the faint buzz of traffic and distant sirens. It was the same background noise that he fell asleep to every night, but now he could imagine his daughter calling out for him, calling out for help. It was a vast jungle for someone so small to be lost in.

"Sod this."

Tired of torturing himself he got up and pulled on his clothes. His watch read midnight. Grabbing his coat he headed out of the front door with the intention of having a smoke and clearing his mind. The moment that the latch clicked behind him, one of the other two flats on the shared landing opened their door.

A face appeared. It was a middle-aged man, red-eyed and skeletal. His thinning grey hair seemed to be the remnants of a Mohican and his ears bore multiple piercings. He looked Shane up and down slowly and nodded.

"So you lost your little girl?"

"I... She's gone missing, yes. I suppose the police spoke to you?"

"Me? No, I don't like talking to the police. I don't live here anyway. Christ, don't you even know who lives next door? What's the world coming to?"

"Well, we..."

"Calm down. I'm just yanking your chain. You're Shane, yeah?"

"That's right."

"Well Shane, I might be able to help you out. The only thing is that you have to do me a few favours first."

"What do you mean help me out? I don't understand."

"With your daughter I mean. You'd like to see her again wouldn't you?"

A wave of nausea passed over Shane.

"What do you mean? Do you know something? Where is she?"

Shane was suddenly in the man's face; ready to do whatever violence it took to get Emma back. The adrenaline headache was almost instant.

"Where is she? Tell me now before I do something I regret."

"Calm down mate, calm down. You need to take a deep breath. She's not here. I can help you but you have to do a few things for me first."

"What? Are you blackmailing me? I'll..."

"Chill. You're not going to like this but you have accept what I'm saying or you'll never see – what was it, Emma? – again."

"What if I go to the police? What then?"

"Then this conversation never happened and you've

lost any chance of seeing your daughter alive again. You can't go to the police; you can't speak to your wife. If you do either one of those things, and trust me I have ways of knowing if you do, then I will just disappear. You could risk it of course, it's a free world, but I guarantee you that this is your one and only chance."

The man shrugged as if to say he didn't care either way.

"What do you think? Can you deal with that?"

"That's... This is insane. You have to tell me where my daughter is. Now."

"Last chance Shane... Will you do what I ask or shall we just pretend this never happened?"

"Wait... I... What do you want me to do?"

"Now we're talking. Keep your head mate and this could end all right. The first thing that I want you to do is sort of a test, a starter for ten as they say. I want you to steal a book for me. It'll be easy. The owner is bedridden, a little old lady. You can just stroll in and pinch it. Wait there, I'll write down the title and address for you."

He kept his head down on the bus, horribly aware that there was bound to be a camera onboard. The leafy avenues of Primrose Hill were not his usual habitat, and just being here made him uncomfortable. *Never mind that*, he told himself; he had a job to do and that was all that mattered. *Focus on the goal, think of Emma.*

His hands were shaking when he got off at his stop. He stuffed them into his pockets and looked around. He was already on the right road so it was just a matter of finding number twenty-three. Odd numbers were on the other side, so he crossed over.

"Good morning."

Shane jumped. It was just an old man and a dog. He mumbled a greeting and walked on. Number twenty-three was much like the others. A low wall sat in front of a small garden that led up to a large creeper-covered Victorian terrace house. Not wanting to draw attention to himself he walked up the path and round to the left as he had been instructed.

There was a locked wooden door at the entrance to the back garden. Taking a deep breath he shimmied up and over it, landing with a thump on the other side. Instead of the neatly groomed plot that he'd anticipated, there was an overgrown mess. He could see various garden implements buried in the undergrowth and a small shed that had half collapsed at the back. *Keep going*, he whispered to himself.

Drawn curtains covered both of the back windows. He stepped up to the back door and tried the handle, fully prepared to smash his way in if it was locked. It opened at first try. Inside it smelled of cats and stale tobacco; it was oppressive and unwelcoming. He passed a kitchen on his left and a small bathroom on his right. The library was next and he stepped in.

The dim room only increased his sense of unease. He pictured getting caught in here. There was only one exit. *Come on Shane, it's just a little old lady. Do it for Emma.* Each wall had a bookcase, resplendent with cobwebs and dust. He peered at the titles, desperate to find what he was looking for. There was no kind of order and he was forced to look through them all. Half were foreign; some had nothing written on their threadbare spines. Eventually though he found it. As he reached out something slithered past his ankles. His chest tightened and he suppressed the urge to scream as he spun round to see a cat running from the room.

"Bloody hell. Nearly gave me a..."

The heavy footsteps on the stairs did not sound like they belonged to a frail old woman. Shane had no intention of waiting to find out. With the book under his arm he dashed out into the hallway and back into the garden.

"Come here you."

A quick glance over his shoulder revealed a bald behemoth striding towards him. Stuffing the book into his jacket he scrambled over the closed garden door and ran.

"Stop thief!"

Shane ran like he had never run before, ignoring the shooting pains cutting through his chest. His legs felt like limp spaghetti and he was concerned that they might just give out from under him. Fortunately they held and he managed to leave his pursuer behind.

Late afternoon shadows were winding their way across the pavement as Shane climbed the steps to *his* flat. He looked around furtively to see if anyone was watching; it would have been difficult to explain what he was doing to Linda and he wasn't sure that *he* would have much sympathy if he were caught by accident. His emotions were a strange mixture of doubt, fear, loss and the smallest amount of hope as he knocked. It was answered immediately.

"Ah, it's you. How did you do? Got it? Well done, well done. Right, that was the easy part. You'd better come in. Time for step two."

"I see. All right. Thank you. Yes, of course. Thank you. Bye."

Shane watched Linda hang up.

"No news. They want us to call them if we hear anything."

"Of course."

"They might do a press conference."

"Jesus."

They stared at their bowls of cereal without enthusiasm, lost in thought.

"I..."

They both spoke at once. Linda frowned.

"Sorry. You go ahead."

"No. It's fine. You first."

"I... I think I'll go and see Mary for a while today. Get out of the flat."

Shane sighed with relief.

"That's a good idea. I might go for a walk. Did me good yesterday."

"Right. Good."

"OK then."

Shane wondered how they could carry on from here, from this specific moment in time. Back to normality seemed such a long way up, he doubted either of them would have the will or strength to make that journey. Even if they got Emma back, their lives had been broken. He could see it in her eyes and he was sure that she could see it in his. Perhaps they would find something acceptable, a state of being that they could settle for, but he doubted it. After what he was going to have to do today, it seemed doubtful that he would even be able to live with himself.

He looked up from the table at Linda. She was watching him but turned away when he caught her eye. There was nothing positive they could say to each other.

"I think I'll go out now. I need some fresh air."

"Alright. I'll see you later."

"Right..."

He hesitated, still hoping to find something reassuring to add, but words failed him. Best he just do what he had to do – perhaps then they could connect again.

"See you later."

Once outside he allowed himself a breath of relief before processing the next nightmare that he had to deal with. The agony that he and Linda were feeling, the bottomless pit of loss that Emma's disappearance had engendered, and the price that he had to pay to try and fix all this; they were not things that he could deal with simultaneously. He was in danger of simply curling up into a ball and screaming if he couldn't find it within himself to compartmentalise these pressures.

His destination was within walking distance. He was glad of that. The bus had made him nervous and that was for a simple theft. This time anonymity was key. Of course this was London, and anonymity seemed ubiquitous, but that was a dangerous mindset for today. Perhaps he should have worn a disguise, but then Linda would have questioned what he was doing. He would just keep his head down and trust that luck was on his side. If he was caught later, so be it. As long as Emma was safe again it really didn't matter.

He arrived outside the office at two minutes before ten. The initial doubt, temporarily washed aside by desperation, had returned, threatening to derail him from his purpose. He leant against the wall and took some deep breaths, pictured his smiling daughter and reminded himself why he was here. It was difficult to reconcile the insanity of such an act with the purity of his purpose, or maybe trying to do so was in itself lunacy, but he had to be strong.

"Right..."

There were three names and three bells next to the tatty black door. The top one read 'Daniel Knight – Solicitor'. He pressed it and the intercom crackled in response.

"Come on up. Third floor."

*We've made an appointment for you at ten. Just go in. Do it and leave. It'll be over in no time.*

This was it. He took the first and second flights of stairs quickly then paused on the third. He pulled the thing that they had given him from his pocket.

*Make sure you give it a few seconds to warm up.*

He switched it on, counted to five and carried on up the stairs.

*Don't feel bad. He's a terrible person. Just think of your daughter.*

"Come in."

Shane put the Taser behind his back and entered.

Knight was sitting at a desk crowded with piles of books and paperwork. The walls were lined with old filing cabinets, some with their drawers half open. The man himself was red-faced and obese, sweating in a pinstripe shirt. He didn't wear a tie.

"Welcome, welcome. You're right on time. Now, let me see. Was this to do with a house purchase?"

Shane's fingers tightened around the weapon. The sound of his own heart beating almost drowned out the man's words. He had to do it now or he never would.

"I'm sorry..."

He stepped towards the desk and pointed the Taser at Knight's chest.

"What the hell is that?"

Knight rose from his seat, inadvertently making himself an easier target. Shane fired and two electrodes shot out and stuck to the astonished solicitor. Electricity arced across the wires and into his body.

*He has a pacemaker.*

The target froze, rigid for a moment, before falling forwards and knocking the contents of the table flying. His head hit the wood with a crunch and Shane could see blood as Knight slumped backwards onto the floor. He walked cautiously round to the body.

*Double check that he's dead. Dead is the deal.*

Daniel Knight was not coming back. His eyes were wide open and motionless; there was pink drool on his lips. Shane flicked the off switch and pulled the wires free from the gun before stuffing it into a pocket. Time to leave. On the narrow stairs he met a silver-haired woman in a business suit coming the other way.

"I heard a bang. Is everything alright?"

Shane didn't answer, just pushed past her and ran down as fast as he could. Once he was out in the street he took off, turning into the first side street that he came to. Nobody appeared to be giving chase but he kept going until, winded, he had to stop and catch his breath. Nobody gave him a second glance, despite his guilt feeling like a neon sign above his head. There was a bus stop just along from him where half a dozen people stood milling about, as if it was simply another ordinary day. How could they not know? How could it not be obvious that he had ceased to be like them, that he was now a killer?

As he walked the rest of the way back home he tried to fill himself with hope. Hope was all that he had now. The return of his daughter was the only thing that could compensate in any way for what he had done. Without it he was doubly destroyed. He tried to imagine what it would be like to hold her again, to lift her up and squeeze her tight, to see her smiling face. He couldn't hold on to the thought though. He kept thinking about what he had done. The path that he had taken might well secure her safety, but he would never be the same.

The door opened before he could knock and his nameless tormentor appeared. His face was twisted into a grotesque smile.

"Here he is, the man of the hour! Come inside, come inside."

Shane stepped into the hallway of the tiny flat and pulled the door closed behind him.

"Where is she?"

"Hold on now mate..."

"Don't give me that, where the hell is she..."

Shane grabbed a handful of the man's shirt, his self-control slipping away.

"Woah there, you need to be careful. You're only one step away from seeing the girl. One step..."

"Really? I'm starting to doubt she's even alive. I ought to..."

"Let me go and I'll prove it to you. Take a deep breath mate, before you hurt yourself."

Shane forced himself to step back.

A small lock of golden hair appeared in the man's hand.

"I thought you might ask, so here you go."

It vanished again, as quickly as it had appeared.

"That's not proof. How do I know it's hers?"

"It's hers. That's all you have to know. Now, the question that I have to ask you is this: how badly do you want her back? Is she that important to you?"

"I've just killed a man for you and you're asking me how important she is to me? Do you have kids?"

"God, no..."

"She means everything to me, everything. I'd do anything to get her back."

"Now we're talking. You might just get to see her again at this rate."

"Might? After what I've done?"

"You've got one more thing to do and then you'll have her back. I swear to you, on my Mother's grave, one more thing. This is what we've been building up to. You're not going to like, it but the choice is entirely yours. Do this one thing and you get to see little..."

"Emma."

"Emma, that's it. Do this one thing for me and you get to see Emma again."

"Name it."

"Bring me your wife's heart."

"What?"

"Cut your wife's heart out and bring it to me. Then we're done."

"You're crazy. I'm not doing that."

"The choice is entirely yours mate. That's the price. You can rant and rave, as I'm sure you'd like to, but that's how it is."

"I can't..."

"Tell you what, have a think about it. Hopefully I'll see you back here shortly with what I want. If not, no hard feelings."


Linda was sitting at the kitchen table. Her eyes were red and puffy and damp streaks stained her cheeks. She watched him come in.

"I didn't expect you back so soon."

"No, I didn't think you would be here either."

Shane walked over to the kitchen sink and leant against it with both hands, his back to Linda. He closed his eyes. His body ached and he felt as if his back might break from the invisible weight bearing down on him. How had he managed to get to this point? Without thinking he pulled open the drawer where they kept their carving knife.

"It's not in there."

He turned slowly. Linda stood behind him, the missing item gripped tightly in her hand. His gaze wavered from her face to the blade and back again.

"So he got to you too? Really? Why didn't you tell me?"

"Why didn't *you* tell *me*?"

"He told me not to. I didn't want to risk it."

"Same."

"Give me the knife."

"No."

"Put it down at least."

"No."

"So you're going to kill me then? Cut out my heart?"

"I don't want to but..."

"Emma."

"Shane, I have to get her back. I have to."

"There has to be another way Linda. I don't want to die."

"Sorry."

Her expression hardened and she lunged towards him. He grabbed her wrist before the point reached him and they struggled for control of the knife. He was larger and had weight on his side, but she was determined. Just when he thought he had loosened her grip, she bought her knee up and he had no choice but to back away momentarily.

"This is madness."

He grabbed a chair and held it out in front of him, swinging it as he advanced on her.

"You can't win, you know. Throw it away."

"Someone has to die."

The blade shook in Linda's grasp but she showed no sign of letting go.

"Look, we could go next door together. Force him to tell us where she is.'

"Someone has to die… for Emma."

"No…"

She tore her own throat open with a vicious slash, cutting through to the artery and sending a spray of crimson arcing over him. He could only watch as the knife fell to the floor and she grasped at the wound, an expression of surprise fading while she bled out in front of him. She seemed to be trying to say something but he couldn't make it out. She made a last desperate gurgling sound and then she was gone.

Shane sunk to his knees and wept, devoid of thought or understanding, drowning in darkness. When he could cry no more he steeled himself to do what had to be done. He butchered her in silence, mechanically, until he held her still-warm heart in his hands. He staggered to his feet and carried it outside.

Next door was unlocked and open, a crack of darkness clearly visible from outside. He elbowed his way into the flat.

"Here it is. I've got what you wanted. I've done what you asked. Give me my daughter."

His voice echoed around the empty rooms. There was nobody there, nor any sign that there ever had been. There was nothing.

# *The Lies We Tell*

## Charlotte Bond

Cathy opens her daughter's schoolbag and finds a letter stuffed down in the back pocket. She opens it, narrowing her eyes as she reads, then strides into the kitchen, clasping it in front of her. She shoves the letter between her daughter's face and the cereal bowl.

"Isabelle, what's this?"

Isabelle looks up. Cathy sees both calculation and fear in her wide blue eyes.

"A letter?"

"It says we've got a parents' evening next week. When were you planning on telling me this?"

"We only got it yesterday," Isabelle says, her voice small.

"Really? It's dated last week." Isabelle looks down at her cereal and Cathy feels anger prickling her skin. "What have I told you about telling lies?"

"That I mustn't," Isabelle says, her voice even smaller.

"That's right. We don't tell lies in this house. You know what will happen if you do..."

Isabelle doesn't reply but shrinks lower in her chair.

Ethan, Cathy's son and Isabelle's older brother, snorts into his tea. "Yeah, right," he says, matching his mother's glare. "Everybody tells lies. Even you."

"No I don't."

*Click*

She glances at the radiator. *Shit. That's all I need. Don't break on me now.*

Cathy turns her attention back to her daughter. "I'm going to fill in this form and give it to you. If I find out that you've not handed it in, there'll be trouble. Understand?"

"Yes, Mum." Isabelle's voice is practically a whisper.

Cathy nods. "Good. Now get ready for school. I've got a showing at nine and I can't be late."

*Click*

Cathy scowls at the boiler then marches to the bottom of the stairs. "Vikram!" she calls. "The bloody heating is playing up again. It must be air in the pipes. Get it fixed, will you?"

Her husband, appears at the top of the stairs. As he descends, he does up his tie. "I'm backed up at work, Cathy. I've got staff appraisals to do. Can't you take an afternoon off?"

"No, I can't. It's much easier for you to take time off."

*Click click*

She points at the radiator in the hall. "There it is again! Did you hear it?" Vikram hesitates. She can see by his frown that he didn't. "Fine. I'll sort it. Just like I sort everything else around here."

*Click*

She glances at her husband, to see if he's heard it this time. It's louder out here in the hall for some reason. But he has turned his back on her, using the hall mirror to straighten his collar. She glares at the back of his head.

His lustrous black hair, which she'd fallen in love with, is thinning and streaked with grey. In his reflection she can see the lines around his eyes: dark crinkled skin showing his age.

*What did I ever see in him?* she thinks as she climbs the stairs. *Whatever it was, it isn't there now.*

Cathy pulls up outside the property at nine o'clock sharp. The viewing is booked for nine-thirty, but she likes to arrive half an hour early. It gives her a bit of time before the rush of the day engulfs her. She has no qualms about the lie she'd told her daughter.

Cathy opens the door, pushing back against the accumulated mail. She scoops the envelopes up and dumps them in the bin. Then she does a walk round of the property, checking everything is in order – although this semi has been empty for about six months so it's unlikely anything has changed. Virtually no one is interested in this place after they've looked around and done a bit of research. The area is a dive, the place is riddled with damp, and although the owners have tried to impress with a brand new ensuite, the plumbing is shoddy and water leaks everywhere whenever you turn on a tap. She finds a dead fly on an upstairs windowsill and disposes of that in the bin as well.

When she is satisfied everything is as it should be, Cathy sits down in one of the few remaining chairs and digs out her phone. She glances at her watch: 09:16. A good amount of time to herself. She opens up the patience app and starts a new game. In a drunken row once, Vikram had told her it was ironic how she loved that game so much given how little patience she had with everyone else in real life. Cathy had retorted with a home truth of her own. She forgets what it was she herself said, but she still remembers his words every time she opens the app.

The viewing couple arrive five minutes early, which annoys Cathy. But she plasters on her best estate agent smile and ushers them into the property. They exchange formalities, information and small talk before Cathy says, "Shall we get started? This really is a lovely property."

*Click*

The sound makes her jump. It's coming from behind the couple. She tries to peer round them.

*That's odd. The radiator's behind me, not them. Maybe there are some water pipes in the walls.*

"Really? How so?" asks the man, leaning to his left slightly to insert himself into her field of vision.

Cathy recovers herself, focusses on him and begins the sales patter. "It's near local schools, if you're thinking of starting a family—"

"No." The woman says it brusquely, indicating there is a history.

Cathy doesn't miss a beat and her smile doesn't slip. "It's only a short walk to the shops and many of the pubs and restaurants around here are excellent."

*Click*

"In fact, my husband took me for an anniversary dinner in a lovely place just around the corner from here. I can highly recommend it."

*Click*

She grits her teeth but the couple are staring around as she talks. They look interested in the property and Cathy doesn't want to lose that, especially if they haven't noticed the annoying clicks. She forces her smile wider. "Shall we start in the kitchen?"

They do a tour of the kitchen, Cathy standing with her shoe over the cigarette burn in the linoleum. Then the lounge, the dining room and finally back to the hallway.

"Shall we venture upstairs? The bedrooms really are the best bit."

*Click*

Cathy gives a nervous laugh. "I'm sorry about that noise. Must be air in the pipes. We have the same thing at home."

The couple exchange a glance then the man says "Sorry? I didn't hear anything."

"That's good then. Must just be my ears attuned to it. It'll be sorted before you move in."

*Click*

"Shall we? There's a beautiful view from the window of the guest bedroom, and the master bedroom has an ensuite, relatively new, all in good working order."

*Click*

*It's okay. They can't hear it. It's not spoiling anything.*

When the upstairs has been inspected, Cathy leaves them alone to discuss their options. She takes herself into the kitchen, firing up her app again and losing herself in the methodical game. It soothes her nerves, on edge from the constant clicking of the heating.

Halfway through her third game, the man pops his

head around the door. "Do you think there's any leeway on the asking price?"

Her fake smile widens.

❖

By the end of the day, Cathy has secured two offers: the couple from this morning have made an offer on the house, and another pair have made an offer on a flat that she showed them round yesterday. She works late, sorting through the paperwork and pinging off emails. She texts Vikram, telling him to pick up the kids, then ignores his replies. She knows he'll do it if she doesn't answer.

The office is empty when she finally shuts down her computer. She is grinning, and feels like she's floating on air as she takes the lift down to the underground carpark. There are no people but plenty of cars; the air heavy and smelling slightly of petrol.

Her heels give off staccato beats on the tarmac. She pulls out her phone and checks her messages. There are six texts from Vikram, each of them piling on more and more anger until he's writing in capitals with an abundance of exclamation marks, telling Cathy how he's had to call in his sister and that Cathy is a terrible wife and mother.

She smirks as she puts her phone away. "Yeah, yeah, Vikram, but you'd be lost without me."

*Click*

Cathy's feet stutter to a stop. She stares around. There are thick pipes running along the walls, but somehow she knows the noise didn't come from them. Some primal instinct, buried deep inside, tells her that she's not alone in this subterranean room.

"Hello?" she calls out. She clenches her fist, ensuring the stones of her engagement ring are uppermost, ready to gouge a potential attacker's face should she be forced to hit out into self-defence. "Hello?"

There's a rasping noise that takes her a moment to identify: it's the sound of something being dragged over the floor. The noise seems to surround her so that she can't tell where it's coming from.

*What the hell is that?*

*Oh god. What if it's a killer and he's dragging the body of his last victim to his car?* The idea seizes hold of her mind and she suddenly knows that this is exactly what is going on.

*There's a killer in here, and he's coming for me.*

"I'm going to call the police!" she calls out.

The dragging noise ceases immediately and the quiet is somehow worse. Her pulse races and her stomach churns. She glances towards her car. It's about twenty feet away. *Can I make it? Is that enough of a head start if he comes after me, wherever he is?*

The silence stretches out as Cathy considers her options, then the dragging sound starts again and it's too much for her. She pelts towards her car, every second expecting a hand to grab her collar, yanking her backwards.

She presses the key to open the doors; the lights flash. She is running so fast she practically slams into the driver's door. As she pulls it open, she risks a glance behind her. The car park is empty. She climbs inside, shuts the door and locks it. Her breath forms fog on the window as she pants heavily. Shaking, she looks in the mirrors, trying to spot her potential assailant. She thinks she sees him in every shadow.

Cathy slides the key in the ignition and, with a screech of tyres, she is flying towards the exit. She presses the button to make the barriers rise and they do so with the awful slowness of a nightmare. She's going so fast she fears she might crash into them, but she doesn't want to slow. As she speeds underneath them, there's a sharp metallic twang as the car's aerial clips the barriers.

Then she is on the main road and driving away, her knuckles tense and white on the steering wheel.

By the time Cathy reaches home, she's just about calmed her nerves. She's poured her fear into road rage, leaving her drained but more mentally balanced.

She parks up and gets out. As she reaches the front door, it is pulled open. Vikram stands there, his face contorted with fury. But then he takes in her appearance and his eyes widen.

"Cathy, what's happened? You look dreadful."

Realising that here is a smooth way to avoid an argument about the kids, Cathy allows her shoulders to slump. She pushes past him, sighing as she drops her keys on the hall table. "I worked late and there was someone in the carpark. I'm pretty sure he was going to attack me. He stalked me and he was dragging something. It scared me shitless." She gives a nervous little laugh that isn't feigned.

"Oh hon," Vikram says, pulling her into an embrace.

She tolerates it because it's preferable to the row that had been brewing.

"Thanks. I just want to get in and forget about it. What's for dinner?"

"Just some ready meals I picked up on the way home." Vikram's face hardens as his mind clearly circles back to his anger. "I didn't have much time, what with you texting at four o'clock to say you couldn't pick the kids up from their clubs."

"Sorry, work was terrible. I just couldn't get away." She reaches out, cupping his cheek the way she did when they were young lovers. His stubble prickles her skin. "You're such a sweetheart. I love you."

*Click*

She snaps her hand back as if electrocuted. "Did you hear that?"

Vikram cocks his head. "No."

"It's the bloody heating again."

He puts a hand on her shoulder and smiles gently. "Well, that's a job for tomorrow. Let's just get some dinner, okay?"

Vikram goes into the kitchen as she hangs up her coat. She glances at the post piled up on the hall table. There's a folded piece of yellow paper with her name handwritten on it. Frowning, she unfolds it. The paper is thick, more like vellum than paper. Inside is written a number.

$$999,887$$

The ink is smudged and there's an unpleasant, greasy feel to the paper. Her frown deepens. The hairs on the back of her neck prickle as if someone is behind her, so close their breath chills her skin. She turns, but the hallway is empty.

Exhaustion sweeps through her then. She goes into the kitchen, puts the letter in the bin and pours herself a large glass of wine.

Two days later, Cathy pulls up outside Ethan's school, tyres screeching as she slams on the brakes. The fury is like a white-hot rod running through her core. She can't decide who she's most angry at: Ethan, for being ill when she was waiting for an important call; Vikram, for not being free to pick up their son; his sister, for not being free either; or herself, for being a shitty mother and putting work before her children. Although she's pretty sure it's not the last one.

"Bloody kids," she mutters as she grabs her bag and climbs out of the car. "Sometimes I really wish I hadn't had them."

She walks to the school office, her back straight, her stride even. She ensures her expression makes it clear just how busy she is and how annoyed she is at having to be here. The receptionist is unfazed.

"Just sign in please, then I'll take you to Nurse Wilkinson." Cathy scrawls her name and details, taking a small amount of pleasure in making her writing so atrocious that it's practically unreadable. The receptionist doesn't seem to care. She signs the book herself then pushes a buzzer that opens the door.

Cathy follows the woman down the corridor, eyeing each watermark or piece of peeling plaster with disdain.

*What's happened to all the bloody taxes I pay? Aren't they supposed to keep the school looking decent?*

The receptionist pushes open the door to the nurse's room. Cathy stares around. It's empty. "What's this?"

A woman in a white top and black leggings steps out from behind a screen and smiles broadly. "Ah, Mrs Chaudhary?"

Cathy nods. "Yes. I'm here to collect my son. Where is he? This had better not be a waste of my time."

The nurse's expression hardens. She glances past Cathy to the receptionist hovering beyond. "I've got this, Rachel. You can go." As the door behind Cathy closes, the nurse smiles reassuringly. "I promise it's not a waste of your time, Mrs Chaudhary. Ethan is indeed unwell, and is currently in the men's toilets."

Cathy wrinkles her nose. "Which end of him is it?"

The nurse gives her a sympathetic look. "Both ends, I'm afraid."

Cathy rolls her eyes. "Bloody brilliant. Just as well I keep some grocery bags in the car. How long will he be?"

The nurse glances at the clock and her forehead creases in concern. "He has been in there a while. We'd best go and check on him."

The nurse leads Cathy to the staff toilets. "We use these for the poorly children. It helps keep them separate from the rest of the school and control infections." She gives Cathy a knowing look. "I don't need to tell you that adults are much better at washing their hands than children, so the risk of bugs spreading is much lower putting them in here."

"Can I just go in and get him?" Cathy asks impatiently.

"Sure. I'll head back to the infirmary. Come find me if there's a problem, but otherwise you can just take him." She smiles again and heads back down the corridor. Cathy glares at her retreating back.

*My, you're quick to dump and run, aren't you?*

She pushes open the door. The sickly sweet smell of urine wafts over her, but there's also something below that. It's just a hint, but it smells like meat gone bad.

*God, just what has he been throwing up?*

"Ethan?"

There is silence. She can see all of the cubicle doors are closed, but only the one next to the wall has a red bar on the lock indicating it's occupied.

She steps inside. "Ethan, it's Mum. I've come to take you home, at great expense to my day, I might add."

"Mum?" The voice is quiet and edged with fear.

"Yes. Who else would it be? Now hurry up. Unless you're throwing up, in which case get it all out of your system. I've just had the car cleaned and I don't want you vomiting in it."

"Mum... there's something in here with me."

"Yes. Me."

"No, Mum. Next to me. In the cubicle. It smells horrible. I can hear it breathing."

Cathy's eyes flick to the cubicle next to her son's. Another waft of that rotten smell assails her nostrils and nausea flutters in her stomach.

"Don't be ridiculous. There's nothing there."

*Click*

"What was that?" Ethan asks, panic clear in his voice.

Cathy can't answer. Her mouth is dry. The sound definitely came from the cubicle, not from the pipes or the radiator this time. Her gaze drifts to the gaps beneath the cubicle doors. She can see her son's feet in one, but the one next to him appears empty.

"Please, Mum. Check. Please." The pleading, frightened tone speaks to Cathy's mothering instincts, buried as they are, and she's walking forward before she even realises she's moving. She halts in front of the door, trapped by indecision: to fling it open hard and fast, or push it open gently?

She reaches out a shaking hand and pushes the door gently. She is convinced she'll see some hulking monster with oversized jaws that click and clack when it moves them. But the cubicle is deserted. Something has been there, however – there's a bloody handprint on the pristine white toilet seat.

Cathy reels backwards, sickened and appalled. She sees a bead of blood trickle to the edge of the seat, forming a droplet, before the door closes on the rebound.

Something is scrabbling at the back of her mind, a memory trying to force its way out. Blood. Bloody... She can't quite grasp it.

"Mum?"

Cathy's tongue feels thick in her mouth. "Can you move?"

"Yes."

"Then let's get the hell out of here."

The red bar turns green and Ethan's pale face peeks out. "What was it? Did you see anything?"

"There's nothing there." Cathy pauses, unconsciously

waiting a beat to hear that click, but it doesn't come. "Hurry up. I want to go home."

They walk down the corridor at speed. Cathy grips Ethan's shoulder tightly, although whether she wants to keep him close for his safety or hers, she cannot fathom. She just knows she needs to get outside and let the fresh air wash the stink from her nostrils. She ignores the receptionist calling after her and waving the signing in book. When they finally step outside, Cathy takes three deep, gulping breaths before she feels strong enough to walk to the car.

Ethan retches three times on the way home, but nothing comes out of him except saliva, which is caught by the plastic bag she's given him. By the time they pull into the drive, he's squirming and making the most appalling smells. Cathy undoes the front door as quickly as possible, then Ethan is pushing past her and racing up the stairs, one hand clamped on his backside.

Cathy scowls after him. *There goes my nice clean bathroom.*

His hasty footsteps have scattered the morning's post all over the hallway. Cathy bends down to pick it up. Her hand hovers over a folded sheet of paper. Her fingertips tingle at the memory of the greasy feel of the last piece. She picks it up, opens it and stares at the number written inside.

$$999,901$$

She crumples the paper, goes to the bin and throws it inside. "Bloody kids. What kind of stupid prank is this?" Her hands are shaking as she goes to put the kettle on.

❖

"Cathy?" Vikram's voice penetrates her dreams. She opens her eyes blearily to see her husband standing over her. "It's nine o'clock. I've let you sleep as long as I can, but you need to get up now. We promised Isabelle we'd take her to the zoo today."

Cathy moans and rolls over. "Can't you do it? You don't need me."

"No." There is steel in Vikram's voice; it's not his normal, placating tone nor the frosty tone he uses when they argue. She twists to look at him. His arms are crossed. His normally soft brown eyes glitter like dark gems. "It's a family day, Cathy. You promised her we could go after she got that reading award. It's her treat and, believe it or not, she loves her mother and wants to spend time with her."

"Fine," Cathy says, flinging off the duvet. "I'm up. Satisfied?"

Vikram just walks out of the room.

Cathy takes her time showering and getting dressed. *I'm the breadwinner around here. It's my weekend too. I deserve some time off. They'll just have to wait.*

When she gets downstairs, she finds Vikram and the children standing by the door, coats on. Isabelle holds up a box. "We made you some toast, Mummy. I put lemon curd on it, just like you like."

Cathy takes the box and stares at it. Then she looks up accusingly at Vikram. "What about coffee? You know I need my coffee."

"We're stopping at the petrol station. I'll get you some

there. Come on." He pulls her coat down from the peg and hands it to her. Her skin feels hot and tight as anger courses through her.

"No. I'm going to have breakfast and—"

But Vikram has already turned away and opened the door.

"Come on, kids," he says, and they head outside, leaving Cathy standing dumbstruck, coat in one hand, box of toast in the other.

"You bastards," she mutters under her breath. "You don't care about me at all, do you?"

*Click*

Cathy jumps so much she almost drops the box. The sound definitely came from down the hall, nowhere near the radiator. Slowly, she walks up the hallway, scanning the carpet and the walls for anything which might give a hint as to where this noise is coming from. Halfway down she stumbles back as a familiar, rotten stench engulfs her. She drops her coat, her hand covering her mouth. Her watering eyes are drawn to the under-stairs cupboard. She remembers a time in her childhood when their pet cat brought in a dead rabbit and left it the broom cupboard where it stank the place out during the heat of a summer day. This smell is similar, only more potent and more putrid.

*Oh god, what if there's a family of dead rats in there or something?*

She opens the cupboard and bends down to see inside. It's too gloomy to make out much. She recognises the tall, thin silhouette of the vacuum and the cluttered shadows of the cleaning shelves. But there's something at the back, a shadow that is completely out of place. It looks like a figure sitting atop a pile of something.

"Cathy!" Vikram's voice is so unexpected and loud that she screams. She turns to him, her heart pounding in her chest, her breathing rapid. He frowns. "What the hell are you doing?"

"There was this noise. Then this smell. And…" She tails off, remembering the strange shape. Vikram's presence bolsters her courage and she reaches into the cupboard to turn on the light. The hunched figure turns out to be a large dust sheet that's fallen over a bucket.

Vikram peers into the cupboard beside her. She steps away. "Sort that, will you? It stinks in there and I need to put on my shoes."

As she walks away, she hears him mutter, "I can't smell a thing."

*Then you're lucky,* she thinks. It takes a good blast of fresh air to clear away the stench from her nostrils.

The cold air nips at every patch of exposed skin. Cathy digs her hands deep in her pockets and tries to stifle a yawn. This is the same zoo that her mother brought her to as a child and it holds little more excitement now than it did then.

*But I did promise Isabelle, I suppose,* she tells herself as she stamps her numb feet.

Besides, she is glad to be out of the house. She hasn't been sleeping well; her dreams are filled with jaws that go clickety-clack and bills from utility companies that have numbers so high she can't comprehend them. The bills come on pieces of paper which bleed onto her fingertips.

She stares at two rhinos that look utterly bored. She tries to push down the dreadful knowledge that is creeping through her mind: she knows where the noise is coming from now. It's coming from under the stairs. She feels it with a certainty that clutches at her bowels whenever she thinks of that dark cupboard.

*The fuses are in there. And the old electricity meter. Maybe one of them is malfunctioning. I'll get Vikram to look at them when we get home.*

The thought calms her and she has enough energy to engage with Isabelle, who is desperate to go and see the octopus in the zoo aquarium. Cathy allows herself to be led in that direction. They step inside and tropical heat washes over Cathy. She lets out a contented sigh, relishing the warmth.

*Click*

Cathy's head snaps round looking for the source of the noise.

*Click click*

It's coming from the darkness of the doorway.

*Click click click*

Cathy backs away, nearly knocking Ethan off his feet. "Hey! Mum! Watch out."

Vikram grips her arm, hissing in her ear, "Cathy, what's wrong with you?"

Cathy stares at the zoo employee who is standing in an alcove by the door. The girl stares back, surprised and wary of this attention, then the door opens again and the girl looks at the newcomers. Her thumb moves, pressing the button on the small tally counter hidden in her hand.

Four people enter.

*Click click click click*

The door opens and a couple come in.

*Click click*

The girl's eyes stray back to Cathy; she gives a slightly nervous smile. "It's for fire regulations," she says. "I count them on the way in, and Mick counts them on the way out. We have to do it when we've got a big exhibition on like the shipwreck one."

"Yeah, sure, not a problem," says Vikram. He tugs Cathy away, demanding in a low voice. "What *is* up with you today?" Cathy doesn't answer; she doesn't know.

❖

By the time they get home from the zoo, the sky is darkening and Cathy is exhausted. It's a struggle just to get out of the car. She staggers to the front door, leaving Vikram to deal with the kids.

As the door swings open, she sees the post on the floor. Sure enough there's a folded piece of yellow paper. She opens it.

*999,992*

The numbers blur as her hand shakes. "Who the fuck is doing this?"

"Cathy! Don't swear in front of the kids," Vikram snaps. The three of them are standing behind her, waiting to come in. Vikram is glaring, Ethan is smirking and Isabelle looks confused.

Cathy's fear morphs into anger and she shakes the letter at Vikram. "Some idiot's harassing me."

Vikram frowns. He ushers the kids into the living room and takes the paper. He studies it for some minutes then looks at her.

"I don't think this is paper, Cathy." He brings the note to his nose, sniffs it. He swaps hands, rubbing together the fingers that were just touching it and she knows he too can feel the grease. "I think it's animal skin."

It feels as if her stomach has dropped to her feet. Her fingertips burn and she rubs them on her jeans. "Animal skin? Ugh. That's sick."

Vikram tries to hand the note back, but she refuses to take it, hiding her hands behind her like a child. He rolls his eyes and places it on the hall table. "Keep this one. If you get any more, take them to the police." Then he walks into the kitchen, as if that settles the matter. Cathy stares at the note, feeling utterly alone in a house full of people.

She starts down the hall, intending to get a very large glass of wine, but her eyes stray to the door of the cupboard. It looks innocuous, but she imagines it opening up, a hand reaching out for her as she passes. A shudder shakes through her and she turns away, walking into the living room.

Cathy spends the rest of the evening in a daze. Vikram has to nudge her whenever the kids ask her questions. When Isabelle asks what's for dinner, Cathy looks at her blankly. Vikram grits his teeth then calls for pizza. Isabelle is delighted; Ethan is smug.

The television is on while they eat, but Cathy can't process what they're watching. There's an idea trying to burrow its way up from the depths of her brain. Something from her childhood is being tugged towards her consciousness every time she thinks of that clicker at the zoo, of that bloody handprint on the toilet.

Bloody...

She can't stop staring at the hallway. It's like the cupboard has become sentient, that it sits there like a hulking animal, biding its time.

"Goodnight, Mummy," Isabelle says, throwing her arms around Cathy's neck. Startled from her thoughts, Cathy hugs her back and sees that Isabelle is already in her pyjamas. She glances at Ethan who is also in pyjamas and reading a comic. She looks to Vikram who is staring at her sternly. "I thought it best if I handled bedtime tonight," he says.

The house is quiet while Vikram is upstairs settling Isabelle and Ethan. Cathy closes her eyes, trying to force some calm into her mind.

*What is wrong with me?*

*It's lack of sleep, that's all.*

*And the bloody heating. That's driving me nuts.*

She holds her breath, listening for the clicking of the air in the pipes, but there's nothing. She exhales and tries to let her mind drift, to find some peace from her raging thoughts. It must work because suddenly she's snapping her head forward, going from sleeping to awake in an instant.

It takes her a moment to take in her surroundings. Vikram is sitting on the sofa opposite, watching her. She gets the feeling he's been there for a while. There's an unfamiliar expression on his face. It looks like fury.

"What's the time?" she asks.

He stands. "It's bedtime. For me, anyway. You can sleep down here, you slut."

Cathy's mind is so anaesthetised the insult causes her no shock or anger, only confusion. "Slut?"

His hands ball into fists. "I was looking for that picture from summer, of all of us by the pool. I knew that my mother sent it to you by text so I went through your phone just now and I found all the text messages from Steve," a glob of spit springs from his mouth as he says the name, "about the two of you, about your meetings, about your..." he pauses, clearly working up to the word 'affair.'

Cathy stands, her legs feeling like water. So many thoughts run through her head but she finds herself inanely saying, "But I have a security code on my phone."

"Yes. And now I know why. If you want to hide a sordid affair, Cathy, I'd recommend having a code that isn't our eldest child's birthday." Vikram's eyes are alive with a dark fire she's never seen before. He takes a step towards her and Cathy takes a step back, almost tumbling back into the chair.

"But that was months ago, Vikram. I haven't—"

Vikram cuts her off, his voice low but somehow more threatening than if he was shouting at her. "I'm going to bed. Alone. While I'm upstairs, thinking about whether I can trust you or even bear to touch you again, I want you to lie down here and think about what the hell you're going to do to make this up to me and the kids, or where you're going to stay if I decide to kick you out."

He stalks towards the door. Cathy calls out after him. "But it meant nothing."

*Click*

"I didn't start it. It was him."

*Click click*

"Damn it, Vikram! Can't you hear that?" She rushes to the door, but can't bring herself to step out into the hallway.

Vikram, one foot on the stairs, shakes his head incredulously. "After everything I just told you, you're more concerned about the bloody pipes? You're a piece of work, Cathy." His normally placid face twists into a sneer.

Cathy watches as he climbs the stairs. She hears the bedroom door open and close. The world seems to tilt around her. She shakes her head, trying to dislodge the feeling that everything's going horribly wrong.

She is desperate to find something that she can control. Her eyes alight on the letterbox and her heart leaps.

"Yes," she murmurs, "that I can do something about."

*Click*

She glares at the radiator in the room behind her. "Just shut the fuck up, okay? I'm not in the mood." She storms into the kitchen, driven by anger and purpose. She roots through the drawer where they keep all the odds and ends. She finds the duct tape and brandishes it with a grin. Then she marches to the front door and kneels down. She tears off strip after strip, plastering them across the letterbox. When a thick mass of grey covers every section of it, she smiles and stands up.

"There. That'll stop you little bastards from pestering me."

*Click*

She spins round. It's dark behind her. The kitchen is dark, the living room too, but she doesn't remember switching off the lights when she left either of them. There's another click, the sound of a door being unlatched. With a gentle creak, the door to the under-stairs cupboard swings open. A sickly yellow light spills from it. The smell of rotting meat quickly fills the hallway.

Cathy is repulsed. She doesn't want to go towards that light, but her feet are already moving that way. The answer to what has been plaguing her is in there, she knows it. Part of her wants to see it, to confront it; the rest of her wants to flee screaming. It feels like she's in a nightmare, and she convinces herself that seeing this through to the end is the only way to make herself wake up.

The boards creak as she walks down the hallway, drawn towards that light.

She places her hand on the cupboard door to steady herself and peers inside. The vacuum cleaner is hidden by a pile of bones. Some are yellow, some are warped, some are a perfect gleaming white and some of them still have shreds of flesh attached to them.

Cathy's gaze travels up the pile of bones to the creature sitting at the top. The creature has the shape of a man, but he's as small as a child, and his skin is wrinkled like a crone. He clearly once wore clothes, but they've rotted away and now only shreds of filthy fabric cling to his wizened body, mimicking the decaying meat that clings to some of the bones. The creature meets her gaze and grins at her, showing a mouth filled with yellow, jagged teeth. Bits of slimy black flesh are caught between them.

"Ah, Catherine. I'm so glad you came. My belly is fair empty." She stares at him and he cocks his head. "You *do* know who I am, don't you?"

Cathy's mouth is dry but the words come out as a croak. "Bloody Bones."

The creature's grin widens. "So, you were listening to your mother. I hope you've told Isabelle and that she listened well. I hope you warned her about how I come in the night to take away naughty children who tell lies.

"Of course, it's not only small children I take," he adds, "but most people ignore that part of the story."

He holds up a piece of yellow paper, like the paper she's been receiving. This sheet is ragged and bleeding around the edges. There is a mole in the bottom corner. But what draws Cathy's gaze is the number scrawled in the middle.

*999,997*

She shakes her head. "This is a nightmare. You're not real."

Bloody Bones lifts a hand. Between his gnarled fingers is a tally counter, just like the one from the zoo. But this one is battered and filthy, clearly very old. His thumb depresses.

*Click*

"You're just a story."

*Click*

"Stop doing that!"

"I'm just keeping track," he says with a casualness that infuriates her.

"This is just a nightmare, it has to be."

He cocks his head, a pitying look in his eyes.

She glares at him and snarls, "You don't scare me."

"Ah! There we are."

He holds the clicker up for her to see, his thumb poised above it. The counter reads 999,999. He presses down.

*Click*

The numbers flick round to zero.

Goosebumps rise over Cathy's skin and she starts to tremble. "What does it mean? What did you do?"

"Don't blame me. *I* didn't do anything," he says, reaching down for his bag. "It was all you, Catherine, all your lies. Big ones, little ones. I just kept count."

He tugs at the cord around the neck of the bag and it falls open – and keeps opening, becoming impossibly wide. The world tilts again and Cathy feels herself falling forward. Her arms pinwheel, her fingers reach for anything that can arrest her progress. But she's not falling towards a bag; what she sees below her is more like a tunnel. There are figures clustered around the walls and they look up at her. Their own personal misery is momentarily forgotten as they raise half-chewed arms in greeting. Those who have skin left on their faces smile as they welcome a new member to their pitiable ranks and Cathy falls inexorably towards them, her screams mingling with theirs.

# Our Lady of Wicker Bridge

## Angela Slatter

There were stories about Wicker Bridge Estate, always had been even before there was an estate. So many stories and for so long that it was hard to tell if what you were being told was new or old. Something that smacked of urban legend might well have its roots in ancient tales of demons and spectres. Sometimes the true tales were worse: folk dying alone, left undiscovered for years, or eaten by beloved pets, only found when some number cruncher realised a gas bill hadn't been paid for far too long.

Tricia had heard them all, retold a few in her time, but the one that occurred most often amongst the children she dealt with was this: if you were suffering, if you were alone and friendless, if you were desperate, a pale lady would appear and offer you a deal.

Hermione Banks, her social work mentor and supervisor, used to joke about that one all the time. Tricia had learned to laugh – at all the woman's jokes, all her hard comments that might have once been humour but had been beaten into a bitter blade by years of working in places like Wicker Bridge. Some days the guiding hand had felt like a hammer.

Still, Tricia's surprised to find she misses Hermione.

Mostly because the people they were supposed to help, the people produced by these dark urban mills, the people who'd spoken to her quite normally when she shadowed Hermione, suddenly acted as if she were so new and fresh out of the packet she smelled like shrink-wrapping.

Now she was knocking on those doors on her own, and the moment they were opened hard gazes fixed upon her – no one knew her, no one remembered, and the estate's population had changed since she was a child here. Dead-eyed women, suspicious children, and angry men all demanded *Where's Hermione?* She explained that Ms Banks had taken some leave – didn't think it a good idea to say 'disappeared' – and didn't they remember meeting her, Ms Parks? That she'd be filling in until Ms Banks returned? It didn't guarantee she'd be let in. She could no longer count on two hands the number of times she'd had to lean her face against a grimy door, with the echoes of 'Fuck off!' in the air, and try in her most patient manner to say there wasn't any choice, they had to talk to her, that she was there to help. There'd have been none of that shit with Hermione Banks there.

Still, she thinks, not much longer.

Tricia pulls her battered Renault into the car park located in the centre of the four ugly residential towers that block out most of the sun no matter what the time of day. There are no other vehicles in the lot, just as the last two times, but it doesn't mean her doors won't end up scratched, the windows chipped with a strange precision, foul words daubed in red and black paint, down low where childish hands can most easily reach.

She taps her palms, then fingers, on the steering wheel, counting to ten, but not really because when she reaches the end she starts over. By the time she's done ten lots of ten under her breath the nerves are almost quiet. She tries to recall why she wanted to do this job; then recalls that *want* didn't really come into it.

*Remember your promise.*

Helping. Helping people. Showing them the way. She puts a hand beneath her sweater, touches the patch of skin crepe-textured from burns left by Billy and his lighter; those marks were old. She moves her fingers to trace the raised, barely healed scar across her ribs, all five inches of it. Not deep, no, but long and needing stitches. A souvenir from three months ago, a mark that Hermione had said she should wear with pride, but it just made Tricia more afraid, less devoted.

She'd got back on the horse, hadn't she? Returned to work as soon as she was fit so Hermione wouldn't be disappointed; returned to banging her head against despair and indifference day after day. She thought she might be able to continue on, too, right until two months ago, the day the man who'd stabbed her – she'd told him he wasn't a very good parent – got out of jail because of over-crowding, ostensible good behaviour, and because some judge said it wasn't really an attempt on her life, just an expression of misplaced anger.

He'd seen her that first day back, and several days since, seen her and laughed and leered; done the same every time she'd come visiting with Hermione, and his gaze made promises that next time he'd do a proper job. Though he never said anything it didn't matter: that gaze was enough to chip away at every bit of strength, every bit of courage she had.

Hermione Banks, thinks Tricia bitterly, had never let something like that discourage her. She bore her scars the way a five-star general wore his medals, with the same arrogant assurance that what she did was right. Her status was legendary: stabbed five times, shot once, beaten sixteen times (and by all accounts gave back as good as she got); minimal sick leave taken even when injured, never went on holidays, just threw herself back and back and back again at the unfeeling wall of social problems, trying her best to rescue the less fortunate and set them on the path to a better life. Coming out of an abusive home, Hermione Banks had done her best to save others from the same fate. As if it was that easy.

*Remember your promise.*

Hermione Banks had never let slammed doors deter her. Nor shouting men and women, crying babies in their shit-filled nappies. Nor feet and knees sore from traipsing up and down piss-infused stairs in buildings where the lifts hadn't worked for years, if ever.

Pressing out a long breath so there's nothing left in her lungs, Tricia grabs her satchel from the front seat, and struggles out of the car as if it's got heavier gravity than she's used to. She closes the door harder than needed, listens to the echo of it ricochet around the courtyard and then has to press the key-lock button three times before it *blips* sullenly. She's five paces away from the vehicle before she needs to breathe again and she sucks in air like a compressor, making roughly the same noise.

Tricia has to check her phone for the numbers –

building and floor and flat. The device, which she levers out of her jacket pocket, flies from her sweaty hand and lands on the asphalt with a *crack*. It hits on a corner, and as she watches the screen becomes a masterpiece of fractures, so many fissures so fine it looks like a spider's web. She bites down on a scream, starts counting again; without the steering wheel to beat time against, she taps her thick-soled boot on the blacktop. Then she realises she's out in the open, anyone can see her, laugh at her. It's hard enough to get people to let you into their homes when they think you're trying to interfere, let alone once they decide you're mad.

She picks up the phone, finding it still works, though it's hard to read the numbers in the notes field. Building three, level seven, flat 748. She knows the lifts don't work. Her back aches. It's late in the day because she spent so much time fiddling around in the office rather than come here, but she needs to be seen doing her job. Now the shadows are long and the sky is heading towards the deeper grey that presages nightfall. Tricia doesn't want to be here after dark. She wants to be at home in her track pants, with slippers on her feet, watching something mindless on the telly. She wants to be eating ice cream out of the carton and not thinking at all about tomorrow or the day after that or the one after that, just knowing she's only got to hold it together a little while longer.

Tricia heads towards the third tower, eyeing the stairwell that's open to the elements but obscured by the late afternoon gloom. Something moves there, something white and fluttery and her heart gives a little kick of panic. Low to the ground, small, frail. A little dog?

Tricia doesn't like dogs no matter what their size. But no, not a dog, a child. A girl in a dress too thin for the back end of autumn, with short dirty blonde hair and bare feet and scratches up her toothpick shins. Tricia smiles in relief, gives a laugh, and waves. The child blinks at her, a slow reptilian motion, but otherwise doesn't move.

"Hello," says Tricia. "Hello, I'm Ms Parks. Do you know if" – she has to dredge up the name – "Mrs Lewis is at home?"

The child says nothing, just stares with one brown eye, one blue, and Tricia decides the girl is probably not all there. In these deprived areas a lot aren't and there's no treatment for them either, not with the NHS being simultaneously gutted and fucked by conservative governments who're no doubt planning to hunt the poor when they run out of foxes.

Tricia takes another step towards the girl in the stairwell, thinks again how uncommonly dark the shadows are behind her, and then realises that those very shadows are moving. Not just shifting as if by a breeze, but rising, rising, rising like a wave about to dump on the sea shore, except what will bear the brunt of it is the child. Tricia lets out a scream, tries to dart forward, tries to grab at the girl's too-thin dress, tries to pull her free – but she doesn't.

She can't.

No matter what message her mind tries to send, her body rebels, and she finds herself back at the car, holding the key fob out, desperately shaking it and pressing the button, praying though she doesn't believe in God that the lock will obey. It does, and somehow she's in the Renault and it starts first go and then she's somewhere down the High Street roaring past a Pret and not stopping for the little old ladies waiting at the crossing and throwing profanities after her.

And Tricia finds she can't pull up any memory of what happened to the little girl. Whether because she was too busy running or because she's blocking it out, she doesn't know or care.

Tricia can't get to sleep.

She'd made it home in record time, miraculously without being pulled over by the rozzers. The hot shower she'd had wasn't just to get her core temperature up, but because she'd peed herself in fright. She'd eaten a microwave meal in front of the television but hadn't taken in anything that moved before her eyes, which might have also had something to do with the three glasses of white wine she'd put away. But when she got into bed, leaving the lights on out in the lounge room so their glow trickled across her bed, she started to think that she'd overreacted.

What had she seen?

A child.

Where?

In a darkened stairwell.

She was tired and grumpy and nervous.

She panicked and she left a child alone.

*Remember your promise.*

The moving shadows were more likely a person in dark clothing.

She should call the police.

Then she'd have to tell them what she did.

And they already thought there was something off about her.

Tricia rolls over, sheets and duvet twisting around her legs until she feels like she's been trussed up like a lamb for the roasting.

She'd run away and left a little girl behind.

A little girl like she'd been.

Hungry, lonely, with no clothes warm enough in any weather.

Tricia had slept in a corner of an empty room, no bed, just an old stained mattress. Her slumber had always been light, one ear kept open for any sounds of drunk parent – her mother – or false stepfather – Billy, who was just the worst of the constant stream of Shelley's boyfriends – or one of their friends making their reeling way along the hall to 'visit'.

Where did that other little girl sleep? Who was supposed to look after her?

*You.*

Who was that child?

Tricia kicks away the covers and sits on the edge of the mattress, her knickers and t-shirt damp with sweat. The heating is up too high, she tells herself. Out on the pale pine table are the files, Hermione Banks' cases. She hasn't been through them all, not in depth, though she's sampled out of sheer curiosity; there's no need, really, it won't matter soon. It was possible she'd read about the girl and it hadn't stuck. Maybe she wasn't a high risk – although given Tricia's memory of the child's appearance that seemed unlikely.

She goes to the kitchen and opens a window to have a sneaky fag. Her housemate's away but she hates Tricia smoking in the flat. Mostly Tricia's good. Mostly. But again, it doesn't really matter anymore. Still, she's careful to blow the smoke out into the night, and not drop grey ash onto the impractical creamy carpet. She selects the first folder.

Two hours and a lost count of cigarettes later – she'd given up trying to herd the smoke out the window fairly quickly and lengths of cinder are piled on a fairly new copy of *Marie Claire* – she'd found nothing. She sits back and ponders her predecessor.

Hermione Banks was meticulous about processes and procedures; she'd have a case file for that child. Somewhere. The old social worker knew every person on the Wicker Bridge Estate. She'd shared all that knowledge with Tricia. So why was this child an unknown quantity?

What had Banks been hiding? If anything...

Everyone had said she was an unlikely candidate to go missing. The police still hadn't found any trace of her; not even her car had been located. A burnt out shell of a vehicle might have pointed the way, given some hint as to her fate, but the lack of it meant there were those who claimed it meant Hermione Banks was still alive. That she'd just had enough and taken off somewhere people didn't yell at her or throw things or try to stab her with cheap stiletto heels. But Tricia knew that wasn't the case.

The child, though, the child bothered her.

If the child wasn't in the system, wasn't in Banks' files, maybe she was recent? Newly moved into the block? Too soon for Hermione to notice her? That didn't seem likely. Hermione would notice anything new, anyone out of place. So: what if Hermione had noticed? What if she'd noticed her two weeks ago and approached the girl? What if whoever had been not looking after the girl in the proper fashion hadn't been impressed by the woman's interference?

What if the girl is alone and in danger?

What if...

What if...

What if the girl had seen something else? Not today, but a couple of weeks ago? What if she knew who Tricia was, though Tricia didn't know her? Was that why she hadn't come when called? Why she'd preferred the grasping shadows to the helping hand Tricia had stretched toward her?

What if...

What if someone else offered the girl help? Not the police, no, because that kind of kid wouldn't talk to the cops. But someone else? The same sort of someone who'd come to Tricia when she was small and cold and afraid?

What if that girl wasn't interested in Tricia's help because a pale woman – *that* pale woman – had come in the night and suggested a bargain, the same sort Tricia had accepted all those years ago? A deal she's not sure was even true because maybe Billy would have died anyway from emphysema or alcohol poisoning or heart attack, only not as fast as the flames that took hold of his bed so swiftly – what if that same woman had appeared from nowhere and held out a hand to the little girl in the stairwell?

*Remember your promise.*

Was that worse or better than if the girl had seen something a fortnight ago?

Tricia goes to the bedroom to dress.

There are parts of London that are never entirely dark; the light from vehicles and streetlamps, factories and theatres, houses and shops, reflects on the smoggy sky and creates a kind of ambient glow that's hard to escape. But there are other areas in the city – their number growing night by night – where the darkness lives and breathes and breeds like viral cells.

The Wicker Bridge Estate is one of those places.

In each block only a few pale yellow beams gleam out from the upper floors, weak as piss. Tricia wonders at that, knowing how densely populated the towers are, knowing that people who don't have to get up and go to work in the morning didn't tend to keep the usual diurnal cycle as wage slaves. Billy had basically been a vampire, coming to life when the sun set, when Tricia's mother came home from work at the factory, smelling like seafood, and cracking the ring pull on her first lager of the evening; that would wake him, that sound of tearing, popping metal. He'd demand a fry-up, breakfast for dinner. The flat would smell like grease and cigarette smoke – same as he did the night the mattress caught fire – that's how she knew he was awake, because he'd spark up a fag as soon as he opened his eyes, before he even sat up. That's when she'd begin to tense, waiting, anticipating a repeat of every night since Shelley had let him into their lives.

Tricia pulls in beneath the sole streetlight and turns off the engine, then listens to it *tic-tic-tic* in the silence. The key is cool, nickel-silver and plastic in her fingers, weighted down by too many other pieces of metal – keys for the office, home, the garage, the storage area to the vacant flat in Wicker Bridge that no one else knows is empty because only Tricia had found the old man dead and desiccated there six months ago; he wasn't on any lists for assistance so he was *her* secret. *They'll bend*, Billy used to tell her, showing her how he only ever kept one key on the ring for his car; showing how he could use it to remove bottle tops, clean the underside of his nails, and tear jagged holes in her skin that her mother refused to notice.

Her hands start to shake; she puts them on the steering wheel and begins to count. Ten lots of ten. Then another ten lots of ten. Then, as she is halfway through a third round, she sees something white from the corner of her eye. Her heart hits hard in her chest and she wrenches her neck to the right. There's the fluttering of a dirty cotton dress, with capped sleeves, a high tie beneath non-existent breasts. Twig fingers clasped in front of a small stomach, dirty blonde hair, badly cut, sticking out like a halo from around a heart-shaped face.

The girl stands a few metres away, staring solemnly at Tricia, waiting. Tricia swallows hard, forces her hands to move, the left to grab her satchel from the seat, the right to open the driver's side door. She swings her feet out, levers herself up, makes herself take the steps that bring her to the girl. Her knees are shaking and so is her voice as she says, "Are you alright?"

The girl nods, the blue eye bright in the light, the brown one looking like a well of night.

"Can you... can you talk?" asks Tricia.

"Yes," says the girl, quite simply, with no judgment or contempt, no offense at being thought mute.

"Do you know Ms Banks? Hermione Banks?"

"Yes."

"Have you seen her?"

"Oh, yes."

"I mean recently?"

"With you before, and again this morning."

Tricia's throat fills with bile; she rocks back on her feet. The girl's lying or mad. Not about the first instance, but the second. Then again, what if...

Hermione Banks was hard enough; her size, the bond they'd forged working together. For all the danger she'd experienced, all the violence, Hermione hadn't expected any from her protégé. The child, thinks Tricia, is much smaller. Tricia feels her fear trickle away, feels warmth flood through her from her feet to her face. Be calm, act normal, don't panic her.

"Can you take me to her?"

"Yes." The girl offers a hand, which Tricia accepts, relieved at the ease. The child tugs her along and Tricia sniffs: the girl smells like smoke and grease. Tricia closes her eyes, sees Billy on the mattress, too drunk to wake, too drunk to move even after she'd set the bed on fire with his own lighter, just like the pale woman had told her to do.

*Trust me*, she'd said, *just the bed, no one else will get hurt. Trust me, it won't spread.* And Tricia did; she did what she'd agreed to and the woman promised freedom in return.

She hadn't lied; Tricia had been taken away, placed with a foster family that looked after her, she'd not seen her mother again. And in return Tricia had promised that she'd assist kids like herself, when she grew up, when she finished her degree; that she'd be shield and sword for them, help them find the way out.

And she had.

Right up until this morning when she'd run away from the girl who now held her hand, left that girl to the shadows.

Right up until the day when she'd seen the man who'd stabbed her.

Right up until that moment after a fortnight of torment, of wordless pressure, of unspoken threats from the man whose eyes promised *worse*, when her nerve broke. When Hermione Banks had tried to calm her down in the stairwell as she, Tricia, wept and shook, blurted out that she was going to run, that she had a plan, that she would leave London, leave Wicker Bridge, leave everything behind. When Hermione had looked at her sadly, knowingly, and said *Remember your promise to her*.

And she'd realised then that somehow Hermione knew everything; her past, her present, her future. The fact there was no escape from the bargain she'd made when she was just a little girl; that the older social worker was somehow an agent of the pale woman. And Tricia knew that Hermione Banks would enforce that bargain unless she was stopped.

So she'd said to Hermione, "You're right, of course. I just panicked. There's something I wanted to show you." She'd led her mentor to the storage area that belonged to the empty flat – not to the home where a man had died all alone, the flat she'd kept up the utilities payments on just in case things didn't work out with her roommate and she needed a place to crash (the body was skeletonised by the time she'd tried the door, found it unlocked, found him, wondered if he'd been murdered, if she should report it, but ultimately decided *no*). She didn't take Hermione to the flat, no, because it would be too easy to discover her; any noises too easily overheard.

She'd led her friend down to the basement level, unlocked the sturdy door, reached in to turn on the single light, then stood aside to let the woman enter first. And, trusting, she did, not seeing Tricia follow her and pick up the old shovel she knew from previous explorations was in the corner closest to the door. What Hermione did see, at that last moment, was Tricia's reflection in the old mirror on the back wall, the downward arc of the shovel that connected with her skull before she had a chance to cry out.

A couple more hits and Tricia was satisfied Hermione wouldn't be exhorting her to remember her promise ever again.

She'd waited until dark and then, Hermione's ugly hat clamped down on her head, driven the woman's car not too far away to an estate that was, unbelievably, even worse than Wicker Bridge. She'd left the keys in the ignition, confident it would be stolen well before daybreak. She'd not even snuck out the alleyway behind the main residential building when she heard the engine; Tricia figured it was some sort of record for the little toerags.

She'd played it cool. Reported Hermione missing the next day when she didn't show up for work. Answered all the coppers' questions calmly, went on with her life and job, only getting a bit wobbly at night and drinking too much. And today, when she'd had to go back to Wicker Bridge. When she'd left the child behind.

But she'd come back. And no harm had been done, the girl was still here, safe as she could be.

Tricia had come back and that counts for something. It did. Surely.

If she forgets what she's planning to do.

The smell of grease and smoke grows stronger the closer they get to the stairwell of Tower Three.

"Where is she?" asks Tricia, testing the girl again, not letting go of her hand even if she does stink like a cigarette butt extinguished in a plate of leftover bacon fat.

"Down. Down in the storage area. You know."

"Oh. Yes."

The girl leads her to the metal grill door that should be locked, available only to key holders, but it swings open under the lightest touch of the child's free hand. The line of fluorescent lights on the concrete ceiling fight a losing battle against the shadows. The girl tugs her forward, seemingly anxious to meet her doom.

"Has anyone..." Tricia begins, stupidly. "Has anyone... offered you help?"

The girl nods.

"Hermione?" she asks hopefully, even though she knows Hermione is in no position to offer anything except an example of how best to slowly decay. She hates to think how the older woman will look after two weeks, even in the cold.

"Almost there," says the girl. In the trickle of light, Tricia recognises the sturdy door that sits ajar, though it shouldn't. The girl pulls her towards it. The door opens without any help, and the child drags her in. The girl's neck is thin, tiny – Tricia's hands won't have any trouble wrapping around it. Squeezing.

"Did you?" the child asks.

Tricia looks around at the storage space; nothing's changed. A discarded mattress, stained and blackened, the mirror against the back wall, the smell of smoke really strong; two broken chairs, an upturned plastic milk crate with a book on it and a camping lantern. Oh, and Hermione Banks propped unmoving in the corner where Tricia left her, neither better nor worse looking than previously. "Did I what?"

"Remember your promise?"

In the mirror, its mercury spotted and peeling, Tricia sees two figures. The tall one is her; the small one... there's something wrong with the small one. The shape is there but not there, not solid, almost as if something shines through it. And it's growing, shrinking, growing again, as if it's making an effort.

"Remember your promise?" repeats the child in a different voice, a voice Tricia recognises from the night the pale lady appeared in her cold room and made a bargain.

Tricia wants to run. She wants to pee herself again. She wants to throw the child as far from her as she can, then slam the door and leave the girl alone until the light dies, the flesh melts from her bones, until her screams stop echoing around the confined space. Until the child is quiet.

But the grip on her hand is far too strong and it drags her forward, until she is only a few feet from the mirror and the figure beside her can be seen clearly: tall and slight as if she feeds on air and drinks only tears, pale and smiling, one moment sad, the next satisfied that her lack of faith has been justified. Tricia meets the gaze only in the mirror, cannot bring herself to turn her head and look at the creature who holds her, cannot bear to stare into the one blue eye and one brown.

"Hermione was one of my favourites, my longest serving. *She* never forgot her promise."

Tricia begins to tremble again.

"Did you forget what you agreed? That if you ever stopped doing what you'd sworn, you'd have to go back. Back to the beginning."

Tricia can't get any words out, her throat is shrinking, tightening, closing over. Suddenly her clothes seem too big, the jeans too long, the belt not cinched tightly enough, her bra straps are falling away. In the mirror there's once again two figures: one tall, bright as bleached bones, slender as starvation, with a head like a skull; the other small, a child shivering with cold and fear. Her, Tricia, once and forever.

Another then a third, behind them: burnt black and fused, leering over the pale lady's shoulder.

# The Church with Bleeding Windows

## John Llewellyn Probert

There was blood everywhere.

It had splashed across the front two rows of pews, soaking the hymn books and turning them into red raw bricks of coagulating clot. It dribbled in broken rivulets down the pine walls of the pulpit so that the place from which God's Word might be communicated now resembled a speaking platform in Hell. It had drenched the gleaming eagle's head of the brass lectern, and now crimson drops were falling from the bird's jutting beak, adding to the spreading scarlet pool beneath.

The vicar's body was in the aisle.

His head was elsewhere.

That was all Martin knew because that was all Martin could see from his hiding place in the choir stalls. Beside him, his sister Alice knelt in shivering silence. He had no idea where everyone else was.

He also had no idea what it was that had killed the vicar. He had seen it, but that hadn't helped.

"Has it gone?" Alice was trembling. Martin didn't blame her.

"I've no idea." How could he? The thing could be hiding anywhere. It was so small it could probably squeeze into any confined space, could hide in any patch of shadow. For all he knew it was clinging to the roof beams above them right at this moment.

Martin quickly glanced up to check.

Nothing.

Just the nice, normal kind of high vaulted ceiling you might find in a church that had been sitting on this spot for the last five hundred years or so.

"Where are the others?" Though she was next to him, Alice sounded miles away.

"I don't know." Everyone had scattered after the attack. Martin hadn't heard the ancient, creaking door open so it was safe to assume they were all still in here somewhere.

Alice's group.

Or rather, the Reverend Cyrus Protheroe's group. The one he held every Thursday night. A kind of drop in thing offering social support for people in the community who suffered from 'dependence problems' and needed somewhere to talk.

Six of them had attended the meeting this evening.

Plus Martin, who had only come along because Alice said she wasn't going otherwise. And she needed this, possibly more than any of them. More than two years on heroin and God knew what else before that, now she was finally clean. The rehab centre had offered her follow-up after her discharge, but the first appointment wasn't for weeks. And Alice needed close follow-up. Very close follow-up indeed.

That was why Martin had agreed to come along with her. It hadn't surprised him that the group had been small, made up of a couple of ex-smokers, someone with alcohol problems and somebody else trying to stay off the cocaine (it wasn't working), as well as one furtive-looking guy who wouldn't admit what his vices were, although the tattoos suggested to Martin that the guy had been in prison. They had sat in a circle, Martin included so he could hold Alice's hand, and talked for an hour before Reverend Protheroe had made them all promise they would return next week. Then he had led them across the church to the exit.

None of them had got that far.

Something had leapt from the shadows and attached itself (Martin could think of no better word) to the vicar's head. The lighting in the church was bad and it quickly became impossible to distinguish between the blood spraying from the man's neck and the thing that seemed to be trying to burrow into it. After that they had scattered.

Martin checked his phone for the umpteenth time. Still no signal.

"We've got to get out of here," said the voice from beside him.

"I know." Alice would be coping with this less well than he was, so Martin bit back his desire to tell her to stop stating the bloody obvious. "I can't see anything between us and the door..." just the entire length of the aisle and what's left of Reverend Protheroe that we'll have to climb over "...so I think we should try to get over there."

"No!" Fingers clutched at his arm. Martin had already prepared himself for the fact that Alice might be too terrified to move, and that he might have to carry her. Then he realised she was pointing at something.

Someone.

Martin remembered her name. Cath. She looked in her mid-fifties but was probably younger, her skin wizened and creased by the cumulative effect of smoking forty cigarettes a day from the age of fifteen. She claimed she had quit two months ago, but Martin wasn't so sure. He had been sitting next to her in the group and the smell of stale tobacco had been pretty overpowering.

Cath was making her way along the back wall towards the exit. She probably thought she was being quiet, but from where he was hiding Martin could hear the crackle of every breath she took.

Now she was twisting the handle and trying with all her might to pull the door open. It wouldn't budge.

She was just stopping for a breather when the thing struck.

It might have been following her, or perhaps it had simply crawled down the aisle from where it had been feeding on Reverend Protheroe. All Martin knew was that one minute Cath was on the verge of freedom, the next a shadowy shape had leapt onto her chest. He heard a fit of strangled coughing augmented by a scream that was all the more terrifying because it was so feeble, so desperately gasped by what little strength her failing lungs were able to muster. After a brief fight, Cath fell to the floor with a feathery silence that just made the sound of the thing crunching its way through her ribcage all the more horrible.

And then the others were rushing to her aid.

Martin saw the remaining members of the group run to help as the monster began to burrow into Cath's chest.

Jane, the twenty-five-year-old cocaine addict, began hitting the thing as hard as she could with the wooden tip of a broom she had found. Kevin, the alcoholic divorcee, had taken one of the heavy brass candlesticks from the side chapel and was trying to knock the thing off the bleeding, wheezing woman. Meanwhile Dave, the man with probable prison tattoos, was tearing a poster from the green baize-covered noticeboard behind them. He rolled it into a tube, set fire to one end with his lighter, and thrust it at the creature.

Martin had to go and help. "Will you be all right here?"

Alice shook her head and grabbed his hand. "I'm coming with you."

They got to their feet and made their way from the choir stalls. By the time they got to the door it looked as if Dave's tactic was working. In the light of the flickering flame, Martin got his first good look at what it was that had been terrorising them.

He had been expecting an animal, perhaps an inner city fox gone crazy, or a cat escaped from some secret animal testing facility. What he found himself looking at was much weirder.

A small heap of what resembled butcher's offal was sitting on Cath's chest.

At first Martin assumed that her killer (for Cath had ceased moving) had gone, somehow escaped without the others noticing. Either that or it was invisible. Then Dave thrust his improvised torch at it once more.

The heap of offal moved.

Alice screamed, distracting the others.

Seizing its chance to escape, the creature slid from

the gaping, empty cavity that had once contained Cath's lungs and trachea, shot across the tiled floor, hit the door, and then slid off into the shadows to the right.

"Come on!" Jane leapt for the exit and tugged at the heavy wrought-iron handle. To no avail. "Why the fuck won't it open?"

"Probably because this is an inner city area and if you don't keep places locked everything gets nicked while there's a group going on." Kevin went over and took hold of Jane's shaking hand, guiding it to her side.

"You mean we're locked in?" Alice was squeezing Martin's wrist so hard it hurt. He ignored it.

"It looks that way," he said.

Dave looked up from his search of the headless body in the aisle. "No keys on him."

"Ok." Martin tried to think. "Why don't we all move to the other side of the church, as far away as possible from where that thing went, so we can work out what we do next."

No-one argued. They were too all busy checking their phones again. Still no signal.

"What the fuck is it?" Jane still had the broom.

"It looked like something out of a lab," said Kevin, hefting his candlestick. "You know, one of those experiments gone mental."

"Too right." Dave no longer had a weapon and looked ill at ease. "Christ knows what they're cooking up in the basements of those factories."

But it was Alice who silenced them. Alice with her tiny fearful whisper as they got to the other side of the church and huddled in a chill corner.

"It's the devil," she said. "We've sinned and the devil's come for us. We don't deserve to live after the lives we've led, and this is how we're going to be punished."

That kept them quiet while they all wondered what the thing really was. It was highly unlikely any of them was going to guess. Not in the entirety of their rapidly diminishing lifetimes.

If Gladys Jenkins hadn't already been dying of an undiagnosed cancer of the gall bladder, it's likely nothing would have happened. If she hadn't been over zealous in cleaning behind the organ pipes at St Gwilym's church it's also likely nothing would have happened. But she was and she did, and that, in essence, is why we have a story to tell.

Gladys was new to Cardiff, having only recently moved from her home in Abergavenny to be closer to her only son, Dennis, who had recently undergone a messy divorce (to those blissfully inexperienced in this particular aspect of the legal system, be assured that there is no other kind). The fact that Dennis had done all he could to persuade her not to come had been gleefully ignored by a woman who had always believed she knew what was best for her son, and that right then what was best was for him to have his mother close by.

But upon her arrival her son had suddenly found himself to be, in his own words, "incredibly busy right now" and consequently Gladys had quickly found herself at a loss for something to do. But, having been a solid – some would say unyielding – member of her church back in Gwent, she had quickly availed herself of the local minister and explained that she would be delighted to give his dusty old church a spring clean. The Reverend Cyrus Protheroe had, not for the first time in his life, raised his eyes heavenwards to thank the Lord for this latest offering of Someone Willing To Do God's Work For Nothing.

"If it's not too much trouble," he had replied to her kind offer, "that would be great."

It wasn't too much trouble, not at all. And so it was that Gladys had spent the best part of that week dusting, scrubbing, polishing and generally making the inside of the little church near the park gleam as if it had been furnished anew. Finally, with the pine pulpit sparkling, the brass lectern gleaming, and the pews positively glowing in their new Mr Sheen-induced radiance, Gladys had turned her remarkable reserves of energy elsewhere.

The space behind the organ pipes was narrow, but not too narrow for a seventy-four year old spry widow to fit into, dusters and all. It was when she was giving the back wall a good going over with the vacuum cleaner that she dislodged some chunks of plaster, which in turn, after due rumbling and the collapse of a couple of loosened bricks, revealed at about chest height a cavity the size of a large earthenware jar.

Which is exactly what was sitting within it.

Gladys reached in and took the container from its resting place, dislodging more dust and fragments of plaster as she did so. Tiny spiders ran to take shelter in the cracked cement between the brickwork whilst larger wriggling things plopped onto the floor and vanished between the floorboards.

Gladys did not notice any of them. She was too busy grimacing at the pot, with its clay seal and its strange writing – more like scratches – around the rim, and oh, such a lot of dust sticking to it that she couldn't possibly show it to the Reverend without first giving it a bit of a clean.

Unfortunately, the pot never got to have what would undoubtedly have been a jolly good scrubbing, because as Gladys tried to back out of the gap between the organ pipes and the wall, one of the wriggling things that still remained in the cavity managed to drop onto her hand and, momentarily startled, she lost her grip on the urn and dropped it.

The clay pot had lasted centuries in its protective cavity. In the hands of Gladys Jenkins it lasted only moments. It hit the floor and shattered; Gladys peered down but it was too dark to see the contents of the pot which, at that stage, just happened to be too invisible to be seen by anyone.

That was not to last for long, however.

Invisible claws tore at Gladys' clothes, razor-sharp talons ripped into the skin on the right side of her abdomen, and... something... burrowed its way past her ascending colon, slipped to the right of her pancreas, found what it was looking for, and proceeded to feast on the aggressively malignant tumour that had arisen in Gladys' gall bladder and common bile duct. Finally, its job done, the creature departed, leaving the ragged, disembowelled carcass of Gladys Jenkins jammed behind the organ pipes, which is where it remained, the icy atmosphere of a Welsh church in February and a significant lack of curious souls during the course of the afternoon meaning it was yet to be discovered.

The creature did not know that Gladys was dead. That is because it had not been designed to think, it had been designed to do, and keep on doing.

Until someone told it to stop.

But only if they knew how.

"Smoke?" Dave had taken out a half-empty packet of cigarettes and was offering them around.

Martin shook his head. "I don't think you're supposed to smoke in here, mate."

"Oh yeah?" Jane had already lit hers and was puffing away as if her life depended on it. "Well you're not supposed to pull vicars' heads off in here either but someone went and did that, didn't they?"

"Something." Kevin's correction earned him a glare. "Something killed Cyrus and Cath."

"Or somethings." Martin was staring at where Cath's attacker had disappeared.

"What?" Jane spat.

"Well I know it's dark, but wasn't what attacked the vicar smaller? Hardly anything at all in fact." Martin looked round for support.

Kevin nodded. "I know what you mean. I thought it was a rat until it started biting so deep that..."

"Don't think about it." Martin waved smoke away from his face. "And the thing we saw on Cath's chest was bigger, wasn't it? Probably the size of—"

"A cat!" Jane had finished her cigarette and was

looking in Dave's direction for another one. "There's a rat monster and a cat monster in here with us! Jesus Christ!"

"Or a monster that's got bigger." Dave had put the cigarettes away and seemed to have no intention of taking them out again, much to Jane's consternation. "After all, it's had something to eat now, hasn't it? Two things in fact."

"So it will be bigger that a cat now." Alice's whisper came from behind Martin.

"Fucking hell," said Dave to nobody in particular, "I fucking knew it was aliens! Fucking alien bastards that want to eat our livers!"

"No." Martin was still thinking. "It doesn't want our livers, but it does want different bits of us. I wonder why?"

"Don't be stupid," said Jane. "It's just gone for the easiest bit to bite down on."

"No." Kevin was shaking his head. "Martin's right. I saw it. That thing climbed up the vicar to get to his throat, but with Cath, it stopped at her chest."

"Maybe it needs different bits?" Martin was stamping his feet against the chill. "Maybe it's trying to build itself into a human being?"

"Fucking body snatchers!" Dave's words echoed around them. "I'm still sticking with aliens, thank you very much."

"If it's building a body why didn't it take more? There should have been enough between both of them to make somebody halfway decent, shouldn't there?"

Jane was right. "It didn't even take good bits, at least not from Cath." Martin scratched his head. "Her lungs were the only part it seemed to want, and I would have guessed they'd be the very worst bit of her."

"So it's a shit judge of organs, so what?" Dave was edging towards the south transept. "I'm off to look for the keys. Anyone fancy coming with me?"

Jane skipped to his side. "I will." She took his arm. "Especially if you give me another fag."

"I'll give you what for in a minute girl." Despite his threat Dave had the packet out and was letting her take one. "The rest of you coming, then?"

"Best try the vestry." Kevin pointed ahead. "I think it's up there on the right. There's some sort of room there anyway, I saw it on the way to the meeting."

Martin nodded. "Sounds fair. Let's all stick together and if anyone sees anything, shout."

"We're hardly likely to keep it to ourselves, are we?" Somehow Jane had already almost finished her second cigarette. She stubbed out the butt and they moved off, alert for every breath of sound, every flicker of movement.

Cath's lungs, and something in the vicar's throat.

It still bothered Martin. He had seen that pulsating thing, and it hadn't been eating that woman's lungs. It looked more as if it had been adding them to itself.

Which was ridiculous. Why on earth would it want to do that?

On the opposite side of the church, behind a sarcophagus that allegedly housed the body of a thirteenth century knight, the creature was resting. This was probably the last time it would need to do so as it reorganised the new organs it had accrued. The bigger its corporeal body, the stronger it became. Soon it would have sufficient strength to keep moving indefinitely, to once again fulfil its purpose after having been locked away for so many years.

For buried deep within that rapidly increasing mass of seething diseased tissue resided a demon, conjured into being by a well-meaning alchemist at some point during the 1600s. Even the demon wasn't sure when, and the alchemist is no longer around to tell us, suffice to say that if it had ever turned up on the demon equivalent of *Antiques Roadshow*, whoever was appraising it would have been very impressed at its rarity, right before it gobbled them up and added their flesh to its own.

Unfortunately for all concerned, the well-meaning alchemist of sixteen hundred and whatever it was had got things a bit wrong. His intention had been to bring into being a spirit capable of curing disease; of gently, definitively and, most important of all, painlessly extracting the 'evil humours' (as the spell in the even older book that dated to well before sixteen hundred and something had described them) from the affected individual, leaving them healthy, smiling, and without the slightest sense that the diseased organ in question had been effectively ripped from them by invisible claws the size of grappling hooks. Which of course is what actually ended up happening, although I imagine you have already guessed that.

The alchemist had immediately become extremely unpopular. In fact he would have been burned as a witch were it not for the fact that the local magistrate was suffering from an acute absence of his cirrhotic liver (too much port), the local sheriff had succumbed to a sudden lack of his entire gastrointestinal tract (a radical but extremely efficient way of dealing with tapeworm) and the local constable was running around screaming and clutching the red raw area where his genitals had once resided. This one was nothing to do with the demon. The constable's wife had caught him in the hayloft with the local witchfinder and had failed to be convinced by the so-called 'learned gentleman' in question – talking at an awkward angle it must be said – that the behaviour between the two men was in fact due to Lucifer having taken up residence within their sheep, Lolly, who was standing nearby. It also hadn't helped that she had been just about to give the very same Lolly a once over with the sheep shears but had been distracted by the unnatural noises coming from the barn.

So as you can see there wasn't really anyone left to torture, behead or burn the alchemist, which was actually a jolly good thing because he was the only one who had any idea how to stop the demon he himself had conjured. He mouthed the words from another page on the spell book and the creature was irresistibly attracted to the earthenware pot he had prepared for it, symbols inscribed into the still-drying clay and all. The demon cast off the diseased body it had begun building for itself, shrank to the size of a fist, and slipped into its new custom-made home, where it found itself a prisoner as the alchemist sealed the lid with a mixture of earth, blood, wax, and something so unmentionable it cannot be reproduced, even in a story of this nature. The book hadn't said anything about holy ground being necessary to keep it imprisoned, but the alchemist had thought it a good idea anyway. A few words and a bag of gold to the men engaged in rebuilding the south-facing wall of their local church, and the alchemist went off with the plan of enjoying a stress-free life elsewhere. He didn't, by the way – in fact he ended up causing quite a bit of trouble throughout Wales, but we shall leave that for another time. Meanwhile, as the years (and the religious movements that held sway over the country) came and went, the demon waited patiently to be let out. Plague, fire and even world wars passed and the creature remained secure where it had been placed.

Until Gladys Jenkins came along with her dusters.

It was the vestry, and it didn't have any keys.

"So where the bloody hell are they, then?"

"Maybe the monster ate them."

Jane looked unimpressed by Dave's attempt at humour. "Where else is there to look?"

Martin closed the desk drawer he had been searching with one hand while Alice held onto the other. "He must have hidden them somewhere."

Jane addressed him as she might a child that Martin would immediately have felt sorry for. "That's what we've been doing, isn't it? Looking for them?"

"I don't mean here." He jerked a thumb towards the doorway where Kevin stood on guard. "I mean out there. Maybe he had some special place he put them that only he knew."

"In that case we're fucked." Dave sat on the lone swivel chair and spun himself round.

"Not necessarily," said Martin. "After all, we were with Mr Protheroe for almost the whole evening, weren't we?"

"Oh my God that's right." Jane was nodding. "He met us all outside the church, didn't he? We saw him unlock the door. Christ, he even made some comment about 'keeping out the draughts' as he closed it behind him."

"He must have locked it as well."

"I don't remember him locking it," said Dave.

"That's funny." Jane didn't sound amused. "I figured you of all people would notice that sort of thing."

Dave got to his feet. "What do you mean by that?"

"Shut up the pair of you." Martin slammed the drawer shut and went to the vestry door. He laid a hand on Kevin's shoulder. "Kevin, do you remember the vicar locking the door behind him when we came in here?"

The man in the doorway didn't move.

"Kevin?"

Silence.

"Mate, are you all right?" Dave had a hand on Kevin's other shoulder now, which was just enough pressure to cause the man to teeter backwards and topple over, revealing the disordered mass of lungs, gall bladder and larynx that was busy adding Kevin's disease-ridden liver to its bulk.

"Run! Now! Or we'll be trapped!" Martin ignored the vomiting noises coming from Jane in the corner and pulled Alice over the mess in the doorway. Dave followed, then went back to get Jane. Having dragged the retching girl out of the room, they were edging away when the creature finished what it was doing and looked around for its next task.

Which apparently was the cocaine-rotted tissue at the back of Jane's nose.

The girl screamed as the mass of sticky, diseased internal organs launched itself at her face. She tugged at it helplessly as the demon thrust invisible claws into her mouth to get at the unhealthy tissues of her soft palate. Her screams took on a higher pitch as it found them and tore them free.

The creature dropped to the ground with a plop while Jane tried to stem the blood spraying from what had once been her face. The monster was looking around for who to cure next while Dave grabbed Jane from behind and pressed a cloth he had found in the vestry to the gaping hole where her nose and upper lip used to be. The white sheet quickly soaked through to red as Dave dragged her away. By the time Dave had caught up with Martin and Alice, Jane was dead.

"Fucking thing!" Dave laid Jane's body on the flagstones with surprising gentleness, then joined Martin and Alice as they backed towards the altar.

As the creature came round the corner and into the light of the choir, the three of them gazed at it in disbelief. The mixture of cartilage and pipes it was using to get around made a slippery scratching sound on the stone, while the bulk of its body consisted of two blackened lungs on top of which sat Kevin's fatty liver. Stuck to front of it was part of Jane's face.

"That's the stupidest fucking monster I've ever seen."

"How many monsters have you seen, Dave?" Martin agreed with him but didn't know what else to say.

"More than my fair share of human ones, that's for sure. What are we gonna do?"

The creature was rearing now, as much as such a thing could, anyway. As it did, they could see there was something else surrounding the mixture of lumped together organs. Something larger, with long, tapering claws that, if viewed at the right angle, was almost corporeal.

"Have you got anything wrong with you?"

Dave blinked at Martin. "You what?"

Martin was nodding at the creature. "I think it takes the bit of you that's diseased."

"You mean it likes to eat cancer?"

"Cancer, infection, bad tissue. Anything."

"But the vicar didn't have anything wrong with him," said Alice.

"Not that we knew, and perhaps not that even he knew. But I bet he had something wrong with his... whatever bit that is that's lodged in there between the liver and the lungs."

"Well I'm fit as a fiddle." Dave flexed his biceps as if that was somehow proof. "Are you saying it won't touch me?"

"I'm not saying anything. But I'm guessing that's the case."

"Right." Dave took a step forward as Martin and Alice took one back. "I've had enough of this." Another step forward. "Come on then, Mr Monster." The creature swung its 'head' towards the sound of his approach.

"Let's see how you deal with someone who can defend himself."

He was only five feet away when the creature leapt and began tearing at his skin.

His tattooed skin, which appeared to cover most of his body judging by the rips in his clothing that were opening up everywhere.

"Fucking run!" Dave was holding it off but it was a struggle. "I'll keep the fucker busy for as long as I can."

"Where can we run to?" Martin didn't know what else to do, where else to go.

"Maybe he hid the key near the door," said Alice. "Maybe it's under the rug or something obvious."

It was worth a shot.

"I said run!" Dave was almost bent backwards now as invisible claws tore strips of skin from his arms and chest.

Martin grabbed Alice's hand and together the two of them hurried through the choir and down the aisle, sidestepping Protheroe's body and reaching the door as Dave's screams echoed behind them.

The key was wedged behind the charity collection box to the left of the door.

"It's coming!"

Martin turned to see the creature, now wrapped in colourful strips of Dave, making its undulating way through the choir like a giant Technicolor leech.

He slid the key in the lock and almost fainted with relief as the key turned.

"Hurry!"

The creature was almost upon them as Martin pulled

the door open, pushed Alice through, and then slammed it shut. Angry wet slurping sounds suggested the creature was too bulky to slide underneath.

"You'd better lock it."

Martin had no intention of doing anything else. He even tested the door just to make sure.

"Come on," he said. "Let's get to a police station."

"Couldn't we just phone them?"

"They'll think it's a prank, and we need to convince them it isn't before that thing gets out. God knows what it could do, or what size it could grow to, in a city this big."

Alice nodded.

It only took a quarter of an hour for them to locate the appropriate authorities, but it was time enough for the creature to have squeezed itself down the church's only toilet and access the sewage system.

Which just happened to be connected to the nearby hospital...

# Sleeping Black

## Marie O'Regan

Black hands on white paint.

Seth blinked and rubbed his eyes, groaning. Not again.

Black handprints on the wall opposite the bed, about two feet off the floor – gaps between the pads of each section of the fingers; a larger gap around the black pad and heel of the hand, white spaces in the gaps. As he watched, the finger marks smeared, as if someone were trying to clean the wall before he woke up.

Too late.

He turned his head and looked across at his wife, Trudy. She was fast asleep; lying flat on her back, mouth wide, snoring for all she was worth. Her eyes were covered by a black satin sleep mask that lay tight against her puffy cheeks, which he'd bought to stop her moaning about the brightness of their bedroom in the mornings. It hadn't stopped her moaning once she was up and about, nothing ever did; but at least she didn't have any excuse for being unable to sleep now. He sighed and rolled out of bed, heading for the bathroom to get a damp cloth and clean the wall before she started to stir. The marks came away easily enough, and he didn't think she'd notice the faint burnt odour – it was already fading, helped along by the lemon cleaning fluid on the cloth. There. It was gone. He straightened up as his wife turned over and sighed, and made his way back to the bathroom to return the cloth before she could ask him what he was up to.

They'd been living here for three weeks now, and – too late – he'd realised his mistake. The house was beautiful, there was no doubt about that – left to him by his late grandmother, the last (except for him) of a long line of Wyers; the house had originally come into the Wyer family when it was bought by his great-great-grandfather, who'd owned a firm of sweeps. It sounded so innocuous, he thought – a firm of sweeps. What it meant, of course, was children. Small boys, mostly, that his great-great-grandfather had bought from the workhouse, or 'saved' from life on the streets, and forced to work for him – sending them up chimneys clad in nothing but rags, or nothing at all, to clean them out, with scant regard for whether they lived or died. The Wyer name was notorious in the sweep trade, and Seth had worked hard when starting out to distance himself from that reputation.

Seth wasn't a bad man. At least he didn't think so. He still owned a chimney sweep firm, the same one in fact, but these days all the work was done by machines. No one had to physically climb a chimney and grub about in the dark, terrified of what might fly out at them, or of falling to their deaths. He felt a deep and abiding shame when he thought of how his great-great-grandfather had built the firm; the conditions those children must have lived in, and the cruelty the great man had shown them. Still, those days were long gone. When his grandmother had died, almost a year before, she'd left the house to him in her will. And what a state it had been in. She'd ordered it locked up years before, after concerned relatives had had her committed. She'd been raving about children, and soot, and something coming for her... but no one had believed her. Why would they? She'd been seventy even then, and had been found running down Upper Street in Islington in nothing but a thin white cotton nightdress, screaming. Her head had been bleeding, clumps of her hair still in her clenched fists when the police managed to hold on to her and force her to lie down on a stretcher. "I'm sorry," she'd moaned, tears streaking her blackened cheeks. "I'm so sorry. It wasn't me."

No one ever found out *what* wasn't her, precisely, but Seth thought he knew. When he'd first come to London to see his inheritance, the house had been unprepossessing, to say the least. The windows and doors were boarded up, the boards themselves cracked and swollen, gaps in between letting in God knew what. He'd hired a firm of builders to come in and renovate, but that first day had been all about getting the boards off and seeing what they were dealing with.

Christ, what a mess. The floorboards on all three floors were warped as a result of holes in the roof letting rain and snow in over the years. The whole place was thick with dust, the floors covered with mouse and rat droppings. Bare slats poked through where large areas of plaster had rotted and fallen to the floor; it wasn't even wired for electricity, and had only basic plumbing – a sink and pump tap in the kitchen. There were fireplaces in every bedroom, and in both receptions – a range cooker in the kitchen. All the fireplaces had been boarded up, rough sheets of plywood nailed into the surrounds. It stank of dust and damp and general neglect, and Seth had felt his heart sink as he surveyed the damage in room after room. It was going to cost a fortune to put right.

He'd had several meetings after that first visit with the building firm he'd hired, armed with his wife's wish-list (she wasn't going to set foot in that house until it was done, she'd told him; God knows what might be living in the walls – you could get eaten alive). Her list was extensive – en suite bathrooms, chandeliers... Trudy liked the finer things in life, and now they'd inherited a big house in Islington it seemed to Seth that she was having delusions of grandeur. Still, they could afford to splash out, and that house was definitely worth it. It would be a thing of beauty once they'd finished. Seth grinned wryly to himself as he remembered Trudy's name for it: "It'll be our forever home," she'd said. Once, that had sounded wonderful. Now it sounded like a threat.

The workmen had grumbled, of course; that went with the territory, didn't it? It was a big house: four bedrooms, two receptions, a grand hall and massive kitchen. There was even a cellar, though Seth had thought more than twice about just boarding that up. He wasn't a fan of the dark, and that space was almost impenetrable; if you stared down through the door in the kitchen that led to the cellar, you saw nothing – just blackness, ready to swallow you whole.

The first job had been stripping everything back to the slats. The plaster was rotten anyway; ripping it all out had been relatively easy, though not exactly uneventful. One of the younger blokes working on site, Nate, had managed to puncture a lung when a slat he'd been struggling to rip out suddenly came free and whipped back, a sharp end stabbing into and between his ribs, straight into his right lung. A thousand-to-one chance, the doctor had said when they'd got him to Casualty. He'd never heard of an injury like that from just pulling a slat out of a rotten wall.

That was the last they'd seen of Nate; always nervous, he'd refused to come back, saying the house was jinxed. "Good riddance," his boss had said, "shown himself for a coward."

No more was said, but Seth couldn't forget the blood. As the boy lay on the floor, moaning, he'd bled heavily – by the time the ambulance got there, he'd been lying in a pool of the stuff. Funny thing, though. Once Nate had been loaded onto a stretcher and the foreman had sent everyone home for the day (no one was in much of a mood to carry on after that), Seth had come back into the room with a big bucket of soapy water, ready to clean up the mess.

Except there wasn't any. The floor was clean, devoid even of dust. The sweeping marks left by a mop crossed the floor, but it was already dry. Seth wasn't entirely sure how that was possible, but made himself let it go. The foreman must have sent someone back while they were all taking care of Nate, he reasoned. Must have. He took the bucket back into the kitchen and emptied it down the sink, absently listening to the water gurgle down through the pipes to the sewer below. Seth shivered. It sounded like something being digested. He stashed the bucket in a cupboard under the sink and made his way quickly out of the house, aware it was growing darker. Was it that late? By the time he got to the front door he was sweating, and he banged the door harder into the jamb than he'd intended, jumping at the hollow bang it generated. He fumbled in his pocket for the keys and then almost dropped them in his haste to lock the door. He fiddled around for the right key and finally he found it, sighing with relief as he pushed it into the lock and turned. The tumblers clicked into place, and Seth heard a faint rumble. Frowning, he looked around and tried to remember the local geography. Did the Underground run under here?

He turned his back on the door, ignoring the itching sensation between his shoulder blades, and surveyed the quiet street. The house had been dark, and growing darker by the minute – he'd thought sunset must be close. Yet here, outside, it was a sunny mid-afternoon – hours of daylight left. He shook his head and resolved to check the windows; he'd thought all the shutters had been removed, but perhaps the foreman had put some back because of broken glass or something. He turned and stared upward, but saw nothing to suggest that; blind glass stared back at him, absorbing what light it could into the shadows within. He stood there for some minutes, watching, but the house was quiet. Finally, he turned and walked swiftly to his car, eager to get home.

The renovation had gone fairly smoothly after that; if he were a superstitious man, Seth thought to himself, he could almost believe that it was satisfied with the blood already spilt. In a matter of six weeks, the plumbing and wiring were in with no injury worse than a stubbed toe or cut finger. The workmen seemed happy, although he'd heard mutterings about this job being jinxed; echoes of Nate on the day he was hurt. "Ignore them," the foreman said, "builders like to moan, you know that."

And he did know that, didn't he. He'd seen enough of it in his lifetime; sweeps weren't averse to a good complaining session either. Still, the job was getting done. Plaster went up and refurbished floorboards went down; the house started to look as if it might make a home again one day.

Seth had wandered into the kitchen early one morning, ready to oversee the installation of the new cupboards and sink. The kitchen was huge, running the entire width of the house at the back, and gave a view of what was going to be a beautiful garden when the landscapers had finished. Right now it was a sea of dirt and rubble, but he had plans that Trudy would love. A deck, for a start, and a pond – she could have those fish she was always on about; what were they again? Koi, that was it. She could have a whole bloody fountain out there if she wanted, he thought, there was space enough.

He heard something rustling behind him, and someone huffing, and turned around. Alan, the foreman, was helping a lad heft what looked like an armload of canvas out of the cellar – soot dropping everywhere onto his nice clean floor. "What's going on?" he asked.

"Sorry, guv," the man answered. He bore a pained expression, as if he'd hurt himself. "These are a bastard to lift, and they've got to come out. No other way, sorry."

"What are they?" Seth asked, moving closer. They smelled burnt, and he stepped back again, not wanting to get dirty himself.

"Canvas sacking, guv," the foreman replied. "Covered in soot, too. There's loads of 'em down there, it's going to take a few trips to get them all up."

The two men were moving in a cloud of soot; it settled around them like ash, and Seth could feel it getting at the back of his throat. He coughed, and moved back once more.

"Oh well," he muttered, "nothing else for it, I guess." He motioned to the two men to carry on, then cried out when something fell from the middle of the stinking heap. "What's that?"

The three of them leant down and examined the object now lying on the kitchen floor. It was a tiny bone, segmented; perhaps a finger, Seth thought.

The workmen dumped the sacks onto the floor and backed off, rubbing their hands against their clothes as if trying to wipe themselves clean. The foreman looked up, his face white behind the patches of soot that spread across his cheeks and forehead. "Better call the police, guv," he said. "That's human, that is."

It was indeed human. The police had responded quickly, several of them making their way down into the cellar even as a forensics officer examined the bone on the kitchen floor, picking it up carefully with gloved hands and placing it into a clear plastic bag. "A finger," the man said, "from a child, I'd say maybe five or six years old, judging from the size. Not much more than that, certainly."

Trudy had gasped at that, and belatedly Seth realised she'd been hovering in the background, waiting for news. "A child?" she whispered, her voice near tears.

They took a moment to digest the information, no one wanting to think about a small child dying down there in the cellar. Had he cried for his mother? Had he even known her?

Finally, Alan broke the silence. "Why was a kid down there?" he asked. "Under those sacks, I mean. What was a kid doing down there?"

Seth cleared his throat. "My great-great grandfather lived in this house," he said. "He ran a group of chimney sweeps."

Alan wasn't getting it. "So?"

Now the forensic officer spoke. "It wasn't like now," he said. "They didn't have machines."

Alan stared blankly at them, seemingly unable – or perhaps unwilling – to understand.

"They used children," the man went on, and turned to Seth for confirmation, his expression vaguely disgusted. "That's right, isn't it?"

Seth nodded. "They did. Small boys, usually." He stared around, gestured at the cellar door. "They would have slept down there, under spare sacking." Now his voice cracked, as he thought about what it must have been like, how scared those children must have been. "There was a name for it," he said, and found he couldn't look at his companions as he went on; and he certainly wasn't going to catch Trudy's eye if he could help it. "They called it sleeping black."

"Christ."

Alan looked as if he was about to be sick, and Seth couldn't blame him. "My great-great grandfather was ruined when the laws protecting child sweeps came in," he said. "And thank God for that. He ended his days destitute; all that was left was this house."

"So, what," Alan said, "you resurrected the family business?"

Trudy snorted. Seth chose to ignore it.

"That's right, except these days it's all done by machine. Much safer."

The men looked at him for a moment, apparently unsure of how they felt about this new phase of the industry. Seth might be blameless, but the industry was built on blood and tears, no matter how far back that was.

"Look," he went on, "I can't help what he did, can I? It's different now, and I run a clean company; my men are happy with their jobs. This house is pretty much all that's left of the old days, and I want to bring it back to what it was, make it great again." He looked around the kitchen, sighed, and added "and my wife will kill me if I don't."

"Too right," she said, and stormed out of the kitchen.

They laughed at that, and the ice was broken. The forensics officer put the bag into a pocket of his overalls, and made for the door. "There'll be officers searching the basement," he said, "just to see if there are any more bones down there, but these are old. My report will show that – barring anything new turning up down there – they'll be done by tonight."

Then he was gone, and the atmosphere in the kitchen suddenly felt warmer. The foreman gestured down at the cellar, where sounds of policemen digging and generally searching the room wafted up to them. "Can't do much down there now, guv," he said, "not till they're done. I could get on with some plastering in the meantime, if you like?"

Seth nodded. "That'll be great, thanks. The cellar can wait a day or two, I suppose."

Something banged in the room beneath their feet, and both men winced.

"Look on the bright side," Alan said. "At least it'll be emptied out for us."

Four days later, Seth stood in the centre of the cellar with Alan and shook his head. "Not so empty after all, is it?"

The police had left a load of canvas sacks piled up in one corner of the cellar; there were footprints all over the floor, tracked in the soot that laid over everything. They'd tracked soot all up the stairs into the kitchen and all over the house while they did a cursory search for anything else untoward; the forensics officer they'd seen had indeed confirmed the bones were over a hundred years old, and no more had been found – eventually, they'd called off the search and left Seth and the workmen in peace, but not before they'd ruined the floors and put them back to square one. It had taken Seth and the whole crew an entire day to clean the floors and walls in the main part of the house, and another to patch up minor scrapes in the plaster, the scratches and scuffs on the new wooden floors left by police boots. Now the house was clean again, apart from the cellar.

Seth took a step forward, reached out and grabbed the handle of a broom leaning against the wall. "I guess we'd better get started, eh?"

Alan nodded and picked up his own broom, and the two men started to sweep.

Two hours later, the floor was clear – they'd swept it and scooped several dustpans worth of soot, fluff and general filth from the floor. The brooms were now leaning against the outside wall, and both men were contemplating the final hurdle: the pile of sacking left in one corner.

"What do you think?" Seth asked, and gestured towards the narrow windows lining the outside wall. "Can we get them all out through those?"

Alan tilted his head to one side, contemplated the window frames. "Might damage the frames opening the windows," he said, "they don't look like they've been used in years. Still, you were going to replace them anyway, weren't you?"

Seth sighed. "I was," he said. "Maybe not just yet, but I was." He stared forlornly at the glass, already cracked in places. "What the hell," he said, "might as well clear it all in one go, I suppose." He moved forward and laid hold of the handles at the bottom of the first window. He braced himself, and tugged upward, hard. The window barely moved, but it was a start. He put his back into it, and the second attempt saw the frame shoot up, making the glass rattle in its frame as it slammed up as far as it could. Mercifully, the glass held, and Seth breathed out slowly, relieved. "Might be able to wait a while after all," he said, and grinned. "Come on."

Finally, the cellar was empty, the floors swept. It looked huge, now that everything was cleared away, and Seth found himself wondering what he could do with it. Cinema room, he wondered? Games room? His musings were interrupted by Alan, who walked back into the cellar wiping his hands on his overalls, grinning widely. Halfway through clearing the sacks they'd found a door leading outside, and the job had gone quicker after that.

"All done, guv," he said, "something like forty canvas sacks piled high in one corner against the back wall. I'll take 'em to the tip tomorrow for you, get 'em out of the way."

He looked pointedly at his watch, and Seth belatedly realised how late it must be – the sun was already sinking down below the rooftops, throwing the cellar into a deep gloom. The temperature was dropping fast now that there was no direct sunlight (not that it ever got much), and there was something more – the atmosphere was changing as the light dimmed, and Seth found he didn't want to be in there anymore.

He forced himself to return Alan's grin, and shook the man's hand. "Great stuff, we've done a lot today. Off you go home, have a pint on me, eh?" He followed the man out of the cellar, the skin at the back of his neck itching as if something was crawling there. He slapped at it, his meaty hand raising nothing more than sweat. It was cold down there, he thought, why was he still sweating?

They reached the top of the stairs and he slammed the door shut behind him, turning the key in the lock and stepping back almost in one move.

"What's the matter?" Alan asked.

Seth felt himself redden, ashamed suddenly of the fear that had overtaken him. "Nothing, just want to let you out, lock up, that's all."

Alan said nothing more, but Seth hadn't been convincing, he could see. Still, he was the boss, and if he wanted to hurry up, he was under no obligation to explain himself. He muttered a goodnight and locked the front door behind his foreman, watching through the spyhole in the front door as the man tripped easily down the front steps and made for his car, parked a couple of doors away.

Then Alan was gone, and Seth found himself alone in that huge, empty house. And he realised with something like shock that he hated it.

Work went on without any further hitches, and Seth had to admit that was at least keeping Trudy quiet. They already had a nice house, a four bedroom detached in leafy Cuffley, but that wasn't good enough now she knew there was a four bedroom house in Islington they could have. That was proper posh, she said. That was class. Seth smiled to himself when he remembered that. She wouldn't know class if it jumped up and bit her, any more than he would, when it came right down to it. He hadn't lied when he told Alan and the forensics officer that all that was left of his great-great-grandfather's business was the house; he'd grown up working class and hadn't had a problem with that, but Trudy had always wanted more than that. She deserved better, she said, and in those days – when he'd been blinded by her looks – he'd been happy to work his arse off to give it to her. Except it had never quite been enough; there was always something for her to moan about. Until now, that was. If he could get this house the way she wanted it, he hoped she'd finally be happy – and he tried very hard to ignore the voice inside his head that laughed at that, that asked him if he actually knew his wife.

Then it was moving day, and Trudy was happy. The house was decorated as she'd wanted, she had her en suites and her chandeliers (all of which she'd been allowed to choose), she'd chosen all the furniture new, rather than bringing anything from home.

Home. Seth looked around at the living room, the huge plump sofas, the carpet you could drown in, the chandeliers... this was home now, for better or worse, and he knew if he valued his sanity he'd better not admit that, actually, he'd preferred their house in Cuffley. Trudy was beaming at him from the other sofa, feet up, fluffy slippers on the carpet at her feet, remote in her hand as she flicked through channels on the obscenely large flat screen TV.

"Comfy?" she asked, popping a chocolate into her mouth.

He nodded and smiled, slightly queasy at the smear of chocolate beside her lip, the sounds she made as she chewed and swallowed.

"Tea?"

He nodded again. "Please."

Then she was gone, off to make yet another cuppa in that enormous kitchen she was so happy with. He heard the distant sounds of the fridge door opening and closing, the kettle being plugged in, and Trudy humming to herself as she pottered about. It wouldn't last. She'd never been particularly domesticated: this was just another new toy to play with till she got bored.

Something nearby rustled, and Seth stiffened. He sat there, barely breathing, listening. For long seconds, there was nothing – and then it came again. It was a soft, rustling sound, as if something were skittering around the floor. Seth leaned forward, searching for the source of the scuffling, but could see nothing. He heard it again, and as he listened, he realised it was coming from the fireplace.

He frowned. He'd had his blokes unblock all the fireplaces and sweep the chimneys clean; there shouldn't be anything in there. He got up and went over to the fireplace, picked up an iron and poked about in the grate. Nothing.

Trudy came back in and glared at him, quick to read his mood. 'What now?'

"Nothing," he said. "Just thought I heard something, that's all."

"What?" she asked. "A mouse? Was it a mouse? Oh God, we've got mice, haven't we..."

"We haven't got mice!" he shouted, then managed to measure his tone. "There's nothing here, I've checked. I must have dropped off, imagined it or something."

"Well," Trudy said, "it wouldn't be the first time, I suppose."

She wasn't convinced, and Seth knew she'd be furious if there did prove to be some kind of infestation and she had to have the house 'fumigated'. "I'll get someone in to check it out, alright?" he said. "Just to make sure."

Trudy humphed, but put his tea down and laid a plate of biscuits down beside it on the coffee table. "Don't let it go cold," she warned, which was as close to admitting he'd succeeded in mollifying her as she was ever prepared to go.

"I won't," he said, and sat back down armed with a digestive. "I'll call them in the morning."

Trudy subsided back onto the sofa, slightly out of breath. "I'll have to do more exercise," she said. "I'm puffed." She picked up another chocolate, examining it closely with something that Seth thought looked suspiciously like love. "I don't want to get fat, do I," she said.

He smothered a laugh. "No," he said. "Course not."

That ship had sailed a long time ago, but he knew better than to fall into that particular trap.

The night had passed without further incident and now, here he was, two in the morning and lying flat on his back staring at the ceiling. He could hear a child crying. He wondered idly which house it was coming from, which of the neighbour had a family... and then, as time went on and the crying persisted, he grew angry at whoever it was that could ignore a kiddie who was obviously upset.

At some point he fell asleep, and when he woke the

house was quiet. Trudy had left a note on the kitchen table that filled him with dread: 'Gone shopping.' He made himself some tea and toast and went through into his office, sat down at the computer screen and logged on, checked what bookings the company had coming up. He relaxed a bit when he saw they were fully booked for the next six weeks; most of the bookings were houses in the posher parts of London, a few were small companies in the area. Work was fine for now.

He turned his chair around and gazed out of the window at the street beyond, watched as the neighbours and passers-by walked in either direction, saw various cars come and go. After half an hour or so, he frowned. He'd seen the neighbours on either side leave, the occupants of the house on their left had left together; a middle-aged couple and a teenage girl, sulky at having to go out with the parents. The house on the right would seem to be occupied by an elderly man, and judging by the cars parked outside, no one had small children. No one had child car seats installed, he saw no sign of buggies being loaded into boots – so who'd been crying?

When Trudy came home that night, laden with bags, he asked if she'd got to know any of the neighbours yet. He declined to mention the bags; he valued his life.

"Not really," she said, busying herself with the joy of unpacking. "They all seem a bit stuck up to me, you know?"

He did know. And he could have told her she wouldn't fit in if she'd asked him, but she'd wanted this house and now she had it. She'd just have to learn to like it. "Any kids around here?" he asked, trying to keep his tone nonchalant.

"No, thank God. Noisy little bleeders."

He smiled. She could try and be as classy as she liked, but he knew his wife.

"Why do you want to know?" she asked, looking up from the shopping.

"Just wondered," he said. "Thought I heard one crying last night."

Trudy shook her head. "Nah. Must have been a cat or something."

"Suppose so," he said, oddly relieved. "Hope it doesn't make a habit of it."

He'd heard the crying intermittently since then, and knew it couldn't be a cat. Cats didn't call for help, or say they were frightened. And they didn't leave sooty handprints all over the wall. He'd got used to rising early, cleaning the evidence away before Trudy woke up – she'd heard the cat a few times, she said, and had taken to knocking back a couple of glasses of wine before going to bed. So she could sleep. He didn't mind; let her enjoy herself. He had a feeling the house was only warming up.

So now he was sitting in the chair at the end of the bed, watching the wall as Trudy slept. He'd got rid of the latest lot of marks, even though the ghost he now believed it to be had smeared them as he rose, apparently trying to grind the dirt into the wall so that he couldn't clean it. He'd lost weight over the last few weeks, and his pyjamas were baggy now; nothing had been baggy on him in years, and it was only a matter of time before Trudy noticed that, too.

As if summoned by that thought, he heard her sit up. "What's up, you sick?"

"No, I'm fine," he lied. "Couldn't sleep, that's all. Didn't want to disturb you."

Trudy heaved herself off the mattress and came over to stand beside his chair. Her hand, when it felt his cheek, was surprisingly tender, and he felt tears pricking.

"You sure?" she asked. "You're getting a bit thin, Seth."

He smiled. "Yeah, I know," he said. "Diet."

She stared at him for a while, thinking about that, and he could see the wheels turning as she decided whether or not to call him out on his lie.

"Well," she said finally, "don't go too far, eh? Otherwise it's the doc's for you."

"I won't," he promised, and did his best to smile. "Want to go out for dinner tonight?"

"Yeah," she answered, and smiled back, true warmth in her expression for what felt like the first time in months. "That'll be nice. Fatten you up a bit, eh?"

He nodded and smiled, let her wander off to the bathroom. "I'll book a table at that new Italian down the road," she threw over her shoulder. "That alright?"

"Fine," he called, and went back to watching the wall. Dinner had been a great success. Trudy had dressed up, and had even gone out and bought him a new suit. "Other one's too big," she said. "Can't have you showing me up."

She'd worked out his size perfectly, just by looking at him, and he felt much better once he was suited and booted and was sitting down with a glass of wine and a dirty great steak. Good times. Trudy could moan, and did, but she knew her husband – and she knew how to cheer him up when he needed it.

They'd laughed and joked, and worked their way through three courses and a couple of bottles of wine before weaving up the road home and to bed. More good times. Then he'd passed out, happy and sated, and all thought of ghosts forgotten.

That night an explosion of soot burst into their bedroom, apparently let loose by a bird trapped in the flue. Seth didn't know where it could have come from; he'd had them all professionally cleaned before they moved in.

The bird, whatever it was (pigeon?), was flapping about in the middle of a pool of soot, one wing broken, crying its heart out as it tried to escape. Trudy had screamed when it happened, then started crying and decamped to the spare room, insisting she was going to stay there till it was fixed and all cleaned up. When she slammed the door to the spare room, the chimney had puffed out another cloud of soot, and Seth had groaned at what it contained.

A little boy stood in front of him; a little boy maybe five years old, wearing nothing but a pair of britches, every bone in his torso standing out in stark relief. There were huge circles under his eyes, and his cheek bones jutted out above deep hollows. The child was crying and reaching out to him, and Seth felt the room start to spin when he realised the boy was missing a finger.

"It's alright," he whispered, and the boy's sobs started to taper off, his chest hitching as he tried not to cry.

"I won't hurt you," Seth whispered again, and he sighed with relief as the child started to dim.

It was dawn, and as the light in the room brightened the child started to fade, but not before he left his mark. Black hands on white paint, dotted all over the room.

Seth cleaned all the handprints off the wall, then went and phoned Mick, the most trusted of his sweeps. He explained what had happened, and waited for Mick to come and sort it out.

Two hours later, Mick emerged from the fireplace covered in soot, echoing the child Seth had seen in the dawn light. "There was a pocket up there," he said. "Some soot had got trapped in it; looks like it all got dislodged when the bird panicked."

He had something in his hands, and now he raised them, holding whatever it was out to Seth. "You'd better get the cops back in," he said. "I found this up there."

'This' was a skull, very small, almost devoid of teeth.

Seth gasped. "There was a kid up there?"

Mick nodded. "I brought this down; the rest's still up there. Thought the police would want it left."

Seth nodded. "Yeah, you did right, Mick. Thank you." He paid the man and called the police, then went to tell his wife.

"There's a what?" she screamed. "In the fucking chimney?"

Seth nodded. "The police are coming," he said, "and Mick's cleaned out all the soot. I'll get the cleaners in once the police take the remains away."

"Remains!" she shrieked. "Oh my God. I can't stay here, Seth. I can't." She was up and flitting about the room, picking up clothes as she went. "I'm going back to Cuffley," she said. "I'll stay there for a few days, okay?"

Seth nodded, dumbly. "Want me to come?"

Trudy stopped what she was doing and stared at her husband. "No," she said, but her tone wasn't unkind. "You stay here and sort things out, love. I don't know if I can live in this house after this." She paused. "Is that bad?"

Seth stared back at her. "What do you want me to do?"

"I don't know. Sell it?"

Seth tried to make sense of what she was saying, but failed. This was the house she'd declared she always wanted. He'd made it perfect for her, just like she wanted. And now she didn't know if she wanted it anymore?

Trudy moved closer; as always, she knew what he was thinking. "I just need to think," she said. "Maybe we could get it blessed or something? What do you think?"

Seth's eyes slowly focussed on her face. Her smug face. "I think," he said, "this is crazy. It's over a hundred years old, and it'll be gone by tomorrow. Call a fucking priest to bless the house if you want, Trude, but I'm not selling. Not after all this."

"Right," she answered, trying to salvage something from the mess. "We'll do that, then. Talk about the rest of it later." Then she swept past him, bag in hand, and clattered down the stairs, leaving him alone once more.

The police had turned up, taken the skeleton away, and when it was confirmed the remains were as old as the finger they'd found, they'd allowed him to finish cleaning the house, putting it right.

Seth hadn't heard the crying since; he supposed the little lad had no need now he was finally found, finally going to be buried. The police were trawling through records from that time, trying to work out who he was – but it was a needle in a haystack, and they all knew it.

The house felt different. It felt lonely. Seth had talked to Trudy a few times in the days since the body was found, but she wasn't ready to come back. "It doesn't feel right," she'd said. So that was that. He'd leave her in Cuffley for a bit; see how things settled. He might even move back there, rent the house out or sell it.

Saturday night, and he was alone. He'd got used to hearing things in this house, whispers and scuffling. He supposed it was haunted by more than one kid after all this time. He thought of his great-great-grandfather and realised he hated him. "All your fault," he slurred, draining his wine glass and reaching for the bottle. "Bastard. Why couldn't you treat 'em right, eh? Why couldn't you feed the poor little sods, look after 'em?"

No answer. Nor had he expected one. The house was cold, and Seth shivered. "Time for bed," he muttered, and drained his glass one last time, shaking the bottle to make sure it was empty before putting it back on the coffee table. "Get warm," he said, barely making sense even to himself. He stumbled up the stairs, stopping twice on the way up to look behind him; to make sure nothing was following. Finally, he reached his bedroom and walked in, then made sure the window was locked and there was nothing up the chimney or in the en suite before he collapsed on top of the bed fully dressed, asleep almost before he hit the mattress.

Trudy let herself in and stood in the hall, listening. The house was silent. She'd been ringing Seth all morning, ready to come home. She felt bad about leaving him there, all alone, but if she knew him he was consoling himself with booze and takeaways. She peeked into the living room through the open door and smiled; empty pizza cartons and wine bottles littered the room, it stank of stale food and alcohol. She made her way to the window and pulled the top of it down, keen to let the room begin to air. Then she made her way upstairs, calling Seth as she went.

When she reached their room, she hesitated, scared suddenly to open the door. *Don't be stupid, Trude*, she told herself. *He's just passed out, that's all. Not the first time.*

But she still couldn't open it. She took hold of the handle, and found herself trying not to cry. She felt so lonely, all of a sudden. Why was that? The air was cold, and she watched her breath furl out in front of her as she shivered. Had he left the window open all night? She steeled herself and turned the handle, finally, pushed the bedroom door open and walked in.

And started to scream.

Seth was lying on the bed, face down, and Trudy could see soot all over him. It had blocked his mouth, his nose, and was pooling on the bedspread around both. His face was black with it, and his eyes – his eyes were staring at her, stretched wide, terrified. Someone had laid canvas sacking over his body, lots of it, and she could see it moving as if someone else were sleeping there, using her husband's corpse to keep warm. The sacking was old, deeply impregnated with soot, black as night. Little hands, barely more than bone, crept over the sacking's edge, and Trudy found herself running, screaming at the top of her voice. She didn't want to see. She didn't want to know what was in there with her husband, sleeping black.

# *Satin Road*

## Gary Fry

Every city, town or village has one: Station Road.

Back at school as a kid, I looked into the history of the one near where I grew up, learning that in the 19th Century there'd been a railway stop there, on a line running between Bradford and Liverpool. After the death of the wool trade, however, it had been closed down and replaced by a strip of terrace housing with no gardens, just characterless front and rear yards.

It was one of these properties that Dean Wetley and his mother rented from the council. Dean was the first boy ever to get expelled from our village school, but it wasn't for any vicious act – no bullying, vandalism or abuse of teachers. His only crime, as far as we eleven year-olds could ascertain at the time, was refusing to kowtow to the institution's policy on uniforms.

Dean was a strange boy, always listening to heavy metal and reading books with garish covers like *The Exorcist*. He'd grown his hair long like his music idols, and this had resulted in conflict with our headmaster, who'd insisted that Dean have it cut. Dean (and his hippy-ish single mum) had disagreed, claiming that hairstyle had nothing to do with the school, ultimately leading to the sixteen year-old being kicked out only months before his final exams.

In other circumstances, such a boy might be seen as a hero among ex-pupils, but that didn't turn out to be the case. On the basis of Dean's particular interests, others hung around his house on bikes and called him things like 'Devil worshipper,' 'black warlock' and similar horror-film nonsense. Then one night some uneducated wit erased a T and an O from his street's name, presumably believing that S ATI N ROAD alluded to the Prince of Darkness rather than a smooth, glossy fabric.

As for me, I actually liked Dean. My parents owned a convenience store just around the corner from his home and he often called in, both before and after he'd been ousted from school, grabbing food, drink and other household essentials. I enjoyed scary stuff on TV myself, and Dean always had a recommendation – maybe reruns of *The Twilight Zone* or new episodes of *Tales of the Unexpected*. Our shop also rented out VHS films, but my dad never let Dean hire any of the 18 certificates. I was glad about that, because some looked frightening and I didn't want Dean tempting me to watch them.

School was full of the kind of kids I considered far worthier candidates for being expelled. This was the 1980s, a period of designer label-endorsed arrogance and petty social warfare. What with our parents' modest affluence, my younger brother and I, both moderate academic achievers, were caught between two camps, with the rougher, poorer pupils calling us 'middleclass,' and the well-to-do, clever ones dismissing us as 'thickos.' There was no way we could win and so, keeping our profiles low, we didn't even try.

The headmaster, Mr Rhodes – the man at the centre

of that Dean Wetley injustice – was a big man, maybe in his early fifties, and with a perfectly bald head. He always wore a pair of blood-red braces over a white shirt, like the actor Michael Douglas in a film called *Wall Street*, which my business-minded dad had seen umpteen times. As the school was such a small institution with only skeleton staff, Mr Rhodes, alongside his other duties, taught both English and PE.

Maybe this was another reason why he and Dean hadn't got along; I remember that the long-haired boy had hated sport, especially football, which in his opinion was only played by 'thugs and vandals.' I could sympathise as I myself struggled in English classes, partly because I was slightly dyslexic but mainly because I preferred watching things to reading about them. I guess I was just a product of my TV-obsessed time.

Whatever the truth was, I dreaded handing in homework, because Mr Rhodes was far from sparing with criticism. Although the sight of blood scared me in horror films, this was more than matched by the amount of red pen regularly added to my class book. He often made cutting comments, as if to drive the humiliation deeper. For instance, if you spelt a word incorrectly – say, 'witch' instead of 'which' – he'd make a big deal of the issue, suggesting alternative readings of a sentence with the erroneous word active ("But what would the *witch* make of this, young man?").

On the day it truly began – the real after-the-event business between Dean Wetley and his former headmaster – I got feedback on a story which my class had been asked to write based on a favourite film. The idea was to explore the differences between visual and written material. None of that meant much to me, but I'd enjoyed – for maybe the first time ever in an English class – composing my version of *Night of the Living Dead*, a movie I'd seen late at night when my scaredy-cat brother and fretful parents had gone to bed.

But Mr Rhodes clearly hadn't enjoyed reading it.

"Quite apart from all the errors," he said, handing across my book parted at my tale, so that I could see what a bloodbath it now was, "I think I need to have words with your parents, who shouldn't allow you to watch such rubbish."

This was something I'd failed to consider while writing the piece, but even so I didn't understand what was so bad about what I'd done.

"It's only a horror film, sir," I replied, assuming he'd understand that – in that day and age, what with bootleg video tapes in circulation – it could have been something far worse. "A lot of us kids watch 'em. They're just a bit of fun."

Mr Rhodes's bald head grew perceptibly redder. He puffed himself up to his striking height, big belly sticking out like a farmyard animal's.

"Perhaps you might tell me what's particularly fun about... well, how do you describe it? Heads exploding and legs dropping off."

A murmur of restrained amusement swept across the class – everyone was afraid of our headmaster – but then I recalled that it could have been Dean who'd recommended the film I'd aped and that Mr Rhodes might remember how much the young man had enjoyed horror fiction. Perhaps he believed that the genre was inherently disruptive and needed to be stamped out.

I glanced down at my story, which had plenty of acerbic comments scribbled in its margins. I wasn't argumentative but was no shrinking violet either, so I found myself half-defending my work.

"We all like scary stories because scary things happen in life. They help us deal with this kind of stuff in our heads."

"Oh, but nightmares are for children, and those considerably younger than yourself," Mr Rhodes shot back, snapping his red braces against his chest so hard that it had to have hurt. "Now kindly go away and redo your homework by selecting a more appropriate source of fiction."

I couldn't be sure, but something about how the man had replied – with an aversion of his gaze, as well as the non-negotiable way he'd concluded our discussion – made me think that bad dreams were something he might once have suffered, back when he'd been a boy himself so many years earlier. All the same, I relinquished my line of argument in case the vindictive teacher, having overeagerly seen off Dean Wetley, started on me next.

Later that day, I went to my parents' shop and hung out with my dad until it was closing time. If the headmaster planned to contact my parents about my choice of viewing, he'd surely call our house number, so I'd figured that I'd be better off here for the time being. But as four o'clock came and went, and then five, and soon six, there was no communication from my mother at home, and so I assumed that Mr Rhodes had more important matters to address.

Just before Dad shut the shop at eight, Dean Wetley strode in, long hair flapping around his leather-clad shoulders and a skull t-shirt lurking under the leather jacket. He and I chatted in the casual way we'd developed over the last year or so, bound by a love of monsters and gore. I often thought that it was odd for a sixteen year-old – very nearly an adult – to be interested in such material, but then realised that this was how the school's headmaster wanted us all to think and dismissed the notion.

I told Dean what Mr Rhodes had said about my story and about the horror fiction we both loved. But I hadn't expected such a peculiar response.

"Don't worry about him," the young man said, taking from a nearby shelf the items he'd come to buy. "I'm gonna sort that man out good n proper before long."

Just as I was about to ask what Dean had in mind, he struck off across the shop floor, dropped the pack of candles on the countertop, paid my dad at the till, and then left the building with haste. Had his out-of-work mother run out of money again, using candlelight because she'd failed to pay the electricity bill? Whatever the truth was, it was surely my beloved horror films which made me entertain an alternative, more sinister reason for her son buying this particular product.

I didn't think much more about Dean Wetley the following week; I was too busy catching up with homework, including rewriting that film-influenced story for my English class (this time I chose something safe: a Burt Reynolds comedy). However, while walking to school one day with my little brother, I strolled along Station Road – or Satin Road, as its sign now declared – and saw what local hooligans had done to the young man's rented home.

Using a green spray can, someone had written 'weirdo' in big letters across the only downstairs window. A heavy object – a brick, maybe – had been lobbed through one of two more upstairs, leaving shards of glass sticking up and down like teeth in the jaws of some monster. I don't know what dead animal had been dumped on the front doorstep but it had been impossible for Dean or his mother to scrub off all the red it had left behind.

I felt sorry for the young man – who by this time I might even have described as a casual friend – but said nothing about the incident at school. Any one of the bigger boys might be responsible for the vandalism and I didn't want them shifting their fickle hatred my way. I also had my younger brother to think about, who was a bit less robust than me, more like our mum than our dad.

All the same, the day I heard from someone at the shop that Miss Wetley and her son had decided to move away to avoid further trouble, I went around to see Dean, hoping I could persuade him that he wasn't disliked by everyone in the area.

When he opened the door after my tentative knock he looked furtive and ghosted, tired and edgy. He didn't let me inside, just came out into his yard, hands clawing with anxiety as if I'd disturbed him in some enterprise he was eager to return to at once. I tried talking about our usual enthusiasms – horror stuff chief among them – but the more I referred to such scary material, the more uneasy he seemed to grow.

Then I remembered something he'd said the last time we'd spoken and asked him about that. His sullen-serious face brightened.

"Just you wait," he said, before heading back inside, long hair swaying in his wake. At that moment I noticed a book hanging out of his back pocket, whose title read something like MAGICK RITUALS. Before he disappeared beyond the front door, he added, "Mr Rhodes will never know he had it in him."

I was troubled for days by this cryptic comment, not to mention the implications of that volume he'd been reading. My concern grew so prevalent that I eventually succumbed to temptation and decided to figure out what Dean was up to. I confided in my brother first, who, with the exception of a few friends in the village, was the person I hung out with most.

Neil hated horror stuff – by which I mean that he was afraid of it – but he loved spy fiction, James Bond and the like, and was always pretending that he was a secret agent, using gadgets he'd invented in the kind of imagination my favourite fiction overexcited.

"We need to put his house under surveillance!" he said, eyes as bright as I'd seen them in years. "We'll have to use binoculars and a camera and other stuff, building up a...a...what do you call it...a *profile* about the place. That's how we'll be able to see what he's up to!"

"Hold on, slow down," I said, wondering how many laws my brother was breaking in one torturous exclamation. All the same, I felt that Neil might be on to something. "That might not be enough, but I guess it's a start."

Judging by my previous visit, I didn't think Dean would allow us inside if we called on him, let alone permit us to look around the place. And so the only option was to monitor the house, looking for signs of suspicious activity. It would be a risky business, but it appealed to my brother's childish fondness for espionage and might even put my mind at rest about matters which grew darker every time I reflected upon them.

A few days before we set our plan in action, Dean Wetley came to the shop again when I was helping out my dad for extra pocket money. He seemed distant and distracted, and our conversation, previously lively, was restricted to mere grunts of "hello" and "goodbye." What he plucked from the shelves troubled me even more. The shop stocked a wide range of products, and when Dean selected a leather football, I could only assume that it was a gift for someone else; after all, he'd always hated sports, another reason why he and PE-teaching Mr Rhodes had experienced so much friction together.

But what was I expected to make of the *braces* Dean also bought that day?

These weren't red like the headmaster's but a standard dull black (the only colour the store had had in stock). All the same, the fact that the young man, who dressed in music t-shirts and lived alone with only a woman, needed them at all worried me, especially in light of comments he'd made recently.

Later that week, Neil and I spent a few days hanging

around Satin Road on our bikes, using battery-operated walkie-talkies to communicate our feeble findings. My brother kept an eye on the rear of the building while I watched the front, but after a whole weekend we had little more than the following few notes in the assignment dossier Neil had prepared for our mission:

- *Saturday, 10am: target's mother puts rubbish out in backyard bin*
- *Saturday, 12pm: target seen at front upstairs window, reading book (title invisible at distance, even with binoculars)*
- *Saturday, 2pm: target spotted at rear downstairs window, carrying narrow white objects (which could be candles)*
- *Saturday, 2.30pm: target's mother has cigarette on front doorstep*
- *Saturday, 4pm, target exits house from rear, walks into village, enters charity shop in high street and emerges with bag full of soft-looking items, possibly clothing; target goes home and re-enters house*

Sunday, by contrast, was a complete wash-out, a real waste of time. Neil and I waited for several hours and saw nothing significant, before going home and watching something on TV, an exciting show which made up for the boredom of our morning. Indeed, we were about to give up on the project when, after returning to school the following morning, an unexpected development occurred.

The Wetleys moved out.

Having seen the removal van parked in front of that terrace house, with two men loading tatty pieces of furniture into its rear, I struggled to see what Dean had been plotting with Mr Rhodes as its target. After all, the moment I stepped back into the school, I spotted the headmaster pacing for assembly, big body as healthy-looking as it had always been, bald head gleaming under the corridor's strip-lights, and those braces holding together his voluminous outfit.

Had the young man's nerve deserted him? Was the savage, black magic-inspired revenge I'd imagined been all brag and no action?

I couldn't be sure what had gone on here, but when I ventured home that afternoon, with my dutiful brother in tow, we saw only a deserted property where our surveillance target had lived the day before. That broken upper-storey window remained boarded up, and the only one downstairs had been left slightly open on its runner. Other than that, there was nothing – just blank silence inside, where little worth stealing could still dwell.

Later that evening, Neil and I talked about the property, and pledged to finish off what we'd started.

"Maybe he's left something inside," I speculated, my mind working like a character in a horror movie. I was eleven years old. "It could be something horrid, something *weird*."

"*Don't*," my brother replied, probably because I was turning his fun spy mission into a dalliance with dangerous forces, and not any of this earth.

As I struggled to sleep that night, with the moon pale and bloated behind my bedroom curtains, I couldn't help reflecting on everything I'd learnt about Dean Wetley. He read books like *The Exorcist*... he was interested in heavy metal music, whose lyrics were often about Satanic practices...he'd bought particular items from my parents' shop, such as candles used in magic rituals, as well as clothing items resembling those worn by his victim...

As my digital clock's blood-red digits flicked to 2:00 a.m., I realised that I was unable to nod off. I got up and changed out of my pyjamas and then snuck into my brother's room. I could hear Dad snoring across the hallway, and so doubted that Mum would detect us exiting the house if we tiptoed. At first Neil didn't look happy with my proposal – maybe *frightened* is a better description of his wide-eyed face – but when I alluded to the fearlessness of James Bond, he agreed to join me. I wanted to believe that I simply needed moral support, but I think even then there was another reason why I'd enlisted his help.

After escaping our nice house on the village's fringes, we ran the half-mile to Satin Road. Nobody else was about this early (or late), and a rough breeze cut in, icing our cheeks with a threat of imminent winter. Down a narrow lane flanked by creaking trees, I noticed something fast scurrying along the pavement, using ragged foliage as cover. I glanced that way, my heartrate so disrupted that all my perceptions trembled, and observed a dark shape, about a foot high and with too many limbs for any wild animal.

But then I realised my mistake. It was just the way the moon and a nearby streetlamp competed over ownership of the thing's shadow, each casting lengthy black strips to and from it. At any rate, whatever it was – a homeless cat, perhaps, or even a predatory fox – was soon gone, and Neil and I finally approached our destination.

I couldn't get Dean Wetley's recent comments out of my head: "Before long I'm gonna sort that man out good n proper... Mr Rhodes will never know he had it in him." I found it difficult to believe that the young man had left the area without at least attempting to exact some kind of revenge on our bullish headmaster. That was why I'd come here in the dark, and also why, as soon as we reached that deserted house, I asked my brother to give me a foot up so that I could access its parted lower window.

"*Don't be an idiot!*" he shout-whispered, as we skulked in the property's shadow-laden front yard.

I promised that I wouldn't be long, taking a quick look around the place to make notes to add to our surveillance report. That settled Neil, and although his face registered grave misgivings, he helped me in the way I'd proposed.

After lifting the runner beyond the narrow opening, I was inside the house. Here was the lounge, a room bereft of furniture, with just a threadbare carpet which felt moist underfoot, as if the building was beset by a creeping rot. The kitchen along a short hallway was little better, suffering a faulty tap whose drip-drip-dripping into a steel sink sounded like a clock clipping away yet more time.

Knowing I must get on, I tried to figure out where Dean might have left some parting gift, an act involving his interests in the occult. *Satin Road*, I thought as I hurried upstairs, and then corrected that misspelling to its intended alternative: *Satan Road*. Trembling with disquiet, I continued searching, but in the young man's bedroom I found nothing other than balls of screwed up paper on bare floorboards, animated only by slivers of wind violating the boarded-up window. There was even less to observe in the one other bedroom – obviously Miss Wetley's – while the bathroom suffered just copious stains and an acrid stench.

That left only one final place to explore: the property's cellar.

As I slowly descended the building's rickety staircase, I tried to imagine where, if I were attracted to darkness, I'd practice a ritual with a view to enacting savage payback. I'd want to be well out of sight, even from those who knew me best, especially family members.

I recalled that book I'd seen Dean carrying one day – MAGICK RITUALS – and was put in mind of too many films I'd watched lately when I should have been asleep. In the house's cloying blackness, anything seemed possible, just as it had since I'd imagined that the young man who'd been expelled from school wanted compensation – not because he'd wished to continue with his studies, but because its bullying headmaster had questioned his character, making Dean feel bad about who he was.

I'd learn later in life that little else was more hurtful, but back then, as I took hold of that final door handle which allowed me access underground, my mind was filled with only demons and monsters.

I'd expected the cellar to be more pitch-dark than the rest of the house but was shocked to discover this wasn't true. Nevertheless, as flickering, ambient light guided me down a flight of stone steps, I experienced anything other than relief at being able to see where I was headed. Was someone still down here, maybe Dean himself, continuing to prepare whatever terrible thing he'd planned to inflict upon Mr Rhodes?

As I reached the foot of those stairs, my mouth felt full of dust while a frisky odour assaulted my nostrils, one I both recognised and couldn't quite place. Then my vision adjusted to take in the chill subterranean room and everything became immediately clear.

Candles (almost certainly those Dean had purchased at my parents' store a few weeks earlier) were stationed all around the cellar, each nearly burned to the stump and whose manic guttering caused uncertain light to lap against the walls like impossible tides. The candles traced the perimeter of a giant circle painted on the ground in thick white paint, but that wasn't the only alteration made to this rented property. At the heart of the circle, running in an unending back and forth line, was the kind of giant five-pointed star I'd seen in horror films. Back then I didn't know the name of such a shape, but realised that it was always involved in black magic rituals.

I glanced into the middle of what I learned later (after researching the issue as a way of making sense of it) was called a pentagram.

A figure was slumped in the centre of that underground chamber. Although ever-shifting candlelight lent it an uncertain structure, I made out clothing stuffed with newspaper: a pair of dark trousers, a white shirt, and, strapped across each side of its makeshift torso, *red braces*.

This was an effigy, and the person it represented wasn't difficult to guess at. I paced closer, my heart a restless object beneath my ribs. Then I noticed that the pretend man's head was formed by a football but that something drastic had occurred to its leather, the top splayed out as if all the air inside had surged upwards, ripping through the object's flesh. Whatever had affected this damage had left a glutinous liquid oozing down the ball's sides and dripping on to the guy's shoulders. At first I thought this must be what had dyed the black braces Dean had bought from the shop, but then, stooping to look closer, I noticed that it wasn't the colour of blood but a sickly, translucent green.

The substance didn't stop at the facsimile headmaster; as I moved fearfully around this human travesty, I noticed that it ran down its back, pooled on the concrete beneath, and then surged in a manic line towards the wall I'd been unable to view upon arrival. But now I observed more of that greenish stuff scribbled halfway up to the ceiling, stopping short at a shadow-filled cavity which, as the wavering light continued to spit and sputter, I realised was a brickless hole.

Had something emerged from that figure's head like some nightmare come to life? Had it then scurried away, boasting enough strength to break out of the room into all the soil around the property, before burrowing up through dirt, and headed – well, where was it likely to venture next?

I thought I knew. A panic-focused mental calculation,

informed by the position of the staircase I rapidly re-ascended, told me that the wall the conjured *thing* had penetrated gave on to the building's rear, the side Neil and I hadn't approached earlier. Then I was back at the lounge window, leaping through, dragging my brother behind with a barked command – "Come on! Follow me!" – before hurrying along Satin Road to gain access to the next street.

We got no further than the property's back gate. Starting from a patch of upturned soil beneath a paving stone just inside the rear yard, more of that horrid, green, icky substance streaked onto the weedy kerb, charging off at a sharp angle towards a bank of trees opposite this side of the properties.

It was the same route Neil and I had taken that night, and this thought dropped something heavy into my gut. Was the *thing* making for *our* house, and would it awaken our parents after reaching there? But no, that was irrational; despite the little effort Dean Wetley had made to say goodbye before he and his mother had departed, the young man held nothing against me. I'd been one of the few who *hadn't* caused him problems while living here, but I could think of many who'd inflicted the alternative.

And after seeing that hideous effigy in the cellar, I had no trouble in deciding who was most culpable among them.

I had just a vague idea where Mr Rhodes lived, but as it turned out such lack of knowledge didn't matter. Although that weird slimy liquid grew perceptibly thinner as we pursued its trail, as if the *thing* from which it leaked was getting weaker as it moved, we traced the path maybe a mile north, in a different direction from our home, to another affluent part of the village where real middleclass folk lived. Although my brother looked fearful beside me, he kept pace all the way, probably because he didn't want to be left alone in the dark with Lord knew what for company.

Running without a break, we reached the headmaster's neighbourhood about fifteen minutes after leaving Satin Road, and although the line of green goo all but died away here, it was immediately apparent which his home was. In front of a detached bungalow with a prissily tended garden, a police car was stationed, alongside an ambulance with blue lights twirling at its solid brow.

Neil and I crept forwards, venturing as far as possible without being spotted, using the parked vehicles as shields. On the property's front lawn stood a police officer, talking to a middle-aged woman wearing a dressing gown and slippers. Perhaps she'd emerged from the two-storey house next-door, because the entrance to that building was wide open and light spilled out across a short dividing hedge. It was now possible for my brother and me to listen to what was being said only a few yards away.

"I thought I heard something prowling," the older lady told the youngish officer, who made hurried notes of her comments in a handheld pad. "I don't sleep well these days, not after several burglaries last year, and when I got up to look outside," – she pointed up at what must be her bedroom window, whose curtains billowed in a soundless breeze – "I thought I saw a...a...well, it looked like a *balloon* – a bloated *black* balloon – gliding across the road the way balloons do, but with a...a kind of *skipping* motion. Then it went directly into Mr Rhodes's garden."

"A *balloon*, madam?" asked the policeman, gazing at his informant with a puzzled frown. "Forgive me, but I think that whatever caused this damage had to be heavier than that."

The officer clearly alluded to the broken window I'd just spotted from my new position closer to the bungalow. The glass was as badly smashed as the Wetleys' had been back in Satin Road, but from the few shards remaining hung more of those gungy green strands, presumably secreted by whatever had forced entry this way: the *thing* from that terrace house's cellar.

"Well, it couldn't be what I first thought it was," the neighbour went on, hands visibly shaking beneath the baggy sleeves of her gown.

"Could you tell me what that might be, madam?" asked the policeman, pen poised again to record the case details.

"A...a human head on legs," the woman finished, and then turned to hurry back next-door, her whole body now conceding evidence of the shakes.

I recalled what I'd spotted earlier, during our dash towards Dean's former home. There'd been some kind of animal in the roadside, entangled amid many shadows of limbs. Or had that been true, after all? In light of everything I'd just heard, might these have been rather *limbs like shadows*?

I didn't dare pursue that thought and soon found myself with a good excuse not to as my brother nudged me. He appeared panicky but held in noise by keeping his lips pressed together. I thought he might even have started crying but when I realised that he pointed with one hand, I flicked my stare away – to the pavement alongside our headmaster's garden.

A darkish object rested there, terminating in what resembled a crow's claw-splayed foot. The limb itself, around six inches long, was as furry as a cat's and yet as angular as a spider's, bending at the middle at a knobbly right-angle. At the end from which it had been severed from its host, it boasted not red gore but the same green I'd first spotted in the Wetleys' former home.

Whatever the neighbour had seen scuttling towards Mr Rhodes's bungalow – a black balloon, a human head, or something even more surreal – seemed to be losing parts of itself, as if, as I'd begun to intuit, it was actually a dream-thing in the process of unravelling.

As much as I wished for it, there was no way we could get inside our headmaster's property, where medical staff from the ambulance must have advanced. This suggested the kind of crime that police alone couldn't deal with, and when one of the paramedics emerged from the bungalow's front door a moment later, she looked deeply disturbed, as if she'd just witnessed something unpalatable, even in her challenging profession.

"What could have done *that* to him?" asked the policeman, who must have spotted whatever injuries the homeowner had suffered after the neighbour had summoned the law's intervention. "The state of his face – what the hell are we dealing with here?"

The woman merely shook her head, clearly struggling to summon words to capture her experience.

"It looks as if some...some *nightmare* has tried to return to what conjured it," was all she said, and this caused me such a surge of horror that I didn't immediately notice what my brother had observed, back on the pavement yards from the two bewildered officials: that crow-cat-spider body-part was slowly dissolving, turning into a gaseous substance and then vanishing altogether like toxic green smoke.

And that was an end to it. Before we could be detected, Neil and I fled the area, arriving back at home about ten minutes later and sneaking inside without our parents being aware. We didn't talk about that episode the day after, preferring to push it to the backs of our minds. A few weeks later, Satin Road was awarded a new street sign, re-establishing it as the historically notable Station Road. I was glad about that, and even more so when new people moved into the Wetleys' former house, brightening it up with coloured curtains and several potted flowers in the front and rear yards.

The school took time to adjust to the appointment of a new headmaster, but gossip and rumour about the previous one eventually died away, as fickle pupils found new trouble to stir up, other people to try and reduce to something less than human. After only a matter of months, it felt as if Mr Rhodes had never existed, his memory reduced to a series of anecdotes and then to nothing much at all.

But *I* remembered him. How could I do anything but when I still had his blood-red pen splattered all over my class book? I regularly looked at that story I'd written, the one based on a gruesome horror film. I also recalled my suspicion that the *thing* I'd tracked was nothing other than a nightmare made flesh.

"This is anatomically unlikely," the nightmare-denying Mr Rhodes had written over my first mistake, and next to another, "Are we to assume that these are also in its eye sockets?" Below a further problem he'd added, "How do we suppose that anything could remain mobile while losing its limbs?" And alongside a final one he'd scrawled, "Surely these entities aren't capable of <u>homing</u>!"

So here are the phrases of mine which, for nearly a year after these bizarre events, destroyed my sleep as I wondered whether the *thing* they unwittingly described had done something far worse to my former headmaster.

"*...mouth as big as its head...*"

"*...teeth everywhere in its face...*"

"*...legs dropped off its body but it somehow kept moving...*"

"*...even though all its eyes had fallen out, it still found its victim...*"

# Non-Standard Construction

## Penny Jones

*Room to let*. The card lay crookedly behind the dusty pane of the corner shop window, resting against an aging silver Christmas tree which was crowned with a lopsided angel whose smile did little to dissuade you of her feelings about where the top of the tree had been wedged. Strangely enough – though it was strange in itself to have a Christmas tree on display in the middle of summer – the tree was surrounded not by presents, but by an array of stuffed rabbits, straw chickens, painted eggs, and a children's plastic bucket and spade.

James nearly walked past, leaving the yellowed parchment to curl up and die on the fly festooned window ledge, but this was London and accommodation was hard to come by, at least in his price bracket. He couldn't afford to ignore even the slightest chance of finding somewhere to rent.

James opened the door to the shop and stepped inside. The bell above the door hung loosely as if someone had tried to rip it from its frame, causing him to duck as he entered. The bell made no noise – whoever had unsuccessfully tried to tear it from its moorings had plucked its tongue out instead – and the bell hung there voiceless. Another step depressed the stained camelhair mat and a buzzer echoed from the back of the store announcing his presence. James made his way towards the counter where an elderly woman stood, watching. He smiled, trying to show he was friendly, that he was harmless. He still wasn't used to the general miasma of mistrust that seemed to permeate every corner of this city. The people who seemed to watch your every movement, each nuance catalogued and assessed as they measured you against a rule. To check you as not bad, or evil, that you weren't going to harm them, rather than whether you were good or kind. *There are no saints here,* their faces seemed to say; *no reason to do good just for the sake of it.* If you committed a good deed, it would be because you had an ulterior motive, that you wanted something in return. *There are no saints here.*

James felt the smile wither on his face under the woman's scrutiny. She opened her mouth to speak and a jumble of words came out in a deep, echoing timbre. The woman wasn't a woman; the dress, some kind of robe; the make-up, dirt encrusted in wrinkles which were too deep to be cleaned by a cursory wipe of a cloth; the breasts, nothing more than the ageing chest of an overweight man who looked ready for his grave. James was glad he hadn't spoken first, that he hadn't named this strange creature made sexless by age as a woman. That he hadn't given the shopkeeper a reason to dislike him more than he already did.

James indicated behind him at the window. The shopkeeper continued to gabble, his peculiar voice given gravitas by James' incomprehension of the words. The man remained where he was, unwilling to leave whatever small amount of security or prestige the counter gave him over his customer.

James reached into the window, past the sun bleached boxes of laundry detergent he was pretty sure weren't even made anymore and the strange display of faded festive cheer. Hooking the card between his fingers, he retrieved it to show the old man.

The shopkeeper held out his hand. James made to pass him the card, but the old man closed his withered fingers as if they were a mouse trap springing sharply back, and whipped his hand away, cradling it protectively against his chest. The card fluttered down from James' slackened grasp and landed prostrate on the scratched and graffitied plastic countertop. James stared at the back of the card; white as a baby tooth it gleamed unsullied against the faded names and announcements scored and gouged into the peeling Formica. James turned his face back to the shopkeeper, whose hand was back again outstretched, his eyebrows raised in silent question. James lowered his hand to the card in front of him. The gnarled face in front of him shifted, the brows drew down, the tattooed grime disappearing into the deepening furrow of his brow, as the shopkeeper slowly shifted his head from side to side before bringing his thumb and forefinger together and rubbing them in the international sign for money. James opened his wallet and peeked into the empty change compartment; the only items his wallet currently held were his oyster card and a five pound note. He pondered for a moment as he stared at the fiver. It was expensive enough living in London and he was in two minds whether to hand over the money for what might end up being a hopeless endeavour. The flat might be too expensive, or in one of the dodgier parts of the city, or even worse it may already have been let. He fingered the slippery material of the note before pinching it between his fingers and offering it to the shopkeeper, hoping that he wouldn't offend the man. He'd heard that the new money was made from animals, and he had no idea whether the note was kosher or not, but then again he had no idea if the man in front of him was Jewish, or Muslim, or Christian – he could be Pastafarian for all he knew. It didn't seem to matter, however, as the five pound note disappeared into the folds of his robes.

The shopkeeper turned away, as if aware that this stranger had nothing of any further worth, and continued to stock the shelves. James picked up the card from the counter and turned it over hoping that it wouldn't be another waste of time, and that this wouldn't be his local shop when he finally managed to find somewhere to live.

*Room to let.* The elegant cursive stated only that, and on the back a number.

James had always wanted to live in the city. He hadn't exactly burnt his bridges when he'd left home, but they were definitely smouldering; his family and few friends fed up of hearing about how everything was shit, and how much better off he'd be once he was out of there. He hadn't been in London long enough yet to be willing to turn tail and flee back to the single bedroom at his parent's house and his (presumably now ex) fiancée. He'd given her an ultimatum, and she hadn't made the right choice, so there was no way he was running back up there. He'd wanted the excitement of the big city and that was what he got. He'd settle in soon enough, he just wasn't used to London yet.

On his first day he'd woken early, excited; with the old adage *the early bird gets the worm* in mind, he'd been up and out, searching for a coffee and waiting for the estate agents to open. But the shutters were down as he walked past row after row of closed businesses, the owners either long gone or asleep, he couldn't tell. The first signs of life he'd witnessed had been the doors being unlocked to a pub on the corner. Its windows boarded, the door, a dark aperture, a mouth that swallowed him whole as he made his way in. Picking up yesterday's paper from a table he'd ordered a coffee, which arrived lukewarm. Sitting himself at a table underneath one of the grimy lights he'd squinted at the newspaper, circling the rooms to let. He tried the first number but the call wouldn't go through; turning the phone so the light shone on the screen, he saw one bar, not enough to make a call. How in the capital city he couldn't get a signal he couldn't fathom. He'd pushed his mug away, the tepid liquid spilling over the stained porcelain, and picked the paper up to head outside and find some daylight and a signal. As he headed out the door the barman cleared his throat and put his hand out. James had wondered for a moment what the man wanted – he'd already paid an extortionate price for the drink, so it wasn't that he was welching on the tab.

"Paper please."

James stared at the barman "But it's yesterday's."

"Papers are for all the customers. Not fair on the others is it? You haven't paid for it, it isn't yours."

James glanced round at the empty bar before reaching into his pocket and bringing out some coins. He dropped a pound into the barman's hand, and it disappeared without an offer of change.

He'd headed outside, the day now warm, but the streets were still empty as the daylight struggled to penetrate through the high buildings and reach the ground, leaving the roads in a perpetual gloom. He phoned every one of the numbers in the paper, and each time he was met with the same answer – he was too late the flat had gone. It didn't matter how small, how expensive, whether it was above a knocking shop or next door to a prison, the answer was always the same; you should have been quicker, the property had been let.

James turned the card over in his hand and took his phone out of his pocket, praying he'd got enough minutes on it to make the call. The last thing he needed with his money running low was a huge phone bill.

The flat wasn't let. The cracked voice on the end of the line had told him the property was still available and given him an address, telling him to be there at nine tonight. So here he was, making his way through this scarred and defaced landscape, visions of violence flashing through his head. He couldn't see how the dregs of society managed to afford houses in London anyway –

for all intents and purposes London should be a haven for the middle and upper classes; the disengaged, the destitute, the deranged priced out of the city. But still he walked along the streets he couldn't afford to live on, saw them thronged with chavs and druggies, leaning over their garden walls, flicking cigarette ends into the gutters that were full of excrement – which could have come from either the dogs or the children that ran amok, unfettered and unattended in the alleys and pathways that threaded their way round the backs and sides of the shuttered and blinded buildings.

Finally he arrived at the address he'd been given. The property sat squatly beneath the surrounding high-rises, the street lights casting shadows on the render causing the ugly house to look leprous, but it had four walls and a roof, and at the moment James wasn't in a position to be picky about where he lived.

Footsteps clicked down the pavement towards him, turning, James saw the woman heading towards him. He expected her to turn and cross to the other pavement as most people seemed to down here, willing to take those few extra steps to avoid confrontation. But instead the lady raised her arm in salute, a clipboard held in her hand. As she made her way closer she called out his name, and as he nodded in response she ticked something on her list before heading down the path towards the house.

"How much is it?" James knew it wasn't smart asking the price straight up, he was sure that the woman would sense his desperation and boost the price to more than he could afford, but he didn't want to get his hopes up again.

"£250 per calendar month." She ticked something else off her list. "Plus deposit of course." She reached a manicured hand past his head and flicked a switch, illuminating the mottled walls with a sickly yellow glow.

"Seems cheap." The words were out of his mouth before he could stop them.

"Non-standard construction." She unlocked the door to the right of the hallway and James squeezed past her and stood by the bed. In truth, wherever he stood in the room he would be by the bed – the room was tiny, with a double bed against the far wall, a single wardrobe to one side, and a single bedside table on the other. The space smelt musty, age had yellowed the paper and damp had patterned it with black curlicues of mould. James opened the wardrobe; the back of the door sported a rust-spotted full-length mirror. James reckoned he'd have to stand outside to be able to use it to any effect, and even then it would still cut his legs off. The wall to his right featured a huge window, overlooking what he supposed was the garden. A row of overflowing bins stood like sentries looking in. "Are the rest of the rooms let?" he asked but the room was empty, a voice echoed from the bottom of the hall.

"The kitchen is down here and the bathroom is upstairs."

He made his way out of the room, switching the light off and carefully shutting the door. Pulling it to make sure the latch had caught, he headed down the dreary hallway towards the kitchen which smelt like socks and week old takeaway.

"Everything you need is here – cooker, microwave,

fridge freezer. You have a shelf each in the fridge," she opened the door, the light shone on her face as she screwed her nose up at the sights that greeted her, shutting it quickly before heading towards a list laminated on the back of the door, effectively cutting him off from seeing whatever was lurking inside the fridge. "These rules are set by the landlord for the benefit of the tenants, as long as you stick to them..." she pointed at the laminated list, her finger touching it for a second before she quickly withdrew it and surreptitiously wiped her hand on her trousers "...you'll have no problems with the others."

"You're not the landlord...landlady then?" James watched as the woman ticked a final box on the sheet.

"Oh no, I'm just his agent, he doesn't like to be bothered with all this." She circled her pen in the air. Turning the sheet over, she thrust it towards him, indicating a line on the back of the paper. "Sign here."

"Don't you want my references?"

"I'm a good judge of character. You can move in tomorrow if you pay cash up front for the first month, or we can wait until the bank has cleared your first cheque."

"Cash is fine." He hoped he had enough in his overdraft to cover the first month's rent – he'd be living on noodles and beans for the rest of the week until he got paid, but it was worth it not to have to fork out the money each day on the hotel. He took the proffered pen and signed his name.

The next morning he was waiting bright and early at the

property; with his belongings stuffed into a rucksack and a variety of carrier bags, he looked like a homeless man. Which he supposed he was at this exact moment in time.

He bit at the skin round his thumb, stripping off tiny strips, a drop of blood welling from where he'd been worrying at the tender flesh.

Once he'd left the property last night, James had stopped at the bank, withdrawing the maximum he could; on the way here this morning he'd stopped at the same cashpoint and done the same. He hadn't checked his balance to see if the money was available, he'd just bitten his cuticles down to the quick and prayed that the machine would spit out his money and give him his card back. It'd been too late, then too early, to actually go into the bank and speak to a human being if his money had been refused, and he didn't think it would have done his cause any good anyway, standing there like a hobo with all his belongings at his feet. Banks didn't seem to give people like him loans, but thankfully he hadn't had to try; he'd folded the wedge of notes into his wallet and stuffed it deep into his pocket, keeping one hand on it to make sure he didn't lose it.

The house was no prettier in the bright light of day; the ageing guttering sagged across the upper windows, which were blinded like cataracts by sheets pinned up inside. He glanced at the naked eye of the window where his room was situated and decided that the first thing he'd do this weekend was put some proper curtains up. He wasn't a student anymore, and as he had no idea how long he'd be calling this place home, he might as well make it feel like one. The sun shone on the pocked grey walls, but rather than making the house more inviting, it instead showed the full degradation of the building; decaying render lay in lumps on the brown grass exposing the inner rot and decomposition of the wall beneath. He headed over and poked at a particularly large patch next to the front door.

"Concrete cancer."

He turned, his finger coated with the white powder residue to see the agent stood behind him.

"Nothing to worry about, it's common in non-standard construction."

"Non-standard construction?" James mused out loud.

"Nothing to worry about, lots of houses round here are non-standard, because of the bombing in the war."

The words meant nothing to James, he had no idea what she meant, but he nodded along, hoping it didn't mean the ceiling was going to come crashing down on his head while he slept. Because this was it, he had to move in, he couldn't afford to live out of hotels for much longer, and he wasn't going to head home so soon after showing his friends and family the finger. Anyway if it was no good he could always save up some money now he wasn't wasting it on hotels and take-outs, and find somewhere better. This was just his first foot on the ladder...

"...and our number's on the back in case of emergencies."

The agent dangled a key attached to a green plastic fob in front of his face. James realised he had been nodding along for ages and hadn't taken in a single word the woman had been saying. He wondered if he should ask her to repeat herself, but instead found himself reaching for the key and uttering "Thanks" as he stepped forward to open his front door.

He'd been on autopilot when he left work, and had gotten halfway back to the hotel before remembering that he didn't live there anymore, turning round to trudge back the way he'd come. He always felt worn out after work. Although he did nothing but sit on his arse and watch screens, he found monitoring the CCTV exhausting. But it was only a stopgap, money to pay the bills, while he figured out what he really wanted to do.

The sun was up when he finally got back to the house; the rooms were quiet as he slipped his shoes off and padded up the stairs in his socks, hoping to grab a shower before the rest of the house stirred and there was a queue for the bathroom. Although he'd lucked out so far – he hadn't seen anyone from the other flats, occasionally hearing a muffled step on the stair or a distant voice, but the other tenants were as elusive as ghosts. He ran the shower and waited for the ancient pipes to clank into action and the trickle of water to heat up. Stepping into the shower he felt the base of the cubicle gritty under his feet – the shower had a thick layer of dust, white patches spattering the lower edges of the glass cubicle where the water had hit it and flicked it up. He used his foot to scoot the now-white water towards the plug hole, waiting for the sludge at the bottom of the shower to clear before ducking under the showerhead and washing.

James towelled himself off and grabbed his

toothbrush. Turning the tap on, he watched as the water spattered against the dusty porcelain, white rivulets running across the grimy sink. James ran his finger through the thick layer of dust, frowning: he was sure that there was only the one bathroom. Maybe, he thought to himself as he spat the minty foam out and rinsed the sink clean, the other rooms had sinks in them which the other residents used.

The house wasn't bad at all, he thought to himself, except for the dust.

James woke while it was still daylight outside, he yawned and wiped the gritty sleep from his eyes. The room was bathed in the auburn warmth of the sun as it peeked over the surrounding rooftops. He allowed the warming rays to engulf him as he lay on his bed – he didn't have work tonight, but he'd got no real idea what he was going to do. He probably shouldn't have slept so late, but he couldn't be bothered to realign his body clock for just a couple of days a week. Anyway since moving down here it wasn't as if he knew anyone, so it didn't really matter whether he was awake during the day or at night. He switched on his phone and flicked through the announcements from the few old friends who still spoke to him: *Going to the local* ☺ *...again* ☹ *bet you're having more fun down in the big smoke. Can't wait for the invite.* James glanced around at the cramped bedroom – there was no way he was going to invite his mates to stay here, they all thought he was living the high life, not stuck in some dead end job and living like a bloody student again. He flicked through to see if there was anything worth going to locally: nothing. He checked the movie listings, and then the prices, and remembered the state of his bank balance. He didn't even have enough money for a pint at the pub, let alone a night out. He switched on his laptop, but without any WiFi it was useless; making a mental note to sort that out first, once his next pay check cleared, he closed the laptop again.

Through the wall he could hear the muttered conversation of his housemates. It wouldn't hurt to go and introduce himself – the worst that could happen would be they'd have nothing in common, in which case he could pretend he was just grabbing a glass of water and head back to his room. But they could be cool, maybe they'd even know of a party or something, anything to get him out of the house – well, as long as it was free. He shoved his feet into his trainers and glimpsed at the shorts and t-shirt he'd slept in; they were wrinkled but he decided not to bother changing, worried he'd miss his chance to speak to the people in the kitchen. He scurried out of the room and made his way to the kitchen for a cup of coffee and to introduce himself. But the room was empty, the kettle cold as he picked it up to fill. Placing it back down in the black circle which was set into the dust on the worktop, he wiped at the residue with his finger before glancing up at the ceiling to find the source, but the swirling patterns which stared back at him appeared undamaged.

The house wasn't all that bad, certainly not as bad as the house he'd shared as a student – the sink was always empty, and apart from a strange smell, the fridge appeared to be clear of rotting food. The only problem was the dust.

The first time he'd gone into the kitchen it had looked as if someone had been baking and spilt flour everywhere. White dust covered every inch of the work surfaces, gummed to a paste under the constantly dripping tap in the sink. He'd wiped the surfaces down before unpacking his meagre culinary delights: some cheapo noodles, coffee, and baked beans, alongside a single bowl, plate, mug, and a mismatch of cutlery.

But wiping the sides down obviously wasn't enough, because the kitchen was covered with dust again.

James rooted about in his cupboard for a bowl and one of the packets of noodles he'd stashed there. Running his finger around the inside of the bowl, it came away white, and when he glanced in the cupboard the contents all had a light dusting of powder on them, as if they were doughnuts sprinkled with sugar.

James ate standing at the sink – he could have sat down, but the table and chairs were all covered with the same white dust, and he didn't really have the money to take his clothes to the laundrette unless he really had to. He hoped that the voices he'd heard earlier would return; standing in the ever-growing darkness, he waited for a sign of occupancy from the house. Finally, after his third cup of coffee, he admitted defeat and washed his plate and mug up, placed them back in the cupboard and made his way back to his room, his shoes leaving footprints in the dust on the tiled kitchen floor.

❖

James woke the next day and wiped at his sleep-encrusted eyes. He was starving – glancing at his phone, he saw that it was just after lunch. "Fuck" he thought to himself as his stomach growled at him.

He'd wasted his day off yesterday. Bored, and with no money and nothing else to do, he'd picked up his book to read, but as the sun set he'd found himself falling asleep, although he'd only been awake a couple of hours. Now here he was awake in the middle of the day – he'd slept for a solid twelve hours and there was no way he was going to manage to fall back asleep, and now his body clock was fucked. He'd be crap at work tomorrow night.

He lay in bed and rubbed at his eyes again, they still felt gritty. He spat on his fingers and wiped at his eyes in an attempt to unglue them, but they felt sore and irritated. Sitting up he ran a hand through his hair, white dust flew like dandruff causing him to cough. He glanced up at the ceiling but there was still no sign of damage to the swirling artex. *Must be old dust I've disrupted, moving my stuff in* James thought to himself as he brushed the powder from his skin. He stood and stretched, glancing at the mess in his room. He edged his way past the bed and over the scattered carrier bags that littered his floor, and made his way into the hall, opening the cupboard under the stairs. "Got nothing better to do" he muttered, pulling out an antiquated vacuum and a plastic bucket filled with some equally ancient cleaning supplies.

It was getting dark by the time James had finished cleaning. He felt better than he had done for ages; the house felt fresher, he felt like he'd gone and done a workout at the gym, and finally he'd managed to eradicate all the dust.

He stowed the vacuum back away under the stairs. Secretly he'd hoped that someone would have heard the noise and come out, but either no-one was in, or – more likely from the state of the place – no-one wanted to get roped into doing the cleaning. James' stomach growled again; he hadn't eaten since the noodles last night and what he really wanted was a pizza, but all he had left to last him till tomorrow was a tin of beans and yet another packet of noodles. James decided to head upstairs, grab a shower and get himself clean, before settling down in the kitchen to his meagre feast.

Turning the shower to its highest setting, James noticed that the metal showerhead was again shrouded in a fine layer of dust. Wetting his hand he wiped it, cursing himself for missing a spot, before he stepped under the tepid water.

James felt drained as he made his way home following work – a twelve hour shift with nothing to eat was bad enough, but with his body clock out of sync, and it being at night, there was nothing to distract him but the ominous creaks and groans of the building. It had been tortuous. At least he'd had coffee, but he'd drunk so much of it, his stomach felt like acid. He'd only gone to the loo before leaving work, but still he needed a wee and he was only halfway home. Trying to hold it in without grabbing himself and looking like a perv, he gritted his teeth as he hurried past the supermarket – where he'd been intending on picking up some food to take home, now he had some money in the bank. Instead he strode down the street, counting the steps in his mind as he hurried home, throwing open the door and running up the stairs to the bathroom. He no longer bothered to remove his shoes and tiptoe up quietly – he'd seen neither hide nor hair of his housemates, and was beginning to think that he was the only person in the house. To be honest, with working nightshifts he hardly saw anyone – he couldn't be entirely sure that he wasn't the only person in London. For a bustling metropolis it could really be dead at times.

He flushed the loo and made his way to the sink to wash his hands. The soap felt greasy as he lathered it between his palms, and glancing down he saw that his hands were peppered with grit. The sink once again had a layer of dust across its porcelain surface. He rinsed his hands and wiped them on his trousers before turning off the tap and opening the bathroom door with the sleeve of his jacket, white streaks contaminating the cotton. He'd been looking forward to stocking his cupboards with food from the shops – for once he had enough money to eat well for the whole week, as long as he didn't live on takeaway – but he couldn't stomach the idea of eating in the house. Gingerly he pulled the front door to and headed towards the greasy spoon cafe he'd passed on his way home.

The greasy spoon wasn't too bad, in fact it wasn't greasy at all, the food was fresh, and the place spotless. James pushed aside his orange juice and toast and powered up his laptop, typing in the café's WiFi code.

The waitress didn't seem to mind him taking advantage of their hospitality as the place was empty following the breakfast crowd, and it would be a couple of hours before the office workers started to make their way in for their lunchtime sandwiches and salads. He clicked on the icon on his laptop and waited for the internet to boot up; he'd been intending to update his CV, but instead found himself typing *non-standard construction* into the Google search bar, hoping he might find out a way to stop the incessant dust from falling. He scrolled through the results with one hand while he picked a piece of toast up with his other, a white residue lining his nails like a French manicure. He placed the toast back on his plate and picked up the fork, trying to squeeze one of the tines down close enough to the nail bed to get out the entrenched grime. A drop of blood fell onto the laptop's keyboard, he winced and went to place his finger in his mouth before thinking better of it and wrapping it in a serviette instead.

He clicked on the first link and read through the article. *A deficit of housing after the war lead to an increase in non-standard housing materials, concrete being the most common.* As he scanned through the article, words such as cancer and asbestos jumped out at him; he grabbed the keys out of his pocket and dialled the number on the plastic fob, tapping his fingers on the table as it rang. He'd heard all the horror stories about asbestos, the scarring of people's lungs and them dying, gasping for breath. He thought about the dust lying thickly on every surface, the dusting on his pillows in the mornings, the grit in his eyes. How much had he inhaled already? Were the walls of his lungs already beginning to thicken and scar?

A voice trilled down the phone line, he fought back the need to cough as he spoke to the agent.

"Of course there's no asbestos."

"But the dust... It's everywhere."

"If there was asbestos, it would have been picked up in the survey. All of our properties have to be properly checked, and if they contain asbestos, we have to put a sign up."

"What about the dust though, it's getting into everything?"

"I'm sorry about that, but cleaning isn't included in the monthly rent. You'll just have to come up with a cleaning rota or something with the other tenants."

James hung up and swallowed his final mouthful of orange juice; his throat tickled as he fought back the urge to cough. Unwrapping the serviette from around his finger, he squeezed the nail between his thumb and forefinger. The skin beneath throbbed at the pressure and a tiny indent in the white infiltrated the pinkness beneath his nail. It felt as if someone had stuck a pin into the tender flesh there.

On his way home James popped into the supermarket, but instead of buying food to stock his shelves, he bought polish and bleach; having filled his basket with every type of cleaner he could find on the shelves, the price had been extortionate, and he expected he'd be eating nothing but beans again for the next week. He passed the cash over, hoping that the new cleaning stuff would finally shift the dust in the house.

Once home he rooted through the under stairs cupboard and pulled out the plastic bucket, tipping the old cleaning supplies in the bin. He filled the bucket with warm water and a liberal slosh of each of the cleaning fluids he'd picked up at the shop. He hoped that the new stuff would work better – the old stuff had probably been there years, looking at the state of the house. It had probably gone off. He hoisted the bucket and headed upstairs to start cleaning.

James was scrubbing the skirting boards in his bedroom when the phone rang, he wiped his soapy hands on his shirt before picking it up and swiping to answer. The screen felt grainy under his touch, a scratch marring the surface where he'd run his finger across.

"Where are you?"

"In my bedroom." James wondered at the question. "Why?"

"Cause you should be here. At work. I was due to knock off half an hour ago."

James pulled the phone from his ear and stared at the time – he was late, it had taken him longer to clean then he'd expected. He apologised profusely to his boss and, grabbing his bag, he rushed out of the house.

"Last warning."

James' boss looked him up and down. James was all too aware that he was wearing the same clothes as he had been when he'd left work that morning, the only change being the splashes of bleach which spattered his trousers, the black material flecked with coral and amber and saffron, like a sunrise on his crotch. Dust sprinkled his shoulders like dandruff: he was a mess, but at least he was here. He couldn't afford to lose this job – what with paying for the hotel and now the deposit and the rent, he had no savings to see him through until he could find another. He locked the door behind his boss, and ran his hand across the rough stubble of his chin before settling down for another long night of work.

He woke suddenly, the vertebrae in his neck popping as he straightened, a cold cup of coffee congealing in front of him. He moved it to see the screens, but they were empty. A hammering echoed further back in the building. James picked up his torch; he didn't need it for its light – the building's fluorescents were on sensors which lit up the corridor ahead of him as he made his way towards the source of the noise – but in lieu of a gun or a nightstick, the heavy metal tube would at least make a decent weapon.

The hammering emitted from a metal fire door at the end of the corridor. James pressed the handle down and the door swung swiftly away wrenching his arm. James stumbled forwards into the ample bosom of the cleaning lady.

"What, were you asleep?" The cleaner barged past him, heavily bundled in her coats despite the mild morning air. "You've made me late." She reached the staff room and turned, her finger pointing at him as if marking him "It won't be me that gets it in the neck." She slammed the door behind her as James made his way back to the reception. Unlocking the front doors he waited for the others to arrive.

James hurried home; his body was weary and ached from all the cleaning, and from falling asleep at his desk. His rucksack bounced against the tight muscles in his arms, sore from all the scrubbing the day before. He'd managed to sneak away without the cleaner tattling on him to his boss. At least if he was going to get a drumming from his boss it wouldn't be until he was rested, clean and in fresh clothes.

Finally home James trudged up the stairs; too tired to shower, he intended to brush his teeth, grab some water and sleep. He squeezed toothpaste onto his brush and turned on the tap. The water ran into the sink, disturbing the thin layer of dust. James ran his finger across the sink, coating it in the white residue. He rinsed his finger and glanced around the bathroom. From a distance it all looked fine, but he was sure that there was a fine coating again across the top of the toilet cistern, and along the edge of the tiles. He rinsed his brush and swallowed some water. It tasted brackish; he'd have to pick up some bottled water to brush his teeth. He just hoped that boiling the water would get rid of any impurities, there was no way he could afford bottled water for his coffee too. James took in the room, his features drawing into a moue of disgust. He lifted his hand to his mouth, his teeth biting into the calloused skin round his nail and pulling a thin strip away. Pain bloomed in his finger, blood welled against the side of his nail, flecks of white slowly engulfed by the red liquid. The white line on his nail bed had lengthened, reaching almost to his cuticle, and the pad beneath was fleshy and hot. He hoped it wasn't infected. He rinsed his finger in the sink, not wanting to put anymore of the white stuff near his mouth.

James made his way downstairs, the banister sandy beneath his palm. He glanced at the closed doors along the hallway – maybe the dust was coming from them. Maybe he should slip a letter under their doors asking them to clean their rooms. Ha! He sounded just like his mum. Maybe he should knock on their doors, wake them up, demand that they keep the house clean. He'd heard that in the city you were never more than ten foot from a rat, maybe he should round some up and plant them in their bedrooms, that'd give them some motivation to keep the house clean. But not today. Now he wanted nothing more than to climb into bed and sleep.

James woke to the muffled sound of his alarm. He rolled over to switch it off and his chest heaved, causing him to cough, a wad of phlegm flying out of his mouth. He didn't feel good, his throat was sore and irritated; he swallowed to try and lubricate it, but every time he swallowed he coughed, which caused his throat to burn even more. He rubbed his eyes and flakes of sleep fluttered to his chest, but still he couldn't open them. Gently he probed at the swollen, hot orbs; wetting his finger with saliva he rubbed at them, carefully prising them apart. He shuffled into the kitchen and turned on the tap; pain flaring through his fingers as he gripped the faucet, he cupped his burning hands under the water and drank. It tasted worse today than it did yesterday. He gritted his teeth and splashed the cold water on his face, hoping that it would do something to alleviate the burning.

James made his way back to his room and picked up the phone; he dialled work and waited for it to be answered.

"Hello, you're through to Solutions. How can I help?"

James opened his mouth to speak but no words would come out. He tried again but his throat burned too much, was too damaged. He tried a third time but his voice was drowned by a barrage of coughs. He hung up and texted his boss instead, before switching his phone off and pulling the covers back over his head.

It was dark when James next woke; a coughing fit wracked his body as he sat up and threw the covers back, dust motes dancing in the moonlight that shone through his still uncovered window. When he rubbed his eyes, the skin on the back of his hands felt rough, flaky. Glancing down, he saw eyelashes clogged with thick clots of sleep caught against the scaly plaques of skin which covered his hands and crept up his arms. His throat burned, he needed to get some medicine, he reached for his phone to check the time. Missed calls flashed across the screen accusingly. He'd been asleep for thirty six hours, he'd missed two days of work, and thirteen calls from his boss. James deleted the voicemails without listening to them, and winced at the last text message which just said *You're Fired*. James switched his phone off – the black screen veiling the condemning words – before he climbed back into bed and pulled the duvet over his head.

"James?" There was no answer from behind the bedroom door. "It's Sally, the lettings agent." Sally hoped that James wasn't in. She hated confrontation, and would rather get the locks changed and his stuff boxed up and out in to the garden before he came back. She didn't really want to be here at all, but the landlord was adamant. The payment hadn't been on time, and there were no excuses. There was always someone more than happy to find somewhere affordable to live in London. She turned the key, and the stench hit her. It reminded her somewhat of the nursing home her Nan had been in – bleach with a heavy undertone of rotting flesh. She stepped towards the window meaning to open it and air the room, her hand covering her mouth as her eyes wept in the stinging miasma in the small space. A body was hunched over in the corner by the wardrobe. Her heart sank as she saw the grimy clothes, the head hung low, the stench of rot – a fetor which emanated from the body. She'd have to call the police and the family; she hated when she had to clean up after the tenants. Then the head turned and red rimmed eyes met hers, a hand raised in greeting. Skin cracked and raw, the hand dipped back into the bucket at its side, tendrils of red mixing into the milky liquid as it squeezed the cloth before returning to scrub again at the sparkling clean floor.

# The Night Moves

## Gary McMahon

**Kata** *(n.)*

*an exercise consisting of a sequence of the specific movements of
a martial art, used in training and designed to show skill in
technique*

Collins English Dictionary

Crouching down in the shadows, Miles eased the well-
worn board away from the window, not even glancing
behind him before slipping through the gap and into the
empty warehouse.

He was never followed here. Nobody knew him; he
knew nobody. He was a ghost, a whisper; a lonely cipher
trudging through the uncaring city streets to come to
this place, night after night, in search of epiphany.

On the other side of the window, he moved the
plywood back into position and set it in place with the
screws: finger-tight, as usual, in case he needed to leave
in a hurry.

He'd been coming here every night – more or less –
for two years now, ever since he'd left the homeless
shelter and been allocated the tiny bedsit on Shallow

Street by the housing association. It wasn't much, that place, but it was his. It was home, of a kind: the best that he could hope for in his current situation.

The sounds of the city were muted but not silenced by these thin walls. He could still hear the night-time traffic, the distant barking of dogs, the shouts and screams and the constant emergency sirens, but when he was locked away inside the warehouse they could not touch him.

Shifting his rucksack to a more comfortable position on his shoulder, he set off through the doorway in front of him and into the main section of the warehouse. At one time the building had been used to store goods for import and export, but now it was as empty as a junkie's promise. There were no working lights but enough ambient light filtered through the various gaps and seams in the ageing structure to allow him to see, once his eyes became accustomed to the gloom.

The concrete floor was stained but the smooth, unbroken finish was perfect for his needs. The columns supporting the roof were spaced so far apart that he had plenty of room to manoeuvre. The lightweight mezzanine floor above him had long ago gone to ruin. The upper half of a steel staircase hung in the deeper shadows to his right but he'd never tried to climb up there. Why would he? Everything he needed was here: space and time and darkness.

He shrugged off his rucksack and set it down on the floor, against the wall. There was a broom in one corner, the one he kept there for his visits. He grabbed it and swept away the dirt and debris that still somehow seemed to gather in empty places, like a bad memory that clings even though you try to forget it.

Once the area was clear he stepped into the centre of an imaginary circle and closed his eyes. Breathing deeply, he performed a series of light stretching exercises. Tight hamstrings were his curse, so he concentrated on them, teasing the muscles into submission as he limbered up ready for practice.

After approximately ten minutes of stretching, he paused, took a long, deep breath, and began to perform the moves an old man had once taught him in what seemed like another life.

As usual, once he started the actual kata his mind broke free from his body and the body took over complete control. By now he knew the moves by heart; they were a part of him, stamped deep inside his tendons and sinews, and he performed them without even having to think about what came next.

It had taken a lot of practice to reach this stage, and he knew he was nowhere near the level of expertise that was required. The pattern of the kata was relatively simple – his steps traced the rough shape of a star on the concrete floor – but it was the individual movements themselves that required so much focus and effort.

Time. Dedication. Application. These were the things that mattered. The repetition of the movements. The intense bodily control. The pacing. The form. The technique. Any improvement he experienced was incremental, which was as it should be.

In his youth Miles had studied martial arts, so his body was used to this kind of exercise. Muscle memory was something for which he was thankful. He'd been rusty at first, yes, and the moves were not at all like the fighting combinations he'd been taught as a child, but with perseverance he had slowly begun to master them.

Kata wasn't the right name for what he did, not really. It was simply the closest approximation to what he understood as a series of ritualised movements whose practice was an end unto itself. The principles of martial kata – form, technique, spirit, rhythm, balance, and placement – all held true for this particular series of movements.

After twenty minutes of practice he was breathing hard. Another twenty minutes and he was starting to sweat heavily. Over time his body had become lean and hard because of the constant exercise. His belly was drum-tight. His arms and legs were as solid as oak.

He would continue all night; he would not stop until dawn.

He paused only for water, and to catch his breath, but always returned to the movements: the form and technique. It had become a part of him, a way by which he could examine himself at the deepest levels while still maintaining a sense of detachment.

Each night, every night, all that existed was the kata. He retreated inside himself, becoming the movements. He was safe, secure, and poised on the verge of enlightenment.

When the sun came up he felt rather than saw the blooming light. The windows were all boarded over but his skin knew, his spirit could tell, that dawn had finally arrived.

He took the towel from his rucksack and wiped away the sweat from his body – at some point he'd shed his t-shirt and jogging pants – and got dressed.

Leaving by the same way he'd gained access, he once again secured the board over the window and walked away across the patch of waste ground to the road. Early morning traffic was building. People were on their way to work; shops and offices were opening up for the day. Miles was exhausted but he felt light on his feet, like a dancer. It would take him an hour or so to come down from this natural high, but once he did he would sleep the morning away in a deep and rewarding slumber, re-energising himself for the following evening's session.

One of these mornings he would walk out of the warehouse having perfected the kata. He wasn't sure what would happen then, or how he would even know he'd reached that stage, but he was convinced that something inside him would click into place. He was sure of it. And until then, he must continue this nightly practice, going through the movements, summoning the passion, focusing on the moment rather than what might come afterwards.

Just as he'd been taught by the old man at the homeless shelter: Hoodoo, the one who had first trained him in the kata and told him that once he performed it perfectly, it would lead him along the road to salvation.

It didn't seem like two years ago. The time had passed by quicker than he could grasp, like water pouring between his outstretched fingers.

Hoodoo had just been another of the homeless dudes in the shelter, a tall, shambling, crooked-shouldered figure who liked to smoke roll-ups and watched everyone through the fringe of his greying dreadlocks. He was tall and thin and his features were womanly: a narrow face, high cheekbones, full lips and the bluest eyes Miles had ever seen.

They had started chatting over breakfast. Their conversation was nothing special, just the usual stuff. Then one day Hoodoo had told him about what he'd called the night moves, and the great promise they held.

It had been as simple as that: no great bonding moment, no earth-shattering revelation. One day he'd simply decided to tell Miles about his theory, and asked him if he'd like to learn the moves.

"It's simple to do," he said. "But impossible to perfect. I see something in you, an aspect of your personality, that makes me think you could benefit from what I have to teach you."

Looking back now, Miles recalled how desperate he had been for something to cling to. His world was dark; his life was a long tunnel that led only downward because the way back to the surface was blocked by memories of abuse, neglect, crime, drugs, drink... Each of these things had marked his existence, leading him to this place, this moment in time.

Perhaps Hoodoo had recognised a fellow traveller, or maybe he was sick and tired of carrying the burden alone. The old man claimed that had never been able to perfect the moves, even though he'd practiced them since he was a teenager. By the time he'd met Miles, he was too weary and battered by life to continue the practical side of his studies. He didn't want to let the moves be lost, or so he'd said, and desired nothing more than to pass them on to someone else, someone who might get closer to the truth than he ever had.

So every night, in the empty breakfast hall, they would go through the moves together. Hoodoo was a fine teacher. He moved like a ballet dancer. Miles thought the man had missed his calling. He should have been involved in education, passing on knowledge and wisdom to eager young minds. Hoodoo never gave away anything about himself, not once did he even try to tell his own story. All they ever discussed was the moves – the kata – and the only thing they did together was practice.

They did this for six weeks and then Hoodoo simply disappeared. Miles asked around, but all he could glean from staff and other residents was that Hoodoo had walked out of the shelter one day and not come back.

No goodbyes. No sentimental note left on Miles's bunk. He was just gone: he was darkness banished by the sun, clouds blown away by the wind.

But he *had* left something behind: the night moves, the kata (as Miles had now come to think of it). This was his gift.

Perhaps the old man had taught Miles everything he felt he could, and had decided that it was time to move on, treading his own lonely path to salvation. Maybe he was dying, and like an African elephant he had set off on a pilgrimage to his own personal death grounds. This was a myth, Miles knew, but wasn't Hoodoo also a kind of living myth? The longer his absence, the more he became a shady figure in Miles's memory, a person who might not even have existed were it not for the evidence of the lesson he'd left behind.

When he woke, Miles made instant coffee and white toast and fired up the battered laptop he'd been given as a farewell gift by one of the girls at the shelter. He had no idea how old the machine was, but it still worked and if he was careful what he ate, his meagre income from benefits stretched to cover the cost of a basic internet connection.

He opened the file marked LOCULUS. There wasn't a lot of information in the file, but what little he'd managed to pull together since meeting Hoodoo told an interesting story. There were snippets of gossip about a place that existed alongside our own version of reality; a scanned Fortean tabloid story about sightings of a dog with a man's face; an article about a housing estate in the northeast of England where trees had grown up through the concrete footpaths and the ground had heaved open, and how the government had built a wall to contain whatever had emerged.

He realised that much of this was about as believable as alien sculptures on the moon and canals on mars, but there was something about these stories, a common thread, which linked them somehow to the kata.

That word: Loculus. It was Latin for "little place". According to his research, loculi were also individual architectural niches in churches that each housed a body; the shelves in a catacomb.

It was a word Hoodoo had used more than once during those initial six weeks of training, and sometimes as Miles worked through the moves in the kata, he saw what he thought was its outline forming in the darkness behind his eyes.

He'd also come across the word several times since parting ways with his erstwhile spiritual teacher: once daubed on a concrete subway wall; again, months later, etched onto the windscreen of a wrecked car after an accident; written on a beer mat in thick black marker pen; tattooed onto the skinny forearm of a wide-eyed Goth girl he'd spotted lurching out of a seedy back-alley shooting gallery...

Was it in fact a real place, and by performing the kata could he catch a glimpse of it, or perhaps even travel there? He remembered his time with drugs, and how he had often felt that by absorbing them he was approaching somewhere that his eyes could not see and his hands were unable to touch. It was the same place, or a whiff of it, he was certain.

Loculus was more than an idea, it was a destination, and people tried different ways of getting there. Some used drink, others drugs. Violence and murder. Rape.

It was the anti-heaven. Not hell, or anything like that, but something all religions strove to reflect in their myths.

The metaphors of Christian dogma were too small, too unsophisticated to even get close to what this was. The other religions fared no better in this respect. Gan Eden, Valhalla and Fólkvangr, Vaikuntha, Jannah, Mictlan, the Elysian Fields. It was all of these concepts and none of them; it was both an idea and a form; silence and sound; being and unbeing; full and empty.

Miles switched off the computer and left his bedsit. He had a few pounds in his pocket; easily enough for a couple of beers. The local pub was full of rough trade but to him it always felt a little like home – at least more than the damp little bedsit or the squalid streets that surrounded him.

The pub was busy when he walked in. After-work drinkers and early diners enjoying a tipple before they headed off towards the city centre. The air was alive with conversation. The wall-mounted television sets in each corner of the bar each showed a different football match: tiny men in bright jerseys running across vivid green backdrops.

"The usual, mate?"

Miles nodded at the young barman, who stroked his shapely hipster beard and proceeded to pull a pint of bitter. He hadn't realised he was coming in here often enough to have a "usual". Miles didn't know if that was disturbing or reassuring, so he settled on neither. Like many things in his life, it just *was*.

"Hey, Miles. What's new?" The shabby figure who sidled up next to him was familiar but Miles couldn't pin a name to the man.

"Not much. Just getting by, you know?"

The man nodded. His age was indeterminate. He might have been thirty-six or sixty-eight or anywhere in between. "I know how that is. Any sign of a job yet?"

Miles laughed. "Yeah. Right."

"I hear you." The man put down his pint and pulled a

mobile phone from his pocket. "See this? I got it from my daughter. See her twice a year when she travels up from Brighton and she gives me a fucking Smartphone I don't even know how to operate. She hasn't even seen my house. If she had, she'd be giving me something I could actually use." His smile was horrible, with something unclean trapped inside, clenched between his yellowing teeth – an emotion that was somewhere between outrage and despair.

"Busy in here this evening."

"Yeah. City types. They only come down these back streets when they want to pretend they've brushed up against the bad times. It makes their annual bonuses and detached houses seem earned." He swiped his hand across the phone and raised it in the air above the bar. "Look at this shit. Someone sent me it but I have no idea who. I don't even have any contacts saved on the thing."

Miles glanced at the tiny screen; then, when he recognised what the image was, he became more interested. It was a fragment of a television news report: shaky handheld footage – probably taken using the camera app on a phone – of a high perimeter wall around the remains of a housing estate, with uniformed figures standing guard at the wall's base.

The man sighed. "I seem to remember this on the news a couple of years back...some northern shithole where trees sprouted up through the concrete and the sinkholes ate up the roads. People died. They built that wall to contain some kind of natural disaster..."

Miles nodded. "Yes, I remember this too, but this is

the first time I've ever seen any pictures. Who did you say sent you this?"

The man swiped the screen again and brought up the sender's details. "I don't know. Don't recognise the number."

Miles felt cold. His lips were dry. There was more going on here than what he could see on the surface.

"Shit. I think I've deleted it. The footage." The man pawed at the screen for a couple of seconds and then put away the phone. "Ah, well. Drink up, eh?"

Miles sipped at his beer. It tasted strange, as if drawn from a bad keg. He had no idea what was happening but it felt as if the kata might be working in some way, drawing events towards him in a way that suggested something was working behind the scenes to aid him in his task. The night moves had begun to open a door and whatever was on the other side was inching closer, sniffing at this world. He couldn't wait for tonight, to practice again.

Two years of training was finally paying off.

Hoodoo had told him that he would barely notice the changes until he was within touching distance of the perfection he sought, the performance that would make things happen.

It was getting close. He could feel it. The winds of another place were blowing against his skin; the sights and sounds of somewhere else were drifting towards him.

Close.

He turned again to his aged companion. "Listen, I know we don't really know each other, just from drinking in this pub, but I want to ask you something."

"Fire away." The man smiled and this time it was warmer, more akin to a recognisable gesture.

"If I said the word 'Loculus', what would it mean to you?"

"Ah...it's a word I've heard before."

"Really?" Miles took a large gulp from his pint.

"Yes, many times."

Miles looked around; nobody was listening. He wasn't sure what he'd expected – eyes turned towards him, fingers pointing – but nobody gave a damn about him and his friend at the bar. "What is it?" he whispered, as if he were afraid to find out.

"I've heard it's the purest drug ever synthesised, the strongest drink ever brewed. I've heard it's the greatest place you could ever see, the most beautiful song you could hope to hear, the greatest book ever written. Someone once told me it was a brand of football – the best ever made. Someone else said it was a car and only one model was ever made, but they destroyed it because it went too fast and travelled too far."

Miles shook his head. "I don't understand."

"It's everything and nothing, my boy. It's the shifting sands and the churning sea. It's a million different things to a million different people." His smile dropped; his bright blue eyes narrowed.

"But what do *you* think it is?" Miles gripped the cuff of the man's overcoat with shaking fingers, holding on tight. He felt as if he was on a ship and it was tilting, tilting, as the ocean heaved like a raging beast around them.

"I think it's a fucking joke. Desperate people cling to stupid ideas, and this is one of those. But underneath the lies and the confusion...who knows? Perhaps it's what we've all been searching for, the ultimate truth of our race?" He shrugged, smiled.

Miles nodded. The world calmed down; the waves died and the horizon settled into a straight line. "What's your name, anyway?"

"You know my name."

"Do I?"

Of course he did.

"My name is Hoodoo."

Of course it was.

"But...but you look different. You don't look like the man I knew."

"We all have many faces, son, and this is just the one I'm wearing now." His eyes seemed to peer right into Miles's centre, and he knew that this was indeed the same man, the shabby mystic who had taught him a way to change into a better version of himself. The eyes did not lie: they said it all, and held the truth within their vivid blue depths.

"Why are you here? Why now?"

"Because you're close, son. You're closer than you realise."

Hoodoo smiled, sadly.

"Do you really think I'd just leave you to it? I've been keeping tabs on you, checking in on you now and again. You're not the only one, you know. There are other places I've needed to be, other students who needed my help, but I've watched you as often as I could and I've been impressed with your progress. I don't know of anyone else who has pushed so hard and come so far."

He paused then, as if contemplating something.

"But I'm here now, and I just wanted to tell you to keep on pushing, keep on doing the moves. Don't let anyone see you or see how near you are. Keep it to yourself. I can see those moves twitching beneath your skin, pushing your bones into new positions in readiness for some final revelation. You've done so well, practiced so very hard, that the moves are now inside you. They're not separate from you anymore."

He touched Miles's hand with his long, cool fingers. "You're almost there."

Then he walked away, into the crowd, and out of the pub, back out into the wide world. He did not turn around.

It was later than usual when Miles got to the abandoned warehouse. He'd stayed in the pub and had a few more drinks, until his money ran out. He'd done the kata drunk before; he usually sobered up after a few repetitions, sweating out the alcohol onto the cold, hard concrete floor.

As usual, he walked to the centre of the space and began his stretching routine. The walls seemed darker, the steel columns more rusted, the floor colder beneath his feet than ever before. This was the same place only different. He took it as a sign that things were changing. Tonight might just be the night when it all became clear.

Starting slowly, he went through the kata, exaggerating the moves, making them big and bold and almost outlandish. It felt good; it seemed right to be starting big in this way. Usually he began in a timid fashion, afraid that he might pull a muscle, and let his body ease into the routine, but tonight he started as he meant to continue: like a champion.

As he worked, he became aware that he was not alone. He thought there might be a dog circling him in the shadows at the perimeter of the space, but it sounded heavier, and as if there were more than four legs moving across the floor. He didn't see the animal, not exactly: he was simply aware of its presence, an unannounced spectator to his grand performance.

He felt stronger than ever before. Each move of the routine was pronounced and the combinations came easily. He knew instinctively that he was performing the kata better than he ever had done in the past; that this was the moment he'd been working towards for two long, hard years.

His mind soared, freeing itself from the flesh so that the body could create and express his desires. He was barely even aware of the movements, only as a slight nagging sensation, a gentle tugging of the flesh as he attempted to free himself from the demands of the corporeal and lift off into the numinous.

He heard Hoodoo's voice in his head: *Keep pushing...*

Each element of the kata became as one: form, technique, rhythm, power. These were no longer separate parts, but different aspects of the whole. Never before had it felt this way. Not once in two years had he ever come this close to perfection.

The muscles in his arms and legs were like steel cables. His belly was a flat board. His chest was a set of bellows pumping oxygen around the engine. He was a kata machine, a mere function of the night moves that he was even now performing to such a high level of expertise that if anyone saw him, they might think he was an angel about to take flight.

The connection between mind and body had been severed completely; he was moving without thought, thinking without being held back by action. The river of time and the universe flowed around him and through him and he let it all carry him away...

He saw images flaring in his mind's eye: a Buddhist enso circle, a triangle of flame, a small grove of trees surrounded by kneeling people illuminated by a light that was produced by something held within a nest of leaves and branches.

The first real tree sprouted right next to him, bursting up through the concrete floor and twisting, arching, forcing its way into this world. Other trees came up out of the floor around him, their roots moving like snakes.

He continued with the kata, too far gone now to even think about stopping. He saw the air blurring about his limbs, felt the warmth of a distant sun on his face, smelled odours that he could not even describe. Leaves rustled around him. He smelled peat and animal dung.

As he worked, he waited for the door to open and lead him from this blighted urban wasteland. The trees, he knew, were a glimpse of another place, mere harbingers of something more.

But it soon became apparent that there was no door. At least not in the way he'd always understood the term.

The walls of the warehouse trembled; the surface of

the world became thin, like ancient skin. Everything *shimmered*.

Without him realising, a tension had begun to invade his body. The kata was deteriorating, the techniques becoming sloppy, the form loosening. It took a few seconds for his mind to catch up with the truth that his body had already understood.

The night moves, the kata, was not in fact a way of gaining access to whatever Loculus represented. Instead, it was a summoning rite, an invitation for something to cross over the threshold the kata created. A call to whatever waited on the other side.

Miles tried to stop but he was in too deep; his body was so disconnected from his mind that he was powerless to control it. He watched in horror as the movements themselves took over, twisting his arms and legs into positions that should have been impossible. But no bones broke, no skin ruptured; no blood was shed. The kata took on a new form.

The world around him started to bleed away, like paint dripping from a canvas, and revealed a wide expanse of short grass, beyond which stood the same grove of trees he'd seen earlier. Only this time, the trees had fallen into decay, the branches bare, the trunks withered and blackened by old fires. Skeletal figures knelt beside the ruined trees.

But even this image was pulled away, like a layer of skin being shed.

Beneath it was only darkness, an endless night that was filled with infinite echoes of the movements he had performed continuously for two years, honing and practicing and working towards something he had never truly understood.

This deep, black universe answered his movements with ones of its own, and they were hideous. The darkness churned, as if invisible horrors writhed within it, lurching and undulating. Outside, the streets and footpaths, the roads and houses and buildings of man crumbled in the sonic pulses and vibrations caused by those movements.

Loculus. The little place. It did not exist, had never existed. All it was, all it had ever been, was a shining lure, a promise that could never be kept.

This was the night, the ultimate night beyond everything: a pitiless darkness without end that was waiting to swallow all time and space.

And, as Miles tumbled head-first towards its ravenous heart, the night rushed forward to meet him.

# /'dʒʌst/

## Carole Johnstone

It's cold. I've only just parked up, and already the windscreen is fogging at its edges. And it's wet. Wet enough that I want to get out of this car about as much as I want to go see a dead body.

"And it's another glorious spring day in the River City, the Dear Green Place. And getting greener by the minute! Taps aff, you lovely, beautiful people, taps aff!" A pregnant pause. The DJ thinks he's a wit. He says the same things in the same way every fucking day (in that, he and the weather are as predictable), and his west-end smarmy smugness sets my nerves on an already brittle edge. I've had about five hours sleep in the last seventy-two, and enough coffee to sink a ship.

"For Christ's sake," I say, turning the radio off with a too-loud click. "Remind me why I let ye listen tae this shite?"

Logan grins. "Gid rock n roll, Boss. Sides, it makes me malleable, right? *Mare* malleable."

"Uh huh." I take another look out the window. It's mid-afternoon, but it might as well be midnight. "Come on, let's get this ower wi then."

Duke Street is busy, nearly gridlocked with cars and vans and groaning buses. Red and white lights bounce off puddles and windows and my skin. I zip my coat up higher, shove my hands inside my pockets. The pavement is completely empty. Anyone with any sense is inside something.

We start heading west, towards three huge twelve-storey tower blocks painted red and beige. The strong yeasty smell of the Drygate and Tennent Caledonian breweries is hardly diluted by the foul weather; behind it I can smell the exhausts of all those gridlocked cars, and coal fires exhaled through brick chimneys.

"Okay, so I've a gid yin fur ye the day," Logan says, nearly shouts, hurrying to keep up with me. He's wearing the ridiculous wax jacket he always wears when it rains; a stone deaf criminal could hear him coming from two streets away. "Guy's sittin at hame, right, when he hears a knock oan his door. He opens it, an sees a snail sittin oan the porch, right?"

"This way," I say, turning onto a narrow path that leads quickly to steps. The change in direction slaps the rain into our faces. I can hear the wind howling around the tower blocks as we get closer, battering against the few trees, rattling the handrails as we climb. *A real bowder*, my granny would have said. A day for staying in bed with another, warmer body. I endure a flash of Nazim's face, and then shove it back inside the wind.

"So." Logan is battling valiantly on. Past events have shown it's easier just to let him. "The guy, he picks up the snail, right, an he flings it away far as he can. An then, one year later, there's another knock oan his door. He opens it, right, an sees the same snail."

At the top of the steps there are two low terraced rows

heading off to the right, and on the left the closest tower block looms: two lower floors of open balconies beneath ten of only windows. An old high brick wall, entirely out of place among the massive blocks and pebble-dashed terraces, runs alongside the road between them.

Logan grins. "An the snail says, 'whit the fuck wis that aw aboot?'" His short hair is plastered to his skull and his face is streaked wet. He looks more like an adolescent boy than usual.

"Ha ha. I know I've said it afore, but ye're wasted in CID, Logan."

He squints, wipes the rain from his eyes. "Where now?"

I turn, start walking towards that nearest tower block. 21 Drygate. There's a single-lane road going through it under a low arch. **NO PARKING** on the tarmac in dirty yellow; a long bike rack alongside. On the wall, two small white signs:

DRYGATE LOCK-UPS
No.s 1-13 ↑

DRYGATE LOCK-UPS
No.s 14-21→

"This way," I say, my voice echoing in the sudden shelter under the block.

Even once we exit the tunnel back into space, the wind stays muted. I can still hear it whistling round the upper floors of the tower block, but this courtyard is small, high-walled. A flat-roofed shop sits on the far side, the metal shutter across its doors only halfway opened. The paint on the sign above is faded, peeling: **NEWS & BOOZE**. Opposite is a row of black-doored buildings.

The Drygate lock-ups, No.s 1-13. I already know that the number we want is 8, but there's only one lock-up currently swarming with uniform and SOCOs anyway.

I walk up to the closest officer – a young guy I don't recognise – writing in his notebook and stamping his feet, soaked and looking pissed off. A middle-aged man in too-big jeans and a too-small jumper stands next to him, arms folded on top of his huge belly, entirely unbothered by the wind and rain and Baltic temperature. A Talker.

"Who's the uniform?" I ask Logan.

"PC Thompson," he says. "Gid centre forward. Scored two ae the three—"

"PC Thompson," I say loud before pressing my lips back together. Chattering teeth don't inspire confidence. "Who's this?"

"Ma'am?" PC Thompson flounders a bit, torn between relief at being rescued, and dismay that it's CID – or more likely, me – that's doing it. "Em, this is Frank Wallace. He discovered the, you know, the..." He looks briefly away, and I resist the strong urge to give him a kick, "body parts."

The man nods hard and fast, and I wonder if he realises he's nearly grinning. "An ah couldnae fuckin believe it, ah'll tell ye whit. Ah'd only just startit openin up, like—"

"DCI Rafiq and DI Logan," I say. I point a thumb at News & Booze. "That yer shop then, aye?"

"Aye."

"Brilliant name," Logan says. And I strongly resist the urge to give *him* a kick.

"Cheers. Ah thought ae it jis when—"

"Who's the LFS on this?" I say to PC Thompson.

"A new guy. I think he's called Harrison."

"Right." It's never the same bloody person twice. I start walking towards the lock-up and all those milling bodies without looking back over my shoulder. "Thompson, I want the exact time and nature ae discovery; whit he touched, whit he moved. And his prints, DNA." How can there be any kind of fucking continuity on a case if it's never the same bloody person twice?

By the time I'm dressed in a Tyvek, gloves, mask, cap, and booties, I'm less mad. Which is better. I don't need the fucking Super sending me on yet another Effective Communication course any time soon. The last one made me want to nail my head to a moving train.

The lock-up smells of fust and something vaguely rotten. Food rather than person. There are at least a dozen black bin bags piled close to the entrance, some broken up furniture in a corner. I step around people and SOC markers to get to the dark rear of the building.

"Harrison, aye?"

He turns round from his hunkered position, looks up. Next to him, one of his colleagues is taking photos with a tripod mount. As soon as they move, I can see it. Them.

A pair of hands. Severed above both wrists, the wounds ragged, untidy. Blood spatter all up the north and west walls, indicating that here was where it was done. There's a lot of blood. It looks just the same as before. My heart sinks, even as that bigger, better tingle starts up in its place.

240 | Carole Johnstone

Harrison grins, starts to take off his gloves. A waggle of what look like landscaped eyebrows. "There's been a murder." An English accent. South East, maybe Essex if I'm really lucky.

"A Taggart reference," I say. "Nothin no tae love aboot a Taggart reference. Top marks for imagination."

He frowns, recovers. Stops taking his gloves off.

"Aye, she's no in a great mood the day," Logan says.

I ignore him. "DCI Rafiq and DI Logan. So, how—"

"D'you have a first name?" I blink at him. His easy smile says this always works even in the direst of circumstances. "Aye. Wis there another note?"

He presses his lips thin. "Yeah. It's in an evidence bag over there."

I hunker down next to the hands while Logan goes to get it. They creep me out, though I'm not about to say so. The severed hands of someone who is more than likely dead because of them are supposed to creep you out. But even so, there's just something else about them – so much the same as the ones we found last week – that leaves me too cold and uneasy. Even whole dead bodies don't make me feel this way, no matter what's been done to them.

Maybe it's *how* they look, placed carefully side by side, fingers touching as if in prayer, while below them the wrists are anything but serene: yellow beans of fat around muscles and white severed bundles of nerves and tendons. Ragged, jagged bones like honeycomb. I can see the two main arteries above both wrists, still bloody where they leaked out: the ulnar on the inside, the radial above the thumb. They look like chewed rubber straws.

"Male," I say. "Looks like a manual worker: callouses, scars, a busted up fingernail. A smoker." Even from this angle, I can see that the finger pads are burnt black, just the same as last time. No fingerprints. There's a tattoo on the right hand in the web between thumb and index finger. Looks professional enough: a seven-pointed star, black. I clear my throat, look back at Harrison, who's still standing, frowning. "Late thirties, mibby? Early forties? Whit d'ye reckon?" A late attempt to make some amends; I do need him on side, after all.

"Bit older possibly. Signs of clubbing, so he probably had some kind of lung or heart disease. I'll know more—"

"Deid?"

"Well, I can't say that for sure yet either—"

"In yer professional opinion," I say, managing not to make sarky reference to his earlier joke. "I'm no gonnae hold it against ye if it turns oot ye're wrang."

"Then, yes," he says, folding his arms, scowling. "Unless his wounds were immediately cauterised or surgically closed, yes, I'd say likely dead." He looks round at the walls, the floor. "There's too much blood here. Probably enough that he bled out, and pretty fast." He points at the lock-up entrance. "And there are what look like drag marks over there, a possible blood trail."

"Want tae estimate a time?"

He furrows his brow. "Big estimate, but I'd say this happened within the last twenty-four hours." He sees my face, and shrugs. "Can't say any more than that, not yet."

"Got it, Boss," Logan says, handing over the note inside an evidence bag. Same paper as the first one:

lined, cheap, ripped from a notebook, so that one side is ragged, uneven. But the words are different. The same, but different:

$$/'smi\theta/$$
$$/d\textipa{Z}i/ \; /'w\textturnv n/ \; /fai^{\textschwa}v/$$

"Great," I mutter. "Okay." I stand up and get my phone out, take a few pictures. I hand the bag back, look at Harrison. "Get everythin tae the lab, and I need aw reports asap. He's got a tattoo on the right hand which is pretty distinctive. I want an ID yesterday, okay?"

Harrison's properly pissed off now, and doing nothing to hide it. "Yes. I do know how to do my job."

*Effective Communication Skills – No.1:*
*Convey respect and you will receive respect in return*
(They don't need to earn it, but you do)

I can already feel the icy whip of the wind as we go back to the lock-up entrance, take off our suits, bag our booties in a paper sack. Logan's grinning hard, but I know it's mostly because he's suffering from that same tingle in his chest where his heart used to be.

"Looks like ye've made another pal there, Boss."

"Shut up."

But he's still grinning even after we've battled through the worsening rain and wind to get back down to Duke Street and our car.

"Gie's yer jaket," I say. "I'm no havin ye stink oot my car wi that thing."

He hands it over easily enough, is *still* grinning when I come back from locking it in my boot.

"Still got that big nine iron in there, Boss?"

My smile is sarky, but he laughs anyway. "Want tae find oot?"

Galbraith is sat at his desk, giving a good impression of someone who wasn't skiving off in the break room seconds ago, except for the slow spreading coffee stain on his shirt. As far as DSs go, he could be a lot worse; he's too impatient, and the devil's always in the detail, in the work, but he'll get that soon enough. As a person though, even Logan thinks he's a dick head – and that's about as low on any scale as you can get.

He throws me a toothy grin. "Heard it wis the same as last week, Boss, aye?"

"Aye. Which means, till we get the go ahead fae the Super for mare bodies, you, Cooper, and MacDonald are on this full time. Pass off whatever else ye're workin on by end of the day, awright?" I look round the open plan office, seeing only empty, untidy desks and a too young guy footering around the water fountain. Another work-exper; just what I need. "Where's Cooper?"

"Assault an muggin aff George Square. Jist went."

"Okay, fine. Tell him the same thing when he gets back. Whit aboot MacDonald?"

"I'm here, Boss," she says, and she's got a cup of tea in her hand that won't be for her.

"Right, Galbraith, I need ye tae keep up the pressure on forensics. The new lead's a guy called Harrison. Chase

244 | Carole Johnstone

up everythin fae the day, and we're still waitin on some outstandin reports fae last week, so we need tae put a fire up their arse." When he frowns, I smile. "But be nice tae him, eh? He's English. MacDonald?"

"Here you go," she says, handing over the mug of tea. The frozen pads of my fingers start to tingle and thaw.

"I want ye on the area aroon Duke Street and Drygate. Find oot if all ae the scheme is Housin Association, and talk tae their officers, see if anythin – or anyone – stands oot. There was a CCTV camera pointin doon Drygate towards John Knox. See if it ever points the other way. Check the footage. I'm goin tae put Cooper on the bodies. They have tae be somewhere."

She's nodding like she doesn't know how to quit. *Stop trying so fucking hard*, I want to tell her, but don't.

"The phoney guy's here, Boss," Logan says from the doorway.

"Funny. And it's aboot bloody time. Where the—"

"Eh, here," the water fountain guy says, his smile small, deprecating. He walks over, and when we shake hands, his grip is a lot stronger than I was expecting. "James Gavin. I'm a leading Scottish expert in IPA and RP."

I let go his hand, smile. "Can ye be an expert in anythin at fifteen?" I feel good and bad at the same time, the usual.

*Effective Communication Skills – No.2:*
*Try to engage in constructive dialogue that does not demean*
(Don't be nippy. It reminds them of their mothers)

I get a flash of Nazim's angry face – more of a montage really – his eyes dark, face screwed ugly. *I'm no one ae yer DCs, Kate. I'm yer fuckin husband.*

Gavin's still smiling. Too young. Far too pretty. "I'm actually twenty-three. I've got a masters in English language and English linguistics from Glasgow Uni, and my PhD in Applied Linguistics involves the systemic analysis of forensic linguistics; the application of its principals to—"

"Aye, that aw sounds…great. An are ye up tae speed?"

"Yeah, I think so. DS Galbraith—"

"Aw I want tae know right now, Gavin, is if that other guy last week wis right? If whit he said last week wis right?"

Gavin's smile vanishes. "Devenny." He leans closer. "I'm way better than him."

God save me from another man-boy who wants me to measure his willy for him. "Well, ye're whit's volunteered tae go the distance, so looks like we're stuck wi ye whether ye are or no. Wis he right?"

"Yes," he says, frowning now, some of the wind gone out of his sails. "What's written on the note is definitely phonemic."

"Like Whisky Tango Foxtrot?" Galbraith snorts.

MacDonald looks up at him, titters into her hand. *Don't fucking titter*, I want to tell her. But don't.

"That's phonetics," Gavin says, unperturbed. "Phonemics is the study of the distribution of sound systems in human languages. At its most basic, phonemes form the basis for pronunciation and language skill. Its alphabetic system, based primarily on Latin, is called the IPA."

"Prefer Kingfisher masel," Galbraith says.

"Awright. Gie it a rest, will ye?" I snap. Just as the slow-moving bulk of the fucking Super pauses at the open office door, shooting me a look of grim disapproval.

Galbraith looks uncharacteristically contrite. "Sorry, Boss."

"Okay, so none ae us need tae understand any ae that, long as ye dae," I say to Gavin. "D'ye agree wi Devenny's translation?"

Gavin frowns. "Mostly." He sits, pulls out a much folded piece of paper covered in scribbles. I recognise what's at its top: the contents of that first note, found one week ago in a doss house in Ibrox. Along with another pair of male hands, and enough blood to likely make them a dead male's hands. Just exactly the same.

/ˈfrɛjzɜːr/
/dʒiː/ /fɔərɔː/

"Okay, so the name is definitely Frazer. But, I think he was wrong about the code underneath it."

He turns the paper upside down. "I think it's a location."

"A location? Whit the hell d'ye mean?"

"See look?" He picks up a pencil, draws three vertical lines through the text. "G and then 4 O. But what if it's zero?" He looks at me, and I see that his eyes are very blue. "Then it could be a postcode region. G4 is the outward area and district, 0 is a partial inward sector."

Nobody speaks.

"Whit wis the location the day? 21 Drygate." I say, but

Logan's already looking up from his phone, and I already know.

"G4 0YE."

Nobody speaks some more.

"Okay, okay." I'm trying not to show how much bigger and badder that tingle in my chest has got. I take my phone out my pocket, bring up my photos, and scroll through until I find the one that's clearest. I turn the screen towards Gavin. "That's the one fae the day. Forensics have it."

/'smiθ/
/dʒi/ /'wʌn/ /faɪ³v/

Gavin grasps the phone eagerly. "G1 5," he says.

"G1 5," I say. "Jesus Christ."

In the space of a little over a week and two, potentially three, murder victims, we've gone from a doss house south of the river, to within walking distance of the Royal Infirmary, Glasgow Cathedral, the Necropolis. Hell, Duke Street's virtually *spitting* distance from the High Street and George Square, and the whole bloody centre of Glasgow. From fucking G1 1.

"Awright," I say. I look at Gavin's still too eager face. "Okay. Dae me a favour, and at least tell me that surname isnae whit I think it is."

He tries to look apologetic, but he can't quite manage it. "It's Smith."

Nazim phones again once I'm back in my office, looking

at a postcode map of Glasgow. It's late, and getting later. No longer gloomy dark, but night. The rain is still lashing down outside, and the old sodium streetlights bathe everything in their off yellow-orange glow. The lights of traffic look like blurry, resigned fireflies queueing to escape. The mobile stops, and then vibrates with a new voicemail alert. I think about listening to it, but don't. I've already heard what he has to say, and Nazim belongs to the school of say something loud and often enough and, like osmosis, it has to pass through even the most stubborn of walls.

Sorry, sorry, sorry.

But he's not saying sorry, I'll stop. Sorry, I'll never do it again. Maybe he thinks he is, but he isn't. He's just saying sorry with a full stop. Sorry you found out. Sorry I'm so fucking weak. Sorry I broke your heart. Sorry me and my midlife crisis have all the imagination of a pond toad.

Fuck it.

I log off, get up, poke my head round the office door. The only one brave enough to catch my eye is Logan.

"Let's call it a night. We cannae dae much till the forensics come back anyroad. Better we get a head start the morra, awright?"

Galbraith is up and out of his chair in seconds. There's no sign of James Gavin. Seven p.m. is probably at least three hours past the vodka-shed. I smile, wondering how quickly he'll regret volunteering as a consultant. Students are even more hard work than police officers. Especially the too smart ones who've managed to somehow turn doing nothing into a career. Logan's probably already running a book.

"Fancy goin tae the pub?" I say, before I know I'm going to. "My round."

❖

The Bon Accord is pretty dead. It is nine o'clock on a shitty cold and wet Tuesday, I guess, although I'm glad all the same. The warm and light and quiet are good; the promise of anaesthesia and diversion even better. There are some uniforms around two tables at the back. They've been here for a while by the sounds of it, but I barely look their way and I know they'll be determined to do the same.

Logan takes my cash and when he comes back, we've sat ourselves down at the best table next to the fire. Two pints of lager for him and Galbraith, a double single malt Talisker, no ice, for me, and a small white wine for MacDonald. And I'm a good girl. I don't say – barely think – anything about that at all. I even manage to smile at her.

"Nae hauf measures, eh?" Logan grins at me, and because it's him, because he's just brought me whisky – albeit whisky I've paid for – I don't bite. I smile.

We chat, we joke about fuck all, because the four of us have absolutely fuck all in common apart from our jobs. Even Galbraith seems happy to stay put. Probably won't last much beyond the first drink, but that's okay. This is, after all, the kind of thing the fucking Super – and all those endless refresher courses – are always on at me about doing. And so I'm doing it. I make the effort. I make nice. Because I know what everyone says about me. What they call me. Except maybe Logan. They think I've risen up the ranks to become DCI in less time than it's taken anyone else because I'm a woman. They're probably dead right. But I'm a better DCI than any of them would be too, so even if they are, I can live with it. Positive discrimination's pretty much the only perk of not having a penis. And the women who get principled or outraged about it are also the kind of women who think not shaving their armpits is one day going to reap the same rewards. That kind of dumb gets you nothing at all. Except itchy armpits.

*Effective Communication Skills – No.3:*
*Be courteous and openminded; always be willing to enter into*
*dialogue, even with people with whom you disagree*
(Make them think you're grateful for half measures, but never ever accept them)

Cooper comes in about half an hour later. Wet through, so it must have started bloody raining again. When he reaches our table, I dig out my wallet, hand over enough for another round. What the hell. I want another whisky, and can hardly just get one for myself.

He comes back, moans at length about his mugging case: the paperwork, the bastard mugger who'll probably never get caught. "Fuckin third time this month. It'll be wee neds or pikeys, like. All ae them stock an investment brokers fae Merchant City ur easy pickins, like." Despite having barely drawn breath since he arrived, he's managed to down most of his pint. "Ye want tae huv seen this poor wanker the day. Right state he wis. They roughed him up, like, pulled a knife, nicked an iPhone an mare than two hunner quid aff him."

They all nod, shake their heads, curse about the curse of neds and pikeys, and I look at them, MacDonald included, and sip my whisky when I'd rather down it. It's not hard for me to separate what muggers, rapists, murderers – criminals – do, say, or think from what these guys do, say, or think. It's easy. But what they do, say, or think about the crimes, about the *victims* isn't. I look at them and I sip my whisky, and I want to ask Cooper: what was the guy wearing? Did he flash the cash? Did he scream? Fight back? How many lagers did he have with his lunch? I won't, of course. You have to pick your battles. You have to be pretty sure you'll win. Especially in the world I've chosen to live in. Not everything's fair. Not everything gets solved. And the fucking Super can send me on as many courses on effective leadership and conflict resolution full of pissed off female execs as he likes, I won't ever complain. Won't say a word. But I won't change the way I speak either, and I won't change the way I think, the way I *do*. I won't stop screwing their spiteful advice so small it could fit inside their arseholes with room to spare, and I won't stop taking my own advice instead. Because doing all those things gets me results. And not even the fucking Super can win against results.

People always underestimate me. They've done it all my career. All my life. They do it all the fucking time.

I drain the last of the Talisker, laugh along with everyone else at one of Logan's lame jokes. Pretend I'd rather be here than just about anywhere else. Or that I don't want another whisky even more than I want to be just about anywhere else. Because the only way – the only way *ever* – is to be stronger, harder, better every single day. And to never believe in their bullshit, not even once; to never start down the road of maybe they're right. Maybe I can't. Maybe there really is no more room to spare. Because there always, always is. As long as they never know that you're pretending.

I wake up choking from a dark dream, scrabbling against my throat, trying to prise free strong and bloody fingers that aren't there. I rear up, grabbing onto the duvet, taking in great and greedy lungfuls of air. I cough, let go long enough to press my palms against the drum of my heart through my breastbone. It's dark, too dark, and I try to think about where my lamp is; my breathing still too fast, brain too slow. I feel lost, alone, afraid. Far too small. It makes me mad.

I lean left, scrabble for the lamp, and my thumb is pressing down on its switch when a loud and urgent *bang bang bang* makes me freeze, and it drops out of reach again. I realise that I heard this in my dream too; it's what has woken me up. The front door.

I sit up properly, wake up properly. Switch on the lamp as I swing round, plant my feet on the cold floor. The light hurts. I squint at my alarm clock until I can see its digits. Five forty-five a.m. For fuck's sake. I suppose I'd been expecting this at some point – just not at fucking five forty-five a.m. Which is probably why he's done it. The *bang bang bang* comes again as I'm pulling on my knickers and bra. Then again – louder, angrier – as I'm trying to pull a hoodie over my head while wriggling into jeans.

The laminated floor is cool on my bare feet. At the door, I go up on tiptoes, peer out of the small glass window above the new silver chain that I keep forgetting to use.

"Ye changed the fucking locks?" Nazim says, looking up at me. The glass is dirty; there's a dead cobweb in one corner. "Come on, Kate, let's talk about this."

He looks as tired as I feel. Dark circles under his eyes, his hair flat on one side, sticking up in random spikes on the other. I still want him though, still feel that familiar pull. And a growing concern that I don't want either. I don't recognise his jeans or coat, and for the first time I wonder where he's been staying the last few days. Probably Phil's. Commiserating. Newly divorced Phil, with his crappy one-bed bachelor pad and endless child maintenance gripes would be a good commiserator.

"Come on!" He gets up close to the window, then stands on the topmost step so that I have to look up at him. His eyes are bloodshot. "Let me in cause I'm no gonnae stop till ye dae." He steps back out of the light, spreads his arms wide. "An I'll keep on making just as much noise as I have tae till ye do an all."

Hot fury burns through me, killing stone dead everything else, because he knows just how much I hate public displays of weakness. I can't bear to think of my bloody neighbours discussing me over their bloody cornflakes. And I'm horribly hungover, I belatedly realise. My stomach growls and churns, and something pulses slow and thunderous behind my eyeballs. When I swallow, my throat is dry enough that it hurts.

I step away from the door, get the keys from my bedroom. Nazim's already started yelling and banging again before I reach the end of the hall, and that hot fury burns brighter, better. He only shuts up when he hears my key in the lock, the dead bolt sliding back. By the time I open the door, he's transformed into smiling, warm, contrite. His familiar photo op pose: the young, hip uni lecturer from Milngavie.

"So, well done," I say, not immediately stepping back to let him in. The cold whips my hair away from my face and feels nearly good. "Now I'm really disposed towards talkin tae ye."

"Disposed towards talkin tae me?" His smile hasn't lasted long. "I'm no one ae yer bloody ned suspects, ye know."

"No," I say, and when I see a light come on in the upstairs bedroom across the road, I go back inside, letting him come in and shut the door. "But ye *are* guilty though, right?" When he doesn't answer, I have to keep going. "How many times?"

His shoulders slump. He turns his sad eyes on full beam. "Not many. And it didnae mean anything, baby, alright? You have tae believe me."

His mum'll kill him, but she'll blame me. She always wanted him to marry a good stay-at-home Muslim girl from Spam Valley, instead of a workaholic, lapsed Catholic from the Drum.

"Ye're never here. And when ye are, ye—"

"Don't ye dare make this about my job again, Naz. Don't ye *dare*. And don't fuckin call me baby." I feel like I might be sick suddenly. I have to put a hand over both my stomach and my mouth until I don't. "How many times?"

He looks set to argue again, to wriggle free, but then

his shoulders drop lower and his eyes focus on the floor instead of me. "A few."

"Define a few," I say, daring him to complain about the way I ask.

"Two," he mumbles, which I know instantly is a lie.

"Where? When? Whit positions?" I can feel the bile coming up from my belly again. I can *hear* it. "Whit wis yer favourite, Naz? Did ye get her on her hands and knees? I know ye like that one a lot."

Sad eyes. Still as beautiful as they've ever been, even bloodshot and self-pitying. "I cannae talk tae ye when ye're like this."

I wonder if I'll change my name back to Campbell. That I'm already thinking that far ahead isn't the greatest sign. Offence is always my best defence, I know. Most tried and tested. And successful. But sometimes it isn't just exhausting, it's self-defeating. Like drinking a bottle of wine just to get to sleep.

I put my palms flat against the lapels of his unfamiliar coat and push him hard back towards the door. "Then don't."

I'm still on my knees on the cold tiled floor of the toilet when I hear my work phone go. I let it go to voicemail, put down the toilet lid and rest my forehead against its cool smooth plastic. The phone goes again. And then straightaway again, with barely a few seconds' gap in between calls.

I get up, wash out my mouth, pick up my phone from the bed.

The voicemail's from Logan.

256 | Carole Johnstone

It's still dark as night by the time I park up on Saltmarket. The wide, four-lane road is dead. No traffic, no pedestrians. I pop some more ibuprofen, and then get out the car, zip up my coat. The vast Greek portico of the High Court of Justiciary looms alongside me, but it's the three police cars across the road that I look at, parked over the entrance into Glasgow Green. I've already googled the postcode for this location. G1 5JU.

I jog over, show the first uniform I see my ID. She's young, torn between being freezing cold and far too excited for six-fifteen on a Wednesday morning. I go around her car, duck under the Police tape that's already been strung between the traffic bollards. The entrance to the Green is vast, the paved path at least forty yards across and flanked by two lines of thin-trunked trees.

It starts to rain. The kind of light smurry that somehow soaks everything through in minutes. The white forensic tent has been set up under the huge sandstone archway that leads into the park proper. McLennan's or McLelland's Arch, something like that. I find room to be glad they got the tent up before the rain started. Doesn't often happen.

Logan turns and waves at me. He's already suited up, so I flag down a passing SOCO, get them to fetch me a Tyvek. I have to take off my coat to put on the suit, and straightaway, I start to shiver.

"Hey, Boss," Logan grins. His mask dangles under his chin, and his nose is bright red. There's a long indent across his forehead where the elastic of his cap has been.

"Gie me a minute," I say, and duck inside.

It's Harrison again. He barely acknowledges me; doesn't look at me at all as I hunker down alongside him. And then there are the hands. Lying side by side on the still-dry ground. Touching. Fingers black. Twin wounds ragged and clean and empty. Same but different. I think of my dream: of me struggling, suffocating, while thick and ugly fingers just like these tried to choke the life out of me. I wonder why that's what I'm always dreaming of; even that first night after the doss house in Ibrox that reeked of landfill in July. I wonder if Logan or Galbraith – or even the fucking Super – ever suffer the same, and when I realise that my own hands are tight, painful fists, I force them flat. My fingers ache with the cold. *Fuck off now. Hangover and cheating husband and shitty boss aside, just do your fucking job.*

"Not dissimilar to the last vic," Harrison says. "No fingerprints. Looks like the same blade too. Male, maybe a little younger. A lot unhealthier." He turns one of the hands from its side onto its back, the fingers like a dead spider.

"Track marks," I say.

"Yeah. And lots of them: scarred and fresh."

"So, our Mr Smith wis a junkie," I say.

Harrison looks up, finally meeting my eyes. "You've already got an ID?"

"No. But the note on the last vic wis for this location and that name. Did ye find a note here?"

He nods. "Your colleague took a photograph of it."

"I'd like a wee look at it." My smile feels as tight as it probably looks. "Please."

He gives a long, low sigh, and then gets up, picks a small evidence bag from a fold-away table. "Here."

/ræfɪjk/
/dʒiː/ /ˈwʌn/ /ˈwən/

"Know what it says?"

"No," I say. "But I know someone who will. Time ae death? I'm assumin ye think he's deid too?" I can't resist giving him some side-eye. "Unofficially."

"Yeah, I do. And again, all I can say is no more than twenty-four hours ago. Likely less, because of the public location. A dog walker phoned it in." He shrugs. "I'll know more once—"

"Let me know then," I say, already ducking back out of the suffocating, too-small tent; only remembering as I'm taking off the suit that I probably should have said thank you. Or goodbye.

"Awright?" Logan says. "Ye look rough, Boss, if ye dinnae mind me sayin."

The wind has changed. I can smell the Chivas Brewery from across the Clyde. The same strong, sour stink as on Duke Street. Is that important? I look up at the fast clouds, shake my aching head. Of course it's not fucking important. It's coincidence. Not even that. There are just a shit ton of breweries in Glasgow. I never like to feel as if I'm grasping at straws, but that's what it's coming to. We have no bodies, no obvious motive, no bloody IDs at all. The only good – and bad – thing in our favour is the escalation. At this rate, a fresh pair of severed hands will be turning up somewhere in the city every bloody day.

And escalators always fuck up. They're like balloons. If they keep filling up with air, it's not long before they explode.

"Whit d'ye think ae the note?" I say, shrugging back into my coat.

Logan shrugs, looks uncharacteristically grim. "The postcode fur this place is—"

"Aye, I know. And I'm no fuckin expert, like bloody *Gavin*, but I think the code on the new note is G1 1." My too-empty stomach squeezes. The Saltmarket is bad enough. G1 1 is going to put this bastard – and his victims – centre stage. And it's going to put us – me – right bang there too alongside them. Every MP, CS, and ACC in the greater Glasgow area will suddenly remember who they're supposed to be serving, and we'll be either the solution or the problem. As SIO, I'll be both.

"Nah, the two ones're different," Logan says, showing me the photo on his phone. "Look. See? They're no the same."

When I don't answer, he puts away his phone, and walks a few feet away from the arch. "Want tae see somethin interestin?" he says into the wind, stopping until I catch up.

"Whit?"

He grins at my expression. "This place used tae be called Jocelyn Square."

"Is that the interestin thing?"

He grins wider, rolls his eyes. "Look."

I come up alongside him. One of the path's stone flagstones is carved with an inscription:

## JOCELYN GATE

I stop, straighten up, look back at the arch. "They used tae hang folk here?"

"Aye, seems like."

Something niggles at the back of my mind, my headache. "I didnae know that."

It starts to rain again. Not smurry this time, but serious in-it-for-the-long-haul rain. I pull up my collar, try to shrink down inside my coat. Logan is looking at me with something alarmingly close to concern.

"A Glasgie wumman goes tae the dentist, an settles doon in the chair."

"Logan—"

"'Comfy?' asks the dentist. 'Govan,' she says."

I manage a sarky smile, but this doesn't make that alarming look go away.

"He still dinghyin ye?"

I glare sharp across at him, but he's looking back at the Saltmarket, the old High Court. "*I'm* still dinghyin *him*," I say. When that wasn't what I meant to say at all.

"D'ye want tae get some breakfast afore we go back tae the office?" he says.

My stomach feels both happy and horrified at the prospect. Logan's still looking back towards the road.

We don't speak again until we're back at our cars. I clear my throat, feel oddly nervous. "Ye know, em, I don't know if I've ever actually said so, but, em, I enjoy workin wi ye, Logan. Ye're a...great DI."

Logan's grinning again. "Aye? Is that number one oan the list ae *Things tae Say tae yer Minions Tae Keep them fae askin ye Awkward Questions aboot Yersel?*"

"I didnae realise ye knew the name ae my last course, Logan. If ye like, I can ask the Super tae sign ye up for the next one." I open my car door, and realise I'm smiling. "Greggs on George Street. Ye're payin."

*Effective Communication Skills – No.4:*
*Always be friendly to everyone. A personal question, or simply a smile, will encourage your coworkers to engage in open and honest communication with you*
(Ask but never answer. Have favourites, but never ever tell them)

The office is too hot. Spring in Glasgow is a confusing time for most HVAC systems. I'm not expecting anyone else to be in yet – it's still only half seven – so I'm very surprised to see James Gavin bent over one of the hot desks, papers and large reference books spread all around him.

He looks up when we come in, waves his hand, and then returns to his books.

"Didnae expect tae see ye here. Thought ye were finished wi the translations?"

"Aye, I was," he says, looking up again. His eyes are bloodshot, reminding me of Nazim before I can apply the brakes quick enough. I wonder how long Gavin has been here. Surely not all night? "But something's been really bothering me about them."

He leans back in his seat, swivels towards me and away from his desk as he stretches. Behind me, I can hear Logan noisily making coffee.

"And I was right," Gavin says, eyes no longer tired at all. "Understanding and even writing phonemics is not complicated. It's very simple. In fact, if you put IPA into google, there are hundreds of example charts, even interactive ones. Or you can download similar apps onto your phone. Anyone could do it."

"Dae whit?"

"Look." He turns his laptop screen towards me, showing a large grid of letters and symbols inside multicoloured boxes. He types Smith into a text box, and straightaway, the phonemic translation appears in another:

/ˈsmIθ/

"Wait. That's no the same as the note."

"Exactly!" Gavin is rubbing his hands together. "It's similar, but it's not exactly the same. So, I looked back at the original note too."

Gavin slaps down a whole sheaf of A4 pages, scribbled with symbols and strike-throughs as Logan comes back from the break room. He raises an eyebrow at me before he sets down three horrible looking coffees.

"Okay, so the first note: Frazer. G4 0. Right? Most of it is bog-standard EPD, OED." When he sees our expressions, he flaps with impatience. "English Pronouncing Dictionary and Oxford English. Okay, so, in Frazer, the ɛj instead of eɪ is CUBE, and the ɜːr is

OALD, and it's not even British English, it's American bloody English!" He looks at us as if expecting more of a reaction than he's getting. He flips over a page.

"Okay, or, look. The partial postcode. You've got the i: in /dʒiː/, right? That's the ee sound in G. EPD, OED, Longman, OALD, all standard. And then, in the next note, the Smith one, the ee is denoted by just i. That's Macquarie, Kenyon and Knott, WL, CUBE." He flaps his hands over the papers and open reference books again. "There are at least a dozen differences. Which doesn't make sense."

"How no?" asks Logan. "Mibby the guy disnae know whit he's doin? He's no an expert, he's jist usin one ae them online interactive things ye were—"

"But that's just it, he can't be. If you type any word you want to phonemically translate into one of them – any of them – their algorithms will source from only one of these dictionaries, not a mishmash of all of them."

"So whit he's doin, it's no because he's doin it wrang—"

"Well, he *is* doing it wrong," Gavin says to Logan. "But my point is he has to know what he's doing very well to do it so wrong."

"So why bother?" I say.

For the first time, Gavin looks nonplussed. "I don't know."

"Mibby it's like gettin the spellin wrang or writin in kiddie handwritin," Logan says. "Ye know, tae put us aff the scent, make us think he's a thick numpty, like the Jack the Ripper 'Juwes' thing."

I roll my eyes, take a big sip of coffee that I straightaway regret. I stand up. "Aye, well, it's interestin.

Make sure ye put all ae that in yer report," I say to an obviously deflated Gavin. I look at Logan instead. "Gie Gavin a copy of the new note, okay? I want to know exactly what it says asap. I need ye tae tell me the next location isnae bloody G1 1."

Halfway to my office, I stop, turn back. Smile. "Thank ye, Gavin."

Less than half an hour later, everyone's sitting in a semicircle facing me and two big boards: one white, one cork. I stifle a yawn, set down my fifth bad coffee of the day so far.

"Okay, just quick afore we get started, now that we've had three vics within three weeks, the Super's given us the go ahead for mare boots on the streets. So, ye can start handin off the grunt work, just make sure ye run it by me first, okay? Second, we're gonnae have tae start splittin shifts; I want one ae us in the office at aw times till this case is closed. I've put a rota up in the break room. Let me know if ye've any objections afore yous go hame the day, otherwise it's no changin. Third, the Super wants me tae remind ye that we're only still lead IS because we were the first available unit tae respond tae that first vic call out in Ibrox. And that obviously, we're gonnae have tae work wi quite a few area CIDs now that the vics are turnin up all ower the place. So, tact, awright? Don't be pissin the wankers off, okay?"

I turn back to the boards, at all the photos, post-its, map grids. "Okay, so let's go through this. MacDonald, did ye get anythin fae Duke Street?"

MacDonald looks up, startled. "Em, no, not really. Nothing on the CCTV; it never films No. 21, or even comes close. And yes, the whole scheme's Housing Association, but I talked to the relevant officers, and there's nothing stands out about any of the residents. Just the usual stuff: alcohol, drugs, domestics, petty crime. Nothing else."

"Galbriath, anythin fae forensics?"

"Aye, some. The first vic wis too decomp tae pinpoint time ae death other than it wis probably aboot two month ago, give or take three, four days either side. But the Duke Street vic's been narrowed doon tae between 4 p.m. Monday an 6 a.m. Tuesday. He definitely bled oot, an pretty fast, Harrison reckons within ten tae fifteen minutes, probably less wi shock. The weapon wis likely a bone saw, ye know, like a butcher's hand saw. One ae the smaller ones, sixteen or eighteen inch, he reckons. Which apparently wid take an awfy lot ae muscle." He winces for dramatic effect. "And aboot twenty minutes max, five tae ten fur each one if the vic was sufficiently incapacitated."

"That it?"

He doesn't answer, and when I turn back round, his smile is just about the smuggest it's ever been – which for Galbraith, is pretty fucking smug.

"Only an ID oan the Duke Street vic."

"*Whit?*"

He gets up, swaggers down to the front. "John Michael Frazer." He takes out a blown up driving license, pins it to the cork board. Frowning, balding, instantly forgettable. "I traced his tattoo tae a right dive in the

266 | Carole Johnstone

Arches; he only got it done last month. Forty-one. An ex-bank manager fae Partick, currently – well, wis – unemployed. Divorced. Nae kids. Nae connections tae Duke Street, Drygate, or Dennistoun in general."

"See next time?" I say, and I wait until he's looking at me. "Ye might want tae lead wi yer best foot, awright?"

He nods, contrite, but I know he doesn't mean it for a minute.

"Criminal record?"

"Aye," he says, smile recovered. "An that's the *really* interestin bit. He served ten year ae a fifteen year sentence in Bar-L fur a two hunner an fifty million pound loans scam. He only got oot end ae last year."

"Fraud," I say. I look back at the board.

"Big fraud."

"So whit the hell wis he doin in a lock-up in Dennistoun? Who's it registered tae?"

"It's not currently registered to anybody," MacDonald says. "The owner lives in Spain, and the last person to rent it now lives in London."

"Awright. Galbriath, keep on diggin up whit ye can on Frazer. Anythin at aw. MacDonald, I want ye tae try and ID the vic fae the day. Smith. That's it. Nae distinguishin marks on him, unless ye count the track marks. Speak tae Harrison. Cooper? Anythin on locatin the bodies?"

"Nothin, Boss. The blood trail fae the lock-up stopped inside the car park, an the rain washed away any tyre tracks. Nae vehicles caught oan CCTV between the time ae death oors." He shrugs, uncharacteristically sober. "Mibbys now we've got the go ahead fur mare uniform..."

"Aye, okay," I mutter. "Keep at it. I know ye're gettin

the shitty end ae the stick – wi nothin else tae go on yet, it's needle in a haystack stuff, but someone's got tae dae it."

He looks up at me, blinks, and then hides his shock inside a big slurp of coffee.

"Okay, so whit dae these places have in common, eh?" I tap the lid of my pen against the map printouts. "Until we ID the first and third vics, that doss house in Ibrox, the lock-up off Duke Street, and Jocelyn Square on Glasgow Green are aw we've got tae connect the gither." I close my eyes, stretch. When I open them again, Logan is typing away on his laptop, but after this morning, I decide to let that go.

"Location, location, location. If we ignore for a minute the phonemic whatsits, because who the fuck knows why the fuck he's usin them, whit aboot the partial postcodes? The one on the first vic matches the location ae the second, as does the name. Same the day: the partial on Frazer matched the location ae who we're assuming for now is Smith. Why? And for whit reason? A partial postcode covers a bloody big area, so whit's the point? And why wis there nothin on the first vic? Wis it because he wis just gettin started? A practice run? Or is there mare significance tae it than that? We're never likely tae be able tae ID him, remember, so my inclination is tae think aye."

"Actually, Boss," Logan says, "I think I might huv somethin oan that as it goes. Jocelyn Square, where the baddies of auld used tae get choked, right? So, that big old wall roon the Drygate scheme, remember?"

"Aye. Whit about it?"

"My dad wis intae aw that genealogy shit, right? An he traced his great great *great* – fuck knows – grandfather back tae a prison called the Bridewell. Also known as the Duke Street Prison. Look."

He turns his laptop round, zooms in on an old pencil-drawn plan. A building with Duke Street along one side, Drygate, High Street, and John Knox along the others.

Another tingle. Not a great big one, but one nonetheless. "Okay, that's good, great. Keep followin that. See whit ye can find oot aboot the location in Ibrox too." I turn back to the first board and Frazer's frowning, forgettable face. "Why always burn off the fingerprints but leave the tattoo on Frazer? Come tae that, if he's worried enough about ID tae get rid ae the fingerprints in the first place, why hands at aw? Why no a leg, a foot, a torso?"

I stop, stretch again, resist the urge to yawn. "Okay, so in summary. One: location – why those locations, and whit, if anythin, connects them? Two: IDs. Frazer. I want tae know everythin aboot him that's worth knowin: how many sugars did he have in his tea, whit shitey football team did he pay tae see lose every Saturday, how ugly wis his cum face?" Some laughs that I definitely feel I've earned. "And Smith, the junkie. Who wis he? Three: Where Are The Fuckin Bodies? He's escalatin. And fast. We need tae start comin up wi the good shit quick smart afore the desk jockeys in mess dress start thinkin they can dae a better job."

Someone clears their throat, and when I glance up beyond the semicircle of chairs, I see a loitering, footering Gavin. I can't stand footerers, and he's beginning to make a habit of it.

"Did ye want somethin?"

He nearly cringes when everyone else turns round to look at him. "So, sorry, em. I didn't want to interrupt."

"Ye translated the note?"

"Yes." He returns his gaze to his boots.

I suppress a sigh. "And?"

"Em, so you were right. The partial postcode is G1 1. He used two different conventions for the checked vowel in the word one, that was why—"

"Whit about the rest ae it? The name?"

"Em, well, you see that's the thing I wanted to—"

"Gavin! Will ye just spit it out! Whit's the bloody name!"

Someone snorts again, probably Galbraith or Cooper.

Finally, Gavin meets my eyes, and I'm struck again by how young he is, how ludicrously pretty.

"Rafiq," he says. "The name is Rafiq."

Someone says *fuck*. I sit down. MacDonald brings me another coffee that my headache wants but my stomach doesn't. I remember to say thank you this time, and get a plate of chocolate Digestives for my trouble.

I'm far too wired, and probably still far too hungover, to even try to sleep. I finish my chippy, open a cheap, too-warm sauvignon. My headache stops shouting halfway through the third glass, and I feel recovered enough to turn on my personal mobile. Twelve texts and two voicemails, all from Nazim. When the first voicemail starts by shouting in my ear, I delete both without listening. I read only the last text.

*If you're never going to forgive me, Kate, then please, just put me
out of my fucking misery x*

*No.* I pick up the wine glass, take a big swallow. I wonder
if I'm just waiting for him to make the decision for me.

A loud bang makes me jump, sloshes my wine. And
then there's another, louder. Outside, I'm pretty sure.
But my belly still flutters and drums when I get up off the
sofa, creep towards the front door. I think I can hear
scratching against wood, and I turn out the hall light,
thinking about black burnt fingers, my own shaking
more than I'd like.

It's just the hangover, I know. That's all. Whisky
hangovers always make me paranoid and too jumpy. And
it's the stress – of work, of Nazim and his wandering
bloody willy. And it's also lack of sleep; I can't remember
when I last slept more than four or five hours in a night.
Or without nightmares about being held down and
choked by bloody hands; suffocated under the weight of
needing to believe in myself and nothing – no one – else,
or that there's still plenty room left to spare, even when
there fucking isn't.

*That's all.*

I hug the wall until I'm at the door. The scratching is
definitely louder, definitely coming from the other side
of it. My hands are tight fists again. I want another
drink. Fear and anger. Anger and fear. Like an old steam
locomotive on a circular track. Making me feel small,
small, small.

I reach up slowly on tiptoes towards the window. That
old dusty cobweb is still there. I half-expect someone –

or something – to lunge into view on the other side when I get close enough to see out. When another almighty bang shakes the glass inside its frame instead, I shout before my view explodes into light and then colour. I blink, see the colours behind my eyes instead. Who the fuck lets fireworks off in March?

The scratching comes again, louder. I crane taller, trying to see what's outside, and nearly crap myself when the dark, sleek shape of next door's siamese darts back into the bushes.

I drop hard back down onto my heels. "Shit." Turn on the light. "Fuck." Slide across the new bloody silver chain.

I'm still angry, still unsteady, as I go back towards the living room. When my mobile bursts into the loud intro to *Lust for Life*, I grab hold of the doorframe hard enough to do it – and my fingernails – some damage. "Fuck!"

I snatch up the phone, nursing my sore fingers. "Whit dae ye want, Logan?"

"Em, pardon me fur wantin tae make sure ye're awright."

I sit down heavily, let go my fingers to pour some more wine. "Well, there wis nae need. I'm fine."

"Ur ye oan yer ane? Aye, course ye ur. Why wid ye think no tae be when there's a murderin, hand-severin madman oan the loose, ye're SIO in charge ae the case, an he just wrote yer name oan the last fuckin vic?"

"Is this ye makin sure I'm awright?" I sigh, drink. "He didnae write my name, he wrote my surname. Have ye any idea how many Rafiqs there are in the whole ae Glasgow?"

"Naw. Dae *you*?"

"Aye, well. No. But it's plenty." I pause for another drink. "It's a coincidence, that's aw. Ye wouldnae be freakin oot like this if the name had been Cooper or Galbraith, wid ye?"

"Aye." His answer's very emphatic. I think I hear the heel of his fist hitting against something; he does that a lot. "An ye can be sure I'd be freakin oot *extra* special if the name had been fuckin Logan."

I sigh. "Whit dae ye suggest, eh? That I phone up the fuckin Super, beg for immediate protection? How good's that gonnae look? 'Lookit the feart wee wumman. Lookit—'"

"Christ." That sound again. "Fur fuck's sake, it disnae always huv tae be aboot ye bein a feart wee wumman. Anyone in yer—"

"Aye, it does, Logan. Because that's exactly whit everyone else will *make* it aboot. I'm no arguing wi ye on this, okay? I'm no helpless, and I'm no in danger. An I'm tired, and I'm goin tae bed."

But of course I don't. I've a bottle of wine to drink.

By Saturday night, nothing has changed. For a repeater in escalation, he's become suddenly reticent. Work shy. There are no more hands. Unless it's just that we haven't found them yet. Just like the bloody bodies.

I'm home alone again. Logan and Cooper are on shift until seven a.m., but I'm not due in until noon. I've had some sleep in the last sixty odd hours, fewer nightmares. I don't feel quite as wrecked. I've turned off my personal mobile, although I've also relented enough to agree to meet Nazim in town on Monday after shift. I still don't know what to think or do about that. More fucking fear and anger, I guess. Maybe I'll just wait and see how I feel on the day. Which wins.

I take a slow sip of merlot while my ancient laptop valiantly tries to open a link sent by Logan. I don't like red wine much, but it makes me feel less like a functioning alcoholic. The webpage loads slowly, painfully. By the time it's finished, so is the glass of wine.

It's from the Scottish Archive Network. *Crime and Punishment in eighteenth to nineteenth-century Scotland.* I skim most of it, reading, as per Logan's instructions, the final paragraph.

> *The Board of Directors of Prisons in Scotland recorded that in 1838, there were 178 buildings functioning as prisons: 20 large burgh or county prisons; 80 small jails or tollbooths, often part of a court house; and 70 lock-up houses, consisting of one small room.*

"So?" I mutter, returning to Logan's email.

> *Checked the Sheriff Court Records for Govan and Ibrox. Looks like there was definitely a lock-up house on Barr Road. We've no way of knowing if it was the doss house at no.14, obv, but odds are pretty good, right? Anyroad, we can chat about it tomorrow afore I go off shift.*

I feel an itch, like a word that's on the tip of my tongue, or a memory that's been lost through drink. It's as familiar a feeling as that tingle in my chest when we get a new case, or in the days, hours, minutes before a breakthrough. There's something. I don't know what it is, but it's something. Something I already know, just don't *know* I know. Yet.

I stand up, stretch. Think about pouring another glass of merlot, and then go into the kitchen for some water instead. My mind keeps going back to that first vic. He's the most important one. The first. No warning note. No name, no location. He was hidden where he might never be found, and he nearly wasn't. The others were in plain sight, and found quickly because they were supposed to be. A city jail. A jail square and gallows.

I hear the ring of my work phone, and get back to the living room before it kicks over into the voicemail service. I look at the number before I answer: Logan's desk phone.

"Aye?"

"Em...hullo?"

"Aye, hullo." I roll my eyes, wish I'd poured that glass of wine. "Who is this?" Although I've a fair idea.

"Em, aye, sorry. Of course. It's, em, James Gavin here. I'm really sorry to bother you, you know, on a Saturday night and everything..."

"Whit're *ye* doin at the station on a Saturday night? Ye ken the university's no goin tae be able tae bill for—"

"Oh, uh-huh, that's...I'm just still trying to work out if there's some kind of pattern to when he uses different IPA conventions. It's just really been bothering me, because there must—"

"Aye, okay, very good. Very...commendable. But I'm thinkin that's no why ye've phoned me."

A short laugh. "No, no, sorry. Em, DI Logan asked me to call you. Him and DS Cooper have had a tip off, and they've just—"

"A tip off?"

"A location."

I put down my water, and stand up very straight. Goosebumps spread along my forearms. That tingling in my chest burns hotter. "Where?"

"A flat above Cibo in the Merchant City."

"The poncey Italian in the old Sheriff Court building?"

"Yes." A pause. "DI Logan looked up the postcode before he went. It's G1 1HD."

"Shite." I shove the phone between my ear and shoulder, start pulling on my boots. "Okay, tell him I'm on my way."

I'm already in my car and driving when it occurs to me to wonder if Logan's gone with more backup than just Cooper, but I let it go. As much as I might want to, I can't micromanage my best DI. He's not a complete idiot. And anyway, the flat above Cibo is probably just another crime scene now. Nearly three days have passed since the last vic, after all. But that something tingling in my chest and on my tongue, and itching deep in the back of my mind says otherwise. And I pick up speed, blowing through a red on Charing Cross.

I rattle along Ingram Street, cutting up slow-moving Saturday night traffic – mainly creaking, barking, lit-up hackney cabs. I ignore about four No Entry signs, and take a sharp right across oncoming cars to drive straight up onto the pedestrian Brunswick Street. Posh pissheads – because this is the Merchant City after all – shriek and jump out of my way, shouting, shaking their fists and oversized phones. I brake to a halt next to a row of stone benches and some very weird looking trees wrapped in fairy lights. Beyond them are Cibo's outside tables and big Kopparberg umbrellas. There's no one there, it's too cold. The warm gold lights inside the stone pillars and archways of Cibo are far more inviting.

I reach down for my own phone, turn it on. I crane up towards the looming red brick and high windows as I realise I have no idea where this bloody flat is. The old Sheriff Court is huge; it has three floors and four entrances, on four streets.

I start to phone Logan, and then stop. It's probably not the best idea to phone him while he's potentially approaching a murder suspect. Even if he probably isn't. I start to phone his office number instead, when a hard rap on the passenger window makes me nearly drop my phone into the footwell.

I press End, and lean across the seat, heart still beating far too fast as I squint against the street and restaurant's too-bright lights. Before I recover even half my wits, the passenger door is yanked open, and someone – a man – gets quick inside, slams it shut in a cold gust of noisy air. Throws a rattling rucksack into the footwell.

I rear back, hitting my shoulder against the window. "Whit the fuck dae ye—*Gavin*?"

He turns, gives me a nervous smile. "I know you hate it when you think someone's trying to get one over on you, and so I want you to know that's not what this is."

"Whit're ye doin here? Did Logan—"

"People think they can mess me about too. They think I'm young, stupid." His cheeks redden. "Pretty. Like I'm a wee girl."

I'm far too wired and confused to give a shit, much less feel guilty. "Gavin. Listen tae me. I have tae go. D'ye know the number ae the flat Logan and Cooper went tae?"

Gavin leans back, looks out my filthy front windscreen at red sandstone. "John Frazer took my mother for every single penny she had."

Everything in me locks up except my chest. My voice. "Oh, aye?"

He closes his eyes. "She was very fragile. And she was an alcoholic. She popped a lot of pills." He turns his head, looks at me, smiles a smile that this time is sad. "Prescription only, of course – we're from Helensburgh. She was very rich. Or, her family was – our family was – and eventually she was the last one left. Apart from me."

"Okay." My phone is still in my right hand, hidden down by my side. "I don't think I know whit it is ye're tryin tae say tae me, Gavin."

"Aye, you do. Ask me any question, Kate, and I'll answer it, I promise."

I swallow, and it sounds far too loud. His smile gets bigger. I take a breath, much quieter. "And Smith?"

"Is that your question?"

I shake my head. "Whit did...whit did he dae? Whit did Smith dae?"

Gavin shrugs, looks back out the windscreen. "He was just a junkie ned who liked to assault and mug suits around George Square and St. Enoch's."

"Oh, God," I say, folding forwards, clutching at my stomach. "Jesus Christ."

"D'you smoke?" he says, holding out a newly opened packet of Marlboros.

"No," I say, still bent over as I shake my head. I risk a look left across at him. "Aye." And then I take one of the cigarettes – fast, like I expect the packet to be boobytrapped. When he produces a zippo and lights it, leans close enough towards me that I can feel the warmth of the flame against my face, I cringe, close my eyes, wait for something really bad to happen.

It doesn't.

I haven't had a fag in nearly three years. The smoke hits the back of my throat, my lungs, and I only resist coughing because I'm determined to hang onto every last bit of that warm, fast kick of nicotine. When I exhale, the smoke curls out across the dashboard, disappears against the already fogging up glass of the windscreen.

"Who wis the first vic?" I say. But this time, I don't look at him.

He doesn't answer. But I can feel his anger. Not hot like mine, but thin and high, untouchable like smoke.

"Wis he yer dad mibby? Yer brother? Partner?" I take another drag, because it gives me the excuse to take a long, deep, calming breath. "Whit did he take?"

Gavin's laughter makes me flinch, and his smile becomes a grin. "You think you've got me all worked out already, Kate?"

"Crime and punishment, right?" I say. Another long, deep drag. "The lock-up, the prison, the jail square, the gallows. Thieves used tae be punished by cuttin off their hands. John Frazer embezzled money, Smith mugged people tae fund his habit. But the first guy. He's whit made ye start, right? He's even mare personal than Frazer wis. An ye made certain that we'd never be able tae ID him, which must mean that IDin him would've led us straight tae you. So, wis he yer dad, yer brother, yer—"

"He was my fucking father!" he shouts, lunging towards me and stopping just short, seething in and out through gritted teeth. I force myself not to react. His breath smells of peppermint and garlic.

"Whit did he take?"

Gavin's eyelids get heavy. I have an absurd urge to laugh when one eye spills a long, fast tear. "Everything." His voice is low, husky. "He took everything."

He suddenly plucks the cigarette out of my hand, and because I'm not expecting it, not expecting *him* to lunge so quickly again into my space, I rear backwards, whack the base of my skull against the window. When I start scrabbling for the door handle, he lunges again, grabbing me round the throat, and this time I do drop my phone; I feel it bounce hard off my knee and then against my boot.

The memory of my dream is too close, too real. Fear and anger. Anger and fear. I scrabble for a hold on his fingers, but he only squeezes tighter. I try to remember everything I've ever learned or put into practice: every defensive move to get out of a choke hold, a corner, a bodyslam. All the ways to fight back. To attack. To win. My vision starts to spot as my lungs start to scream out for air. I can't move. I can't even open my eyes, never mind lever my own body forward. And this is what all that fear and anger has always come down to. This. It doesn't matter who I am, or what I am. What I do, or believe, or think, or achieve. *He* is stronger. *I* am weaker. Small, small, small.

And then he lets go.

I cough, still choking, as I try to drag in any small amount of breath. For a terrible moment, my throat closes up completely, and then it opens in an ugly loud rush. The black spots in my vision diminish, become pinpricks, disappear.

Gavin doesn't look at me, but reaches out to pick up my still smouldering fag from the dashboard instead. When he cracks the window to chuck it out, I get a blast of cold air and distant shouts, music. A flash of white light – the weird looking trees wrapped in fairy lights – make me realise just how isolated – how hidden – we've become. Every window is fogged up completely. When he shuts his window again, all outside sound is instantly muted. Far away. And even though he's not choking me anymore, I'm still inside my dream. I'm still lost, alone, afraid. Small.

"Logan and Cooper. They're no here, are they?" My voice is hoarse, ragged.

His smile is back. Benign, patient. "Is that what you really want to ask me, Kate? *Really* really?"

I cough, and it hurts enough that I know I won't do it again. "Where are the bodies?"

He shakes his head. His smile dims a little. "I know that's not what you really want to know either. I didn't take you for such a coward." He sighs. A weary, but still patient sigh. "Okay. I'll help you a wee bit. I had a girlfriend, Kate." Smile. "She wasn't a bit like you. She was shy, vulnerable. Easy led. But I still loved her. I still wanted to marry her."

He stretches out his legs. The bag at his feet rattles ominously, and he shoots me a toothy grin. I wonder if a sixteen or eighteen inch bone saw would fit inside a Nike rucksack. "So, with that in mind, what's your question, Kate?"

*Effective Communication Skills – No.5:*
*Nonverbal communication – Pay constant attention to your*
*body language, eye contact, hand gestures, and tone.*
*Nonverbal signals convey how a person is really feeling*
(Always, *always* seek to hide every one of your natural
weaknesses and desires)

I let my shoulders slump. I try not to catch his manic stare and end up looking down at my feet instead. "Whose hands are up there in that flat?"

His laugh is more like a bark. Delighted. Over-excited. "Yes! Right fucking question!"

When he lunges towards me again, I force myself not to react, to move.

"You want to know what *he* took from me?" Another warm breath of peppermint and garlic. "She was doing it with him. Behind my back. For fucking months. He took *that* from me." Then just as quickly, Gavin's back to rage. Like flicking a switch. He spits it into the space between us. The gearstick, the plastic drink holder, the handbrake. My sleeve. My skin. "He made her have an abortion. He took *that* from me. She got an infection, that's how I fucking found out about any of it, and now she can't have kids at all. He took *that* from me. She hates me, because I Hate Her." Blink. "He took *that* from me."

"Who did?"

He has a very slight overbite. Too-sharp canines. "Her fucking English lecturer. What a fucking cliche, Kate. Right?"

My stomach clenches, and my throat threatens to close up again. I forget to hide. "Rafiq." My voice is a whisper.

"Rafiq." He leaves teeth marks in his bottom lip.

"I don't believe ye."

"Ah hah! Well, I've prepared for that likelihood." He reaches down for the rucksack, and my next breath catches and stutters inside my chest, until he brings out only a phone. "It's hers. Do you want to listen to some of his messages?"

When I don't reply, he turns it on, its screen light moving sickly shadows across his face.

"Okay, this is a good one."

And then Nazim's voice fills the cold, dark, choking space between us. Something terrible rushes up from my belly. My chest. Fizzes inside my bones. My cold fingers press against my mouth.

*"What the fuck is wrong with ye, Shona? Ye're a grown up. I trusted ye tae take appropriate precautions. What the fuck are ye thinking, leaving hysterical messages on my phone? I'm a married man. I love my wife. And ye're too young. Ye've yer whole life ahead ae ye. Take care ae it. I'll pay."*

Gavin goes on grinning in the wake of the recorded voice asking if we want to hear the message again. "If it makes you feel any better, Kate, he leaves a few other, nicer messages after that one. Even says sorry."

I take my hand away from my mouth. Let all of that something terrible out. I launch myself at Gavin, not with my fists but my nails. "Ye wee shite! Ye fuckin useless bastard *shite!*"

I don't know who I'm shouting at. Him or Naz. Gavin looks momentarily worried until he's able to grab hold of my wrists, push me backwards against the better balance of his own weight.

I let go, remember to hide. Close my eyes. Cringe back against my seat. When I look again, he's still smiling, but it's not a good smile. I've drawn blood. Not a lot. A trickle down his cheek from his left temple. A shorter, deeper gouge in the side of his neck.

"I'm going to let that go, Kate, because I was pretty angry too. When I found out. But that's your lot, okay?"

I nod.

"And like I was saying before, I don't want you to think all this time, I've just been trying to get one over on you, because I haven't. I really haven't. That's not what this is about, okay?"

When I still don't speak, he sighs, gives me sad eyes that remind me so much of Nazim I want to scream. "I used phonemics in the notes because I knew you'd have to come to the uni and the School of Critical Studies. And I knew I was the best available student, the most qualified. All I had to do was volunteer. I added in all that non-conventional phonemic stuff because I needed to be around longer than it would take just to translate the notes."

*You bigged up your part.* I glance at him, turn my face blank. *You probably have to do that a lot.*

He keeps on looking at me with his earnest, sad eyes, but I refuse to ask him why.

"I wanted you to see what he was like for yourself. I wanted you to know what it feels like to find justice. To take back what was taken from you."

That's not what he wanted. He wanted a power trip. He wanted involvement. He wanted to peek. He wanted to *share*. He wanted big, and then he wanted bigger.

"He's not dead, you know."

And I can't help it. I slap that hand hard across my mouth again before I can even think past the words. Their implication.

"I thought I'd leave that up to you." He gives a one-shoulder shrug.

"Naz is alive?"

Quick nod of the head. Another half shrug. "Like I said, I want someone else to know what it feels like to *take* justice. Apartment number 4A – your lucky number, right?"

I breathe. Breathe. Don't waste any time in wondering how the fuck he knows everything he knows about me. I look down at his Nike rucksack. "So, whit? Ye want me tae go up there and dae it?"

He laughs again. Rolls his no longer sad eyes. "No, of course not. *I'll* do it. All you have to do is say yes to me doing it."

"And if I say no, ye'll no dae it?"

Smile. "I'll no do it."

"I don't believe ye," I say. And when he frowns, leans quick towards me, I make myself flinch backwards, hit the back of my head hard enough against the driver window to make me see those black spots again.

"I know you're going to say yes."

I breathe. Breathe. "Ye expect me tae sit in this car while ye murder my husband? And then, whit? Ye expect me tae let ye go?"

"You can try and get me if you like, Kate," he smiles. "Come up after me yourself, phone for backup, whatever. I'll be long gone either way. He's the last one on my list. And you can say it was me or not me, it doesn't matter. I know you always want a neat end, a closed case, but the murders will stop, I can promise you that. And I'll never come anywhere near Glasgow again."

"No," I whisper. "I say *No*."

I get a flash of those too-sharp canines again, a warm blast of breath, and I rear backwards again, whacking my head against the window again, until I realise he's only thrusting his girlfriend's phone into my face again. Subjecting me to Nazim again.

*"Fuck, I miss ye, baby. I miss the way ye smell, the way ye taste. Just thinking about ye makes me so fucking hard. But ye know what I love the most about ye, baby? More than how beautiful ye are, or how interesting and funny and fun? It's that ye get me. Ye just get me. Ye get when I want tae fuck or talk or just be left alone. Ye love me no matter what. An I can call ye baby — Hell, I can call ye a fucking girl — and ye won't lose yer shit or lecture me about patriarchy and misogyny for an hour. God, dae ye know how much I miss yer hot, wet—"*

I grab the phone, press down hard on the power button. "Stop."

Gavin takes back the phone. He reaches down into the footwell for his rucksack. It rattles and clunks.

"I'm going to go now, okay?"

I look at the foggy windscreen. Try to remember what must still be on the other side of it.

"Last chance to stop me!" His childlike sing-song voice sets my teeth on edge, so I just grit them harder.

I hear the passenger door handle clunk down, the door creak open. The outside rushes in. The wind. Distant shouts, music. Clacking stilettos, squeaking brakes. White bright light. I hear his weight shift. Hear one boot meet the pavement. Then the other.

And still I say nothing. Look at nothing.

"Okay, Kate. I'm going now. I understand. You don't always have to say yes to mean yes."

For one moment, I feel the warm, sour breath of him against the side of my face, and then he's gone. The passenger door slams shut, briefly rocking the car.

And I'm alone.

I expect to start shaking, but I don't. I expect to want to move, to want to get out. But I don't.

I breathe. Breathe. Breathe.

Nazim asked me once what it was that made me so angry all the fucking time. And I wanted to say, injustice. I wanted to yell it right into his face. *Injustice!* The fucking injustice of endless, inevitable, preventable, predictable fucking injustice. That what gets believed and accepted and investigated and solved always depends on *what*. On *why*. But most of all, on *who*.

It starts to rain. It drums against the car roof, the windows. I reach down the side of my seat for my dropped phone. Now my hands start to shake; hard enough that my teeth want to chatter. The car stinks of garlic and smoke, and I wind down my window, breathing in the cold city air. Gavin is nearly at the Brunswick entrance of the old Sheriff Court, his dark coat flapping wide against the weight of his rucksack. He's so certain, so fucking sure of me, that he turns left and disappears inside without once looking back at the car.

You always have to play to your strengths. But better *their* weaknesses. And that's nearly always ego. Like Naz thinking that fucking a teenage girl and leaving her to clean up his filthy, selfish, *oh baby, just thinking about ye makes me so hard* mess is okay as long as he doesn't get caught. Like the fucking Super thinking that he can promote one lone woman up through the ranks and then punish her with snide stares and snider memos, and weekend long courses on how to try to be a leader. Or like a pretty, bright-eyed little mentalist thinking that he can flirt with me while he's threatening to kill my husband. While he's choking the fucking air out of me.

I drop the phone into my lap, turn on the radio, look at the digital time display.

And it feels fitting somehow, that it's the smug and smarmy west-end DJ who fills up the dead silence with his anodyne noise.

"Now, here's something to make your Saturday night complete, guys! Listen to this – it's absolutely mental! If you say Space Ghetto in an American accent, it sounds exactly – *exactly*, if ye dinnae mind – like saying Spice Girl in a Weegie accent! Try it! I am *not* having yous on. It is mental! Absolutely pure dead brilliant!"

I turn on my phone. Bring up the switchboard number of the closest police station, one that I know has the best response times in the city.

288 | Carole Johnstone

Not everything's fair, not everything gets solved.

Except for this thing. This time. This now.

James Gavin can think he's getting away and never coming back all he likes, but it isn't going to happen. I look out at the rain, the windscreen wipers, the parking permits stuck in the left hand corner, the blurry red sandstone and pillars and fancy architraving. The trees shacked by twinkling fairy lights. I rub the sore spot on the back of my skull; listen to the shriek and shout and stamp and beep and creak of the city centre.

And I wait just long enough for long enough.

No half measures.

*Effective Communication Skills – No.6:*
*Ego vs Cohesion – Be Generous and Gracious. There is no I in*
*Team*
(Grab every opportunity as your own. Claim every victory as your own. Be stronger, harder, *better*. Every single day.)

I get out of the car and go around to the back. Open the boot and take out the golf club. It's not a nine iron. It's a driver called Big Bertha. And behind it there are half a dozen cans of the Defender pepper spray that all those desk jockeys in mess dress long ago deemed too effective. I pick up two, put them in separate pockets.

I allow myself one more long, low breath, and then start walking towards that Brunswick entrance.

The rain stops. I glance up at all the tall lintels and sash windows. The glass door feels like ice; the corridor beyond like a warm, dark cave.

I take out my phone. Press Call. I don't stop walking. I do start smiling. When I put the phone to my ear, my hands aren't shaking at all.

People underestimate me. They've done it all my life. They do it all the fucking time.

Charlotte Bond
**charlottebond.co.uk**

Paul Finch
**paulfinch-writer.blogspot.co.uk**

Andrew Freudenberg
**angelicdistortion.com**

Gary Fry
**gary-fry.com**

Cate Gardner
**categardner.net**

Carole Johnstone
**carolejohnstone.blogspot.co.uk**

Penny Jones
**penny-jones.com**

Gary McMahon
**garymcmahon.com**

Marie O'Regan
**marieoregan.net**

John Llewellyn Probert
**johnlprobert.com**

Angela Slatter
**angelaslatter.com**

**blackshuckbooks.co.uk**

Also Available

GREAT BRITISH HORROR 1

# Green and Pleasant Land

edited by
Steve J Shaw

Jasper Bark - A.K. Benedict - Ray Cluley
James Everington - Rich Hawkins - V.H. Leslie
Laura Mauro - Adam Millard - David Moody
Simon Kurt Unsworth - Barbie Wilde

Lightning Source UK Ltd.
Milton Keynes UK
UKHW040731130122
397072UK00001B/45